A Fat...

FAITH MARTIN

ONE PLACE. MANY STORIES

HQ
An imprint of HarperCollins*Publishers* Ltd
1 London Bridge Street
London SE1 9GF

1
First published in Great Britain by
HQ, an imprint of HarperCollins*Publishers* Ltd 2020

ISBN: 9780008348748

MIX
Paper from
responsible sources
FSC
www.fsc.org
FSC™ C007454

For all my readers who remember the 1960s with affection. And to all my readers too young to remember them!

PROLOGUE

Oxford, 1961

The firework that was later to be accused of killing a man was just an ordinary rocket, made by the Standard Company of Huddersfield. Along with others of its kind – such as Catherine wheels, Roman candles, the ever popular bangers, and more exotic beauties, such as Mount Vesuvius, short fountains, air bombs and star shells – it had been purchased for Bonfire Night. It had been manufactured to do nothing more controversial than contribute to a half-hour or so of noisy, colourful entertainment for one and all.

That year, November 5th fell on a Sunday night, which many couldn't help but feel was an ideal time for such celebrations. It meant that the man of the house didn't have to worry about getting home from work as fast as possible and then gulping down his tea, thus risking incipient indigestion. Rather, he could take his time before doing his duty for his clamouring, over-excited children by setting light to the bonfire and then overseeing the traditional letting off of the fireworks, and all just before their bedtime.

Alas, that year, the weather didn't deign to co-operate, and instead of producing the cold, frosty, clear night that everyone had been hoping for, brought torrential rain and high winds.

Some wisely opted to put off the celebrations until the following night. Most, being British, gamely ploughed on. After all, if the odd firework, caught by the wind, veered off and broke the window of someone's new conservatory … well, there was no real harm done, was there? Rattan furniture, if it caught fire, could easily be replaced. Except that there was nearly always going to be an exception to prove the rule.

And in the suburb of Headington, set high on a hill, overlooking the beautiful city of Oxford, one firework was fated to be accused of doing something very naughty indeed. In fact, it was to be accused of ending the life of a certain Mr Thomas Hughes, a retired businessman of some standing in his community.

Ironically enough perhaps, Guy Fawkes, who was responsible for instigating Bonfire Night celebrations in the first place, might well have appreciated the murderous consequences of the aforesaid rocket. After all, his gunpowder plot in the basement of Parliament had been intended to help quite a number of people into the after world.

But of Guy Fawkes's guilt there had been no doubt.

As to that of the rocket … well, some people, when all the facts about what had happened that night were examined in the cold light of day, had their doubts. Some people, in fact, began to seriously wonder if the rocket might not have been innocent all along.

Chapter 1

Dr Clement Ryder, Coroner for the city of Oxford, looked out over his courtroom feeling distinctly satisfied. The start of any new and potentially interesting case always gave him a sense of anticipation. Not that investigating the circumstances of some poor unfortunate's death was something to look forward to exactly. However, there was something to be said for overseeing the necessary telling of a sad and significant event.

A handsome man in his mid-to-late fifties, he looked around, noting that the press bench was almost full. He recognised some of the various reporters from the *Oxford Times*, *Mail* and *Tribune*, and wasn't surprised to see representatives from other county newspapers as well. It wasn't often one of the city's more prominent and wealthy members burned to death in the family shed.

It was a wet and cold Monday morning in November, lending the courtroom a grey and melancholy air, and for some of the more superstitious in attendance, the fact that the date was the 13th only added to a general sense of foreboding. The coroner's usher, however, showed no sense of unease as he called the first witness.

Mrs Alice Wilcox, née Hughes, eldest daughter of the victim, rose from her seat and took the stand, going through the usual formalities with a firm, low, but thankfully quite carrying voice.

Clement regarded her thoughtfully. He knew from his preliminary reports that she was forty-two years old, but she looked rather older. She was about five feet six and slightly plump, but she was dressed in a smart powder-blue skirt and jacket outfit, with a plain white blouse that did its best to hide the fact. Her greying, auburn hair was held up in a firm, no-nonsense chignon, and when she turned to look at him, Clement became aware of how pale she was under her make-up. She also clutched her handbag tightly, showing the whiteness of her knuckles, and her large hazel-coloured eyes were wide with trepidation.

Clement gave her a gentle smile. No doubt she'd been dreading this moment for some days now, and he wanted to put her at her ease as quickly as possible.

'Thank you for your attendance, Mrs Wilcox, I understand how difficult this must be for you. I'll try to be as brief as possible. If you need some water, or at any time feel like you'd need to rest, just say so,' he informed her kindly.

'Thank you,' she murmured.

'Now, I understand your father, Thomas Hughes, lived with you at your family home in Headington? Is that right?'

'Yes. Father was widowed a while ago, and found it lonely to go on living alone. So he sold his house and bought a larger property in Headington, with the understanding that myself, my husband and my children would also live there. Since we were beginning to feel rather cramped in our own house, which we were renting, it worked out well for everyone. And it meant I could look after Father too, of course.'

'I see. That sounds very sensible,' Clement said. 'Your children are Olivia, aged fifteen, and Lucas, aged twelve?'

'Yes.'

'And on the 5th of the month, Bonfire Night, you held a bonfire and fireworks party for all the family in your back garden?' he prompted.

'Yes. Father always put on a big display for us when we were children, and he kept it up for his grandchildren. That's why all the family was there, not just those of us with children of our own.'

Clement nodded. 'The other children belonged to your brother Matthew …' He looked down to check his notes. 'Benjamin, Clarissa and Helen?'

'Yes – they're a fair bit younger than my own, and so were very excited at the prospect. Grandpa's fireworks parties were always a big event for them. He threw one every year.'

'Also present were your brother Godfrey and your sister Caroline?'

'Yes, it was always very much a family affair,' Alice agreed, her lips firming into a thin line. She was so obviously determined not to break down, that Clement felt he could now safely ask her to tell them what the jury and the members of the press were all so eager to hear about.

'In your own words, can you tell us what happened this particular Bonfire Night, Mrs Wilcox?'

The dead man's daughter drew in an audible deep breath and nodded. She also turned slightly, so that she was now looking at the jury, rather than the coroner.

'Yes. It was Sunday, and the weather had been pretty bad all day. Rain and wind, and all that. At about five o'clock, just as it was getting fully dark, I asked Father if he thought we should cancel. Although the worst of the rain had abated a bit, it was still showery, and the winds were distinctly blustery.'

As if to underline this, outside a spatter of rain was suddenly thrown against the window by a wind that had been gradually building up overnight, and Clement saw several members of the public look up at the windows and shiver.

'But Father wouldn't hear of it,' Alice carried on, her voice clear in the silent room. 'He said he'd been at bonfire parties in the past when it had actually been thundering and lightning, and it had … never done him any harm.'

As the sheer inappropriateness of these words hit her, she faltered slightly, coughed and then ploughed gamely on. 'He said he couldn't let the children down, but he'd be careful to make sure that he picked a really good and sheltered spot in the garden from which to light the fireworks.'

'Were there a lot of fireworks?' Clement put in, knowing he needed to make the point for the jury.

'Oh yes. Father was a fairly wealthy man, and whilst he was always very careful with money, he did, on occasion, like to indulge in certain things. And the annual bonfire party was one of those. So he'd bought boxes and boxes.'

'And these were stored in the wooden shed at the back of the garden?'

'Yes.'

'Thank you. Please continue.'

Alice Wilcox again took a deep breath. 'Well, when Father had got an idea fixed in his head, it was no use trying to talk him out of it,' she said, then aware that this might sound disloyal, forced a brief smile to her pale lips. 'Father was always a very strong-minded man, and he liked things just so.'

'I understand,' Clement soothed her. He could see she was getting flustered, thinking she'd said the wrong thing, and he helped her out with a brisk question. 'Did the other members of the family ring to ask if the festivities would be cancelled?'

'Oh no,' Alice said. 'They knew I would have telephoned them and let them know if Father's plans had changed.'

'I see. At what time was the fireworks display due to start?'

'Six-thirty. Joan – that's my brother's Matthew's wife – wanted to make sure her little ones were in bed by seven-thirty at the latest. So we lit the bonfire at about quarter past six, and then father went into the shed to begin collecting the fireworks.'

6

Again, the room became very quiet, with not even the odd shuffle of feet or the rasp of clothing against clothing to mar the stillness.

'Was this the usual routine?' Clement asked encouragingly.

'Yes. We've lived at the big house in Headington since 1958, so we'd had three previous parties there, and that was always how Father did it. He wouldn't have fireworks in the house, he said it wasn't safe. In case of … fire.'

Alice dipped her head and faltered again on the last word. Somewhere, someone in the public section gave a soft gasp of sympathy.

'He sounds eminently sensible,' Clement said, keeping his voice both crisp and calm. He glanced down at his notes and said, 'Your father was a retired businessman I understand?'

For some reason, this brought her head up sharply. She turned her attention from the jury back to the coroner, and Clement could see that she'd gone almost white. Her gaze, too, was definitely startled – and alarmed.

'Well … yes, that's right, yes he was,' Alice mumbled, after a visible hesitation.

A handsome young man on the press bench smiled somewhat grimly at this, and made a quick, predatory note, his pencil digging deeply into the notebook on his lap.

Clement, not sure why such an innocuous question – which again he had asked only to help her out of an uncomfortable moment – should cause her such unease, moved on briskly.

'Did you have difficulty lighting the bonfire? The wood and detritus must have got thoroughly soaked during the daytime rain?'

'Oh yes, Godfrey and Kenneth had a real job getting it going. In the end, I think they used a little paraffin.'

'This paraffin was normally kept stored in the shed?' Clement asked gently.

'Yes, I believe so,' Alice acknowledged miserably.

'And can you remember if the paraffin was returned to the shed once the bonfire was lit?'

'I think so. Yes, I'm pretty sure I saw my brother put it back, just inside the door.' Again, his witness responded unhappily, and he cast the jury a quick look to make sure they'd got the point. The garden shed, as well as containing a large stack of fireworks, was also the repository of other, very flammable materials.

'What happened then?'

Alice squared her shoulders and lifted her chin. 'Once the bonfire was going, I went back into the kitchen and began wrapping up some sausages and potatoes to put into the base of the bonfire. Father liked to make use of the fire to cook the food, as they did when he was a boy. Caroline, my sister, helped me with this.'

'And then?'

'I took them out, all piled onto a tray, and left them on an old iron garden table that we keep near the kitchen window. Later, when the bonfire wasn't so fierce, I was going to push them into the base of the fire with an old shovel or something to bake. So I went in the shed for something to use, and, yes, I'm sure I remember Father coming up the path towards me as I left with an old rake. I assumed it was to get the fireworks. I smiled at him as he passed.'

Here she paused, then took another deep breath and pushed on. 'I went back to the bonfire … no, wait, sorry. I went back into the kitchen again to fetch the hot chocolate for the children. That's right. I'd just bought out the jug and mugs, and had put them on the table, when I heard a big bang behind me. It made me jump. Of course, I realised right away what it was,' she said with a nervous smile. 'It was a banger going off. I thought at first that it must have come from one of the neighbour's back gardens. Children do so love bangers, don't they?' She managed another smile and shot a quick glance at the jury.

One or two of them smiled back at her and nodded.

'But then I heard someone – I think it was my brother Matthew – shout something about the shed, and I turned around and saw flames were coming out of open doorway.'

'The door was open?' Clement emphasised.

'Yes. Yes, I'm sure it was. As I watched, something colourful – all blue and red – started fizzing about inside, and I realised it was a firework.'

Clement glanced around the room. On a grey, wet, Monday morning in November, his courtroom looked chilly and dull, but the atmosphere was as tense as he'd ever seen it.

'What did you do, Mrs Wilcox?' Clement asked quietly.

'Nothing,' Alice said simply. 'I didn't know what to do. At first, I couldn't understand it. I couldn't think why Father would have let off a firework inside the shed.'

She looked down at her hands and shrugged. 'I think I turned to Godfrey, who was standing closest to me, and asked him where Father was. I couldn't see him, you see. I thought at first that he must just be standing in the dark, outside the light thrown up by the bonfire. But then I realised I couldn't see him in the light from the kitchen window either. Then suddenly, there was this huge explosion of bangs and whizzes and coloured sparks, and it looked as if the shed trembled.'

The shed in question, he knew from the fire inspector's report, had been a standard, six-by-ten foot wooden shed, common to gardens all over the country, where they were used to store garden tools, wheelbarrows, sacks of potatoes, winter logs and other odds and ends.

'We all sort of … screamed. And then the shed roof began to really blaze,' Alice said, gulping out the words now. 'The smoke was really thick, and my husband, Kenneth, shouted out Father's name and ran towards the shed, but as he did so, a rocket shot out of the door and veered off into the neighbour's fence. It didn't hit him, but it only missed by a few inches. I called at him to come back. I was afraid … You see, I didn't want … I didn't know, then, that Father was in the shed, and I didn't understand why he was going so close and putting himself in danger like that.'

Her jerky words echoed around the silent room, as everyone digested her words – and the horror of the scene.

'My brother Godfrey said something about Father not coming out of the shed, and then I realised … But by then, the whole shed was ablaze – the heat was infernal. And fireworks kept going off, explosion after explosion … It was like being back in the Blitz. I visited London once as a child during the war and I never forgot the air raid …' She trailed off and shot the coroner a look of mute appeal.

'Thank you, Mrs Wilcox, I think we'll hear about the rest of the events from your husband now.'

'Oh, thank you,' Alice said and left the witness box with such alacrity, Clement had no chance to ask the jury if they had any further questions for her.

He looked curiously at the man who stood up to reach for his wife and help her back into her seat in the front row. Her spouse then said something soothing to her, before striding across to take his place on the witness stand.

In stark contrast to his wife, Kenneth Wilcox looked very business-like and calm. If he felt at all nervous at having to give evidence, it didn't show as he was sworn in.

Clement knew his age was fifty, but unlike his wife, he wore his age much better, and could easily have passed for a decade younger. He was around five feet ten inches tall, and huskily built. He had an abundance of sandy hair, which showed no signs of silvering, and bright, almost electric-blue eyes. A neatly trimmed beard and moustache, just beginning to go salt-and-pepper, only added to his overall attractiveness.

'You're Mr Kenneth Wilcox, son-in-law of the victim?' Clement began mildly.

'Yes sir, that's correct.'

'You've just heard your wife's testimony. Perhaps you can now tell us what you saw the night her father died?'

'I'll do my best. Like Alice said, we had a little trouble getting the bonfire to catch light, so in the end we had to use a sprinkling of paraffin.'

'Whose suggestion was that?' Clement slipped in.

The witness blinked slightly, then shrugged. 'I'm not altogether sure. I think mine – or else maybe Godfrey's?'

'Go on,' Clement said.

'Yes. Well, we got the bonfire going. The kiddies were pleading with their grandfather to start letting off the fireworks, and I think he was teasing them, pretending he was going to make them wait or something, but I saw him eventually head off to the shed to collect them. He usually brought them out in a wheelbarrow.'

'Were the fireworks stored in tin boxes, for safety?' Clement asked sharply.

'I have no idea, but I doubt it,' Kenneth said flatly. 'Otherwise, I can't see how so many of them would have gone off like they did when the shed caught fire,' he added logically.

Clement made a note and sighed. If only people would be more careful! 'And how do you think the shed *did* catch fire, Mr Wilcox. Did you see anything strike it – say, another firework from someone else's display?'

'No, I don't think so. The only thing I can think of is that some burning newspaper from the bonfire must have blown in on the wind, through the open door, and landed on one of the exposed fireworks. I wish now we'd never used that damned paraffin. Mind you, it wasn't only the embers from our fire floating about – the wind was so strong, I think plenty of other bright orange bits and bobs blew in from the neighbours' bonfires too.'

'Did you actually *see* any burning newspaper or embers blown into the shed?' Clement asked sharply.

'No sir, I didn't,' his witness admitted honestly. 'But then, I wasn't really looking or taking much notice. I didn't realise at the time that it might be important, unfortunately. Hindsight's a wonderful thing, isn't it?'

Clement nodded, acknowledging the truth of the man's wry comment. He also knew from the police statements that none of the family there that night could tell them how the shed had caught fire, with such tragic consequences.

'I see. Did your father-in-law carry an electric torch with him? It must have been dark inside the shed.' Clement tried a new tack.

'Yes, he did. A big, heavy, black rubber thing. He certainly didn't go in there with a box of matches or a candle or an exposed flame, if that's what you're thinking,' Kenneth Wilcox said smartly. 'No one could accuse the old man of being such a fool!'

Out of the corner of his eye, Clement noticed someone, he thought on the press bench, make a sharp movement of some kind, but when he turned his head to look more closely, saw only industriously bent heads as they took down the witness's words in their best shorthand.

'I see. Did your father-in-law seem himself that day?' Clement asked next.

'What do you mean?'

'Was he in good health? Did he have a cold, or was he in any way breathless?'

'Oh, do you mean could he have been taken ill suddenly and somehow done something to set things in motion? No, I don't think so,' Kenneth Wilcox said, frowning thoughtfully. 'He was always in good, hearty health as far as I know.'

'I see. When were you first aware of there being a problem?'

'When someone – I think it was Godfrey – said something like, "hoy, watch out, the shed's on fire" or something along those lines. I looked, and sure enough, I could see smoke billowing out. Then the roof caught, and everything seemed to explode at once – whizzers and bangers, and what not. Rockets started shooting out – bloody dangerous it was, I can tell you. I realised at some point that my wife was asking everyone if they knew where her father was. And I suddenly realised that he wasn't anywhere around, so he must still be in the shed. But it was impossible to get close to it. I yelled to Caroline to go inside and call the fire brigade. They arrived quickly, I'll give them that, but by the time they arrived and hosed it down … well, they found my father-in-law's body inside. Bloody awful it was, I can tell you.'

Clement didn't think there was any point, in the circumstances, in upbraiding the man for his use of bad language, so instead merely nodded.

'I think, at this point, that we should hear from the Fire Brigade, and then we'll have the medical evidence,' he said instead.

Chapter 2

The Chief Fire Officer was a tall, lean, calm man in his mid-fifties, who'd testified before Clement many times before. He was a clever man but he spoke plainly, so that the jury could understand even the most complicated evidence, which sometimes bedevilled arson cases.

Not that there was anything to suggest deliberate arson in this case, as was quickly made clear. In the Fire Officer's opinion, the worst of the fire had started more or less in the middle of the shed, but with burn patterns that suggested multiple points of contact, consistent with fireworks shooting off in all directions and starting mini-blazes wherever they landed. These small fires were quickly acerbated by the likes of paraffin, bottles of white spirits, some bags of fertiliser and a supply of winter logs, which the family had all admitted were stored inside. Added to the fact that the walls, floor, roof and shelves were all wooden as well, it was hardly surprising that the shed had been reduced to a pile of ashes and bits of burned wooden planks.

When asked how, in his opinion, the fire was most likely to have started, the Fire Officer was reluctant to give any definite opinion. In his view, too little remained of the shed to provide any positive answer – but he saw no reason why either a stray spark, firework or ember blown in by the wind shouldn't have ignited a firework and set off a chain reaction, as suggested by so many witnesses.

The coroner thanked him warmly and called his next witness.

Dr Marcus Borringer took the stand and glanced at Clement with a brief nod. The two men knew each other, of course. Clement had been a surgeon in the same hospital as Borringer before his own health problems (which he'd been careful to keep concealed from everyone) had made him retire from the medical profession and retrain as a coroner. Since then, Doctor Borringer had regularly been called on to give medical evidence in his court. Whilst the two men weren't friends exactly, they each respected the reputation for professionalism which they both enjoyed.

'Thank you, Dr Borringer,' Clement greeted him cordially. 'You performed the autopsy on Mr Thomas Hughes?' he began briskly, confident that the pathologist would have done a fine job.

'I did – two days after he was presented at my mortuary.'

'And can you tell the jury about your findings as to cause of death, please?' Having asked the question, he leaned back in his chair slightly, prepared to put in a clarifying question if need be, but confident there wouldn't be too much to puzzle or flummox his jury.

'Yes. Mr Thomas Hughes was a well-nourished male, seventy-one years of age, in reasonable health. That is, I found no signs of advanced heart or liver disease, or anything of a serious nature, that would normally have been causing him distress. He showed the usual signs of wear-and-tear as it were, for a man of his age – the first indications of arthritis in his wrist and elbow joints, for instance, and he had probably been diabetic, but had not been taking medication for this disease.'

'I see. In other words, you found no evidence that he had suffered a heart attack or a stroke of anything of the kind that might account for his death?' Clement clarified smoothly.

'Quite so.'

15

Clement nodded and indicated him to continue.

'Naturally, the body had been very badly burned indeed – not to say blackened – and had adopted what we term 'a pugilist pose'; that is, his arms seemed to have been drawn up and his hands were fisted, as if he were about to start a boxing match. This, as you know, is due to the heat tightening the tendons in his arms.'

Clement nodded and turned briefly to explain – and demonstrate – the pose to the jury. 'And what else did your autopsy discover?' he prompted.

'We found traces of scorching and evidence of smoke damage in both Mr Hughes's throat and lungs. Also in his blood samples …' The medical man proceeded to give a technical but clear account of a man who had died, most probably, from smoke inhalation.

'You think then, that he was probably unconscious before he would have felt any pain as a result of his burns?' Clement said, with one eye on the victim's family, who were now sitting extremely pale-faced in their seats.

He caught the pathologist's eye, who then gave a slow nod. If, privately, he wasn't so sure that the victim wouldn't have felt anything, he, like Clement, was in no hurry to cause pointless distress by lingering on the fact.

'And was there anything else that caught your attention?' Clement asked next.

'Yes. I found a head wound on the back and to one side of Mr Hughes's skull.'

At this, there was a quick stirring in the court, as Clement had expected there would be, when this particular snippet was announced. It was always the so-called 'dramatic moments' that people responded to most readily, but he (who'd already seen the doctor's report) wasn't taken by surprise.

'Can you tell us more about this injury please?' he asked, almost placidly, his matter-of-fact tone doing a lot to settle the mood in the room.

But he noticed that one of the journalists in particular was fascinated by the medical man's testimony, and had been taking down every word verbatim, with an intense look of concentration on his face. He was a handsome young man who looked to be in his late twenties, with a thick head of black hair and pale eyes that Clement thought would, on closer inspection, probably turn out to be pale blue or grey. Perhaps he was less experienced than his more grizzled and world-weary colleagues, Clement mused. Or perhaps this was his first big story and he was keen to make a splash?

His attention quickly turned from the reporter to his witness as Dr Borringer began to speak once more.

'Yes, the wound was fairy long but narrow, and angled along the right-hand side of his temple.'

'Would it have been enough to kill him?' Clement asked flatly.

'Oh no. There was no actual fracture of the skull – or to be more precise, no fracture of the skull due to *impact*. As you know, the results of a fire can sometimes cause fractures in bones *after* death,' the pathologist emphasised carefully. 'I would say the blow would certainly have stunned him – and quite possibly have rendered him unconscious for a short period of time.'

'I see. And do you have any evidence as to what might have caused this blow?'

'I'm afraid not – there was too much damage done to the body.'

At this, there was a general sigh of disappointment from the onlookers, who probably felt cheated. People liked to have their facts dished up to them on a silver platter, but the coroner was far too experienced to expect things to always be cut-and-dried.

Clement nodded, but not without some sympathy for the pathologist, the police and the fire investigators. What with the near-total destruction of the shed, and the badly burned condition of the body, they were struggling to come up with any physical evidence at all.

'It has been suggested,' Clement began carefully, 'that the deceased was in the shed when fireworks were going off in very close proximity to him. Is it possible that the long thin narrow wound you describe could have been caused by a firework – a rocket, for instance – grazing his head?'

Dr Borringer didn't answer right away but clearly thought about it. He frowned slightly. 'Well, it's certainly possible,' he said, a little uncertainly. 'I'm not an expert on fireworks, naturally, nor am I overly familiar with the science of propulsion. But I imagine something like a rocket would be designed to exude considerable force, in order to lift it off the ground and high into the sky. So I imagine, if it hit someone a glancing blow, it might be powerful enough to cause significant injury.'

'Did you find any foreign bodies or material in the wound?' Clement asked.

'No, I'm afraid not – the burns went too deep. Although we did find tiny fragments of burnt wood – but given that the man died in a wooden shed, that was only to be expected. I understand that there was not only firewood stored inside, but roughly constructed shelves of wood also.'

Clement knew when to take a hint. He smiled slightly.

'Are you saying the blow might more likely have been caused by the victim hitting his head on such an object?'

'It's certainly possible,' the pathologist said, 'and in my opinion, rather more probable. If the deceased had heard a fizzing sound and seen a firework explode, he would very likely rear back or duck instinctively, and thus could have hit his head on something wooden inside the shed. But that is pure speculation on my part.'

'I see.' Clement glanced at the jury and saw one or two of them nodding their heads. The pathologist finished giving his medical report, but nothing of any further sensational nature was forthcoming, and Clement dismissed him with a word or two of thanks.

Next, he called the local police officer, a sergeant at the

Headington Police Station, to give his evidence. But since he spoke of little more than the routine aspects of any investigation following an unexpected death, there was now a distinct sense of anticlimax settling over the court.

The officer reported on the removal of the body by ambulance and touched on the witness statements. However, as none of the dead man's family had taken particular notice of the dead man's movements, they could add little to the proceedings.

By the end of the day, all that was left was for Clement to sum up by giving the usual warnings that people should take sensible precautions with fireworks, and encourage people to store such dangerous objects in fire-proof tins, before asking the jury to retire to give their verdict.

It didn't take them more than five minutes to return a verdict of death by misadventure. The police looked satisfied, the family looked relieved and the usher looked happy to be able to bring the proceedings to a halt well in time for him to get home for his tea.

Clement gave his brief but sincere commiserations to the Hughes family for their misfortune, and there the matter ended.

Or so he thought at the time.

Chapter 3

Two days later, DI Jennings sat at his desk, reading the headlines of the *Oxford Tribune*, the local daily that had once been his favourite of the city's three newspapers, and swore bitterly under his breath.

Superintendent Henry Malting, sitting opposite him, pretended not to hear it. In fact, he'd indulged in his own fair share of such swearing shortly after coming in to his office and getting waylaid by the Chief Constable.

Unlike his DI, Malting tended to read only the *Oxford Times*, so he'd been unaware of the 'scoop' in the more downmarket, but very widely read newspaper that liked to appeal to the more scurrilous-minded of the city's population.

It had taken his CC to point it out to him, and then demand that something be done about it. In true, pass-the-buck style, Malting was now passing the order down to Jennings.

Now, as he gave his man time read the article, he wondered, not without some amusement, whom *Jennings* would choose to pass the problem onto. Whoever it was, the poor sod would probably not be impressed.

The whole thing was clearly a mare's-nest dreamt up by either a bored or gung-ho journalist, designed to do nothing more than stir up interest and gain the paper yet more readers. Never mind that it caused trouble for the police! Or needlessly harassed a family already touched by tragedy.

DI Jennings was thinking much the same thing, as he glumly perused the offending article. From the deliberately eye-catching and mischievous title, to the sly innuendoes peppering the text, it was as aggravating and unnecessary a piece of reporting as he'd ever read. And in his time, he'd read a few doozies!

WAS THE DEATH OF LOCAL 'FINANCIER' THOMAS HUGHES REALLY AN ACCIDENT?

Many of our readers will probably know the name of Thomas Hughes. A life-long resident of our fair city, he was the son of a local shop owner who rose in prominence to build a modest but nevertheless impressive empire for himself, starting out first with a series of chandlers' shops, before quickly moving on and diversifying into coal, aviation and shipping. Many of our older readers will remember the 'golden age' of aviation fondly, when Hughes Aircraft provided shuttle services across the country, back in the years between the wars, for the more well-heeled traveller.

Since then, of course – many readers will remember rather less fondly – there have been two other offshoots of Hughes Enterprises, the ill-fated Hughes Radio and Hughes Premium Bonds Consortium, both of which folded after six and eight years respectively, with considerable losses to their investors. But not, as the authorities made a show of pointing out at the time, with any personal losses to Mr Hughes or his other business interests.

So is it likely, this reporter found himself asking, whilst attending the inquest on the death of Mr Hughes during last week's bonfire festivities, that such an unpopular but canny and careful man should have met his death in such a lackadaisical manner?

What man, I found myself asking, when confronted by a shed burning down around him, or a barrage of fireworks going off right past his face, wouldn't simply run for safety?

Why was the medical evidence of a 'blow to the head' allowed to pass with barely a raised eyebrow?

With the man's entire family gathered together in one place, how is it that not one of them saw anything of how the fire started? Or could give the authorities even the most uninspired of guesses as to what could have happened? And just how likely is it that not one of them noticed when Mr Hughes went into the shed or came out of it, before it was too late to save him?

Rumours have been spreading of ructions in the dead man's immediate family for some time now – the same family that has just inherited the vast wealth so ruthlessly accumulated by the businessman.

Which leaves us at the Tribune *wondering whether the police might not have been altogether too quick to close this most suspicious of cases without even a proper investigation. Could it be that some discreet pressure might have been exerted in certain places to let the matter rest before being properly investigated? If so, we at the* Tribune *protest – and in no uncertain terms. After all, no matter how prominent a person or family, the law applies to us all equally.*

But rest assured, even if the authorities are prepared to look the other way, we at the Tribune *will continue to ask questions – as unwelcome as they may be. So if any of our readers have any information at all about Mr Thomas Hughes (perhaps you were one of the many who suffered financial losses after investing in any of his defunct schemes?) we would be pleased to hear from you.*

We would also like to take this opportunity to humbly suggest that our local constabulary takes a second look at this most outlandish and distinctly odd death of one of our city's more controversial figures.

Jennings glanced at the byline, but didn't recognise it – which made him think that it was probably a new reporter, anxious to make a name for himself.

'I don't know this Duncan Gillingham chap,' Jennings grunted.

'Seems to me he's flying close to the wind in some of his statements, too.'

'Hmmm, but he's been careful to refrain from saying anything definitely libellous,' the Superintendent replied with a cynical smile. 'The paper's legal eagles would have made sure of that before allowing it to go to press. It's all innuendoes and "ifs" or sly suggestions.'

Jennings sighed heavily. 'Do you know the owner of the paper, sir?' he asked cautiously. In his experience, most of the city's movers and shakers belonged to the Masons – as did most senior police officers, come to that. And if a discreet word could be had in that gentleman's ear, it was possible that all his unpleasantness could be made to just fade away.

Superintendent Maltings caught on at once and gave a weary smile. 'Only vaguely, I'm afraid. See him on the golf course too from time to time, but have never played a round with him. From what little I know of him, though, he seems a sound enough chap. This –' he tapped the newspaper with a slight sneer '– doesn't seem to be in his line at all. Which makes me wonder.'

Jennings eyes widened slightly. 'Wonder, sir? Do you mean – he might know something that we don't? You surely can't think there can possibly be anything in it?' he asked, his voice rising a notch.

'Personally, no. I've had a look at the case file, of course, but even at a quick glance, it looks open-and-shut. Even better, it was one of Dr Ryder's cases as well, which helps enormously. Whether you like or appreciate the old vulture or not, Jennings, you have to admit that he's not the sort to let anything much slip past him.' He broke off and eyed his DI quickly. 'He *hasn't* mentioned anything to you about it, has he?' he added sharply.

In the past, and whenever he'd smelt a rat, the curmudgeon of a coroner had been known to stick his nose into the odd closed police case or two, and (much to everyone's annoyance) been proved right.

But already Jennings was shaking his head, his relief clear on his face. 'Not heard a squeak from him, sir,' he said, with heartfelt satisfaction. 'So I think we can take it that this is just a bit of muck-raking and tub-thumping on the part of this Gillingham chap?'

The Superintendent smiled grimly. 'No use trying to wriggle out of it, Jennings,' he advised him sardonically. 'I'm afraid the powers that be are fuming over the suggestion that we've been asked to sweep it under the carpet, as it were. I've been ordered to give the case another look over – officially, and obviously, as it were. Not that it will come to anything, you understand. It'll turn out to be a complete waste of time, you mark my words. But with public scrutiny now on us, we have to be seen to be taking a proper interest.'

Jennings knew what was coming next and sighed. 'You want this station to check into it, sir? Strictly speaking, shouldn't that be Headington's job?' he asked hopefully.

Maltings grinned. 'Another good try, Jennings, and *my* first thought too,' he admitted, unabashed. 'But the powers that be want an "independent" eye cast on it, and since it was Headington Station's baby to begin with, and they conducted the initial investigation, it falls to us to pick up the baton where they left off. The high-ups don't want this rag –' he nudged the paper again disdainfully '– to have any excuses for slinging more mud our way.'

But Jennings wasn't going to go down without a fight. 'We're hard pushed at the moment sir,' he complained. 'Sergeant O'Grady is hot on the post office robbery in St Ebbes, and my other officers are still investigating Roddy Blackwood and that business over Littlemore way. We're sure he's using his fleet of lorries to—'

The Superintendent held up his hand in a pacifying gesture. 'Good grief, man, you don't have to put any of your *best* people on it,' Maltings said, a shade wearily now. 'Surely you have some dozy spare constable or other that you can hand it over to? He doesn't need to be all that experienced. He just needs to be seen

24

asking questions and doing something to reassure the public that we're doing our job properly. And it needn't be for long either – a few days, a week at the most. Just until the paper loses interest and goes on to the next big story. You must have someone who fits the bill?'

At that, DI Jennings began to smile. It was such a happy smile that, for a moment, Superintendent Maltings couldn't help but smile himself.

'Well, there's always WPC Loveday, sir,' Jennings said blandly.

'WPC … Oh, the girl who … Ah. Yes, I know the one you mean,' the Superintendent said thoughtfully. 'Hasn't she just finished her probationary period as well?'

'Yes sir,' Jennings confirmed, a shade morosely. In truth, he'd been hoping that WPC Trudy Loveday might have left the police force before completing her two-year probationary period. But now he was slowly becoming resigned to the fact that they were stuck with her.

'Actually, you know, she might just be the ideal choice, Jennings' Maltings said, suddenly warming to the idea. 'After all, she had all that good publicity not so long ago concerning that case with the Earl's son, so handling the press should be right up her street. What's more, the reading public already know her name. And the bloody papers can't say we aren't taking them seriously if we assign the case to her. Even though we aren't – taking them seriously, I mean!' he laughed.

Jennings could see his superior's point. A little while ago, his WPC, with the help of Dr Ryder, had helped solved a murder and in the process, Trudy Loveday had prevented an attack on a Lord of the Realm. His grateful father, the Earl, had then insisted on holding a dinner in her honour and presenting her with a letter of thanks. The papers (including the *Tribune*) had covered it closely and had helped make the WPC a bit of a local heroine, praising both her bravery and professionalism. So they could hardly cry 'foul' now if she was given the Hughes case.

'I'll call her in now, sir, and give her the good news,' Jennings said, with a brief grin that was as much grimace as smile.

'Well, I'll let you get on with it then,' Maltings said, rising quickly to his feet and mentally washing his hands of the matter.

'Sir,' Jennings said dryly.

Chapter 4

Two hours later, Trudy Loveday collected her police-issue bicycle from the shed and trundled it reluctantly out onto the street.

At five feet ten, she was a slim girl, with masses of long dark brown curly hair that she kept tightly restrained in a bun and mostly hidden under her police cap. Having finally reached the age of twenty, she was glad to leave her teenage years behind her, but as she mounted her bicycle, checked behind her for traffic and started to pedal energetically towards Carfax, she felt considerably older than a mere score years.

Her last big case, when, with the help of Dr Clement Ryder, she had tracked down the killer of a young boy, had definitely left its scars on her – mostly mental ones, it had to be said. But she was well aware of all of them as she turned left at the famous clock tower and headed down St Aldates, past the beauty of Christ Church college and its cathedral, and towards St Ebbes and Floyds Row, where the coroner's offices and the morgue were situated.

It had been some months since she'd last seen Dr Ryder, and she was not sure how she felt about seeing him now. Such ambivalence almost shocked her.

When she'd first met Dr Ryder, he'd been unhappy about an old case and had relentlessly harassed her senior officers into letting him investigate it, with the aid of a police officer to make it official. And she had no illusions as to why her DI, Harry Jennings, had chosen her for the task.

She'd been just eighteen then, on probation, and considered pretty much a nuisance by all her male colleagues. Reduced to filing, making the tea and walking her beat, she'd been little more than a glorified clerk. So she'd jumped at the chance to do an actual investigation – even if everyone thought the coroner was on a wild goose chase.

But the old vulture was too wise and wily to indulge in such a foolish pastime, and by the end of the case, they had laid a murderer by the heels. It had been a heady, exciting time, and she had felt vindicated and full of enthusiasm for her choice of career.

A second case, again with Dr Ryder, had also ended with success. As had a third, although that had not ended as she'd expected.

And then had come the incident last Easter – and the death of a young boy. Although she and the coroner had again succeeded in solving the crime, both of them had nearly died. And Trudy, for one, was still feeling the fallout from such a near miss.

Ever since, she'd been worried that she might have lost her nerve, but as every day passed with her fulfilling her usual duties without incident, she'd felt her confidence returning. But now her doubts came flooding back. It annoyed her – and scared her.

As she nimbly dodged around a red bus with the familiar pale lime-green stripe down its sides, she was pleased to note that it wasn't her father driving. Frank Loveday's route covered the Cowley area as a rule. No doubt, though, if he *had* been behind the wheel, he'd have given her a good talking to when she got home about the somewhat cavalier way that she'd been cycling. And no excuse that she'd had her mind on other things would have been accepted!

She sighed, stuck out her hand to indicate right and dodged

inside some black wrought iron gates and into the cobbled court-yard of Floyd's Row. Like a lot of the city, it had probably been there, in some form or other, since medieval times. She dismounted and carefully propped her bicycle against one of the red-bricked walls that composed most of the single-storey complex before slowly trudging across to the offices.

It felt odd to be coming here solely to pick the coroner's brains as a potential witness, and as she forlornly made her way to his office, she actually found herself wishing that it had been another coroner who had handled the Hughes case. The echoes of their last case together still weighed heavily upon her, and she felt a creeping sense of shame wash over her at her reluctance to meet Dr Ryder again.

The coroner's secretary looked surprised to see her, as well she might. There wasn't much of Dr Ryder's official business that she didn't know about, and since she wasn't aware of any case he was working on that needed Trudy's input, she looked a little put out to find herself in the dark.

'Hello WPC Loveday,' she said crisply. 'Is the doctor expecting you?'

'No, sorry. I don't have an appointment,' Trudy admitted, making the older woman look a shade happier. 'I just called in on the off chance that I could see him. It's police business,' she added, a shade unnecessarily. Although she regarded Clement Ryder as a mentor and, to some extent, a friend, she was well aware that they weren't exactly social with each other, and she felt compelled to make it clear to the man's secretary that she knew her place.

'Of course. I'll just check to see if he can spare you a few minutes,' the secretary smiled gracefully.

Trudy nodded, and began to pace up and down. This was going to be the first time that she and the coroner had got together since Easter, and she couldn't help but think that nothing good could come of it, whilst a more robust part of her was telling herself off for being so lame.

'Dr Ryder can give you ten minutes, Constable,' the secretary said, holding the door open with a friendly smile. Her eyes, however, narrowed slightly as she took in the young girl's pallor and the tight look around her mouth, and as Trudy passed her, the older woman shot her a sharp, speculative glance.

Trudy, unaware of the scrutiny, forced a smile to her face as she entered the familiar office. 'Dr Ryder. Thank you for seeing me,' she began formally.

Perhaps her tone had been a bit too official. Or perhaps her tension was palpable, for she saw the happy smile of greeting that had been about to rise to his face freeze and then retreat.

'Trudy, how lovely to see you again,' he said cautiously. 'Please, sit down.'

Trudy took a deep breath and pulled out a chair. She reached into her satchel and rummaged through her accoutrements for her notebook and pencil.

'Thank you, Dr Ryder. I'm here about the Thomas Hughes case.'

Chapter 5

Clement leaned back in his chair with a slow frown. He was dressed in a dark grey suit with a discreet navy stripe, and a navy and red tie. His head of thick, white-and-grey hair gleamed in the grey November light coming through the curtains. In the fireplace, a large coal fire glowed invitingly. 'Would you like a cup of tea?' he asked.

Trudy shook her head. 'No, thank you. This shouldn't take long,' she said with another forced smile. 'DI Jennings has been asked by our superintendent to cast a second, more detailed look over the death of Mr Thomas Hughes. It was your case, I believe?'

Clement smiled briefly. He felt a little hurt by her rather chilly, brusque manner, but he was wise enough not to let it show. Clearly something was bothering his young protégé and until he learned what it was, he was prepared to tread carefully.

In an effort to lighten the mood, he decided a compliment probably couldn't hurt anything. 'Don't say Jennings has finally seen the light and begun to give you more responsibility? That's wonderful, Trudy.'

Trudy forced yet another smile. 'Thank you.' She wished the coroner wasn't being so friendly and informal. She wanted to get this bit over and done with and leave as quickly as possible.

'Did anything strike you as odd about the case, Dr Ryder?' she asked, finally looking up from notebook and for the first time, properly meeting his eye. She felt herself flush as she recognised both concern and bafflement in his look.

It was obvious that he was picking up on her reticence and she quickly looked away again, quashing a feeling of irritation. It wasn't as if she'd asked to be put in this position!

'No, I can't say as it did. Not at the time,' he added, making her blink.

'That sounds as if you've had second thoughts, sir. Any particular reason?' she asked eagerly, pencil poised.

Clement shrugged. 'I read the papers, along with most of the city. I have to say, the *Tribune*'s contribution did take me by surprise a bit. It almost felt as if the writer had been taking things a bit too personally. But you know the old saying – where there's smoke there's fire. So I *did* just wonder if something more might be afoot. I take it the headlines in the *Tribune* are what lit the fire under the powers that be over at your station?'

Trudy opened her mouth to deny it, then realised there was very little point.

'When certain … accusations are made, they have to be investigated as you know.'

'Quite right too – and by us, no less. Well, it's about time we had another case, isn't it?' He leaned forward to pick up his telephone and Trudy watched in horror as he rang through to his secretary. 'Ah, yes, Jean. I'm afraid I'm not going to be in the office quite as often as I thought this week, so you can please cancel any non-urgent appointments and re-arrange my schedule to leave me, say, three hours free every day until further notice.'

He hung up and beamed at Trudy, who continued to gape at him, appalled.

'Is something wrong, Constable Loveday?' Clement asked mildly, deciding abruptly to take the bull by the horns.

She gulped, knowing that she was going to have to tell him

that she would be working this one alone and didn't need his input. Why oh why, she wondered desperately, had he assumed that she'd come to him to ask for his help?

She saw him lean back with a happy and content smile on his face, and felt her heart fall even further. She sat up a little straighter, searching to find the right words that would let him down without hurting his feelings.

Clement, aware of the lengthening silence and something of the mental battle that was obviously waging behind her face, watched her with unfathomable, grey eyes. 'Is there a problem?' he asked mildly.

Trudy nodded, relieved to have such a perfect opening to set things straight dropped right into her lap. But even as she opened her mouth to tell him that he wasn't needed, she felt the words dry up.

Apart from anything else, she suddenly realised that it wasn't actually true. She knew (none better) how intelligent this man was. How experienced, and how thorough – and just how much of an asset he'd be. For another thing, nobody knew the case better than this man, who'd have any relevant details already at his fingertips.

So why was she so determined not to work this case with him? It didn't make sense … until suddenly, in a blinding flash of awful self-awareness, it did, and she knew just why she was feeling as jittery as she was.

Since Easter, she'd been doing her job and slowly dealing with her inner demons. She'd found the courage to walk her beat alone again, and stalk purse-snatchers, and question witnesses, and do all the daily routine things that she'd once feared might be beyond her. After each of the little milestones that she set for herself had been successfully reached and passed, she'd come to believe that the crisis was over. Her self-belief and self-confidence had been restored, and everything was all right again.

But now, as she sat here in this room, she had to acknowledge that only half the battle had been won. For completing her regular police duties was only a part of her professional life and career. Her cases with Dr Clement Ryder were something entirely different.

On their last case, she'd nearly lost her life. And until she worked with him again on another case, she could never be truly sure that she had – once and for all – conquered all her demons. What's more, the time had now come when she had to do just that. No wonder she felt as if she was all over the place!

She felt her heart thumping in her chest and swallowed hard. She took a deep breath and said – not quite truthfully – 'Of course there's not a problem. Everything's fine, Dr Ryder. And thank you for agreeing to help me.'

In his chair, Clement felt his shoulders suddenly relax. For a second there, he'd wondered if she was actually going to reject his offer of help. Not that it took a genius to figure out why she might have felt reluctant to take on another case with him. The attack they'd both suffered during their last case had shaken even him, and he had served in the war!

He'd wanted, many times over the past months, to call on her and see how she was doing, but instinct – and experience – told him that it might not be a good idea. Sometimes, life's hardest lessons had to be learned alone – or they were never learned at all.

But he'd always known that Trudy was a woman of rare courage as well as brains and ambition, and he'd had faith in her – faith that was now being justified.

But even as he picked up the telephone again to ask his secretary to bring him the Hughes file, something else began to worry him.

What if something *else* was making WPC Trudy Loveday question whether or not she wanted to work with him again? Was it possible that she had, in fact, guessed that he had a serious illness?

Once or twice in the past he'd wondered if she had noticed

some of the physical symptoms of a person with Parkinson's disease. Although he was still in the early stages, he sometimes stumbled, and from time to time his hands trembled uncontrollably.

And Trudy was a trained observer.

On more than one occasion in the past, Clement had wondered if she was going to ask him outright about the state of his health. He'd been prepared to lie to her face and tell her that he was fine.

In the end though, she hadn't asked. Perhaps it was out of respect for him, or perhaps she simply hadn't been confident enough of the accuracy of her observations. But did she still secretly wonder about him? Did she wonder or fear that he wasn't up to another case?

The thought made him go cold.

Because if that was so, he'd have to make sure that he gave her no cause to regret bringing him in on this latest investigation.

Trudy, blissfully unaware of her mentor's state of mind, looked up with a resigned sigh as his secretary deposited the Hughes file on his desk.

All right, so she was feeling a certain amount of trepidation about working with the coroner again. But really, she was just being silly. It was not as if there was any rational cause for it. She'd done some research before leaving the station, and she knew that the likelihood of anything truly sinister having happened in the Hughes's family back garden last Bonfire Night had to be virtually nil. It had been a tragic and awful event, yes, but nothing about it suggested that a crime had been committed.

Just because, so far, each time she and Dr Ryder had joined forces it had turned out to be a case of murder, it didn't mean that it would always be so. Especially on such a flimsy case as this! As Dr Ryder himself had just pointed out, her superior officers only wanted the case looked into at all because some silly man writing for the papers had been doing some muck-raking.

No, surely they'd just do a quick but thorough investigation, she'd write up her report for DI Jennings and that would be it. It would probably take only a few days at most and turn out to be downright boring!

Duncan Gillingham read his article again and smiled grimly. Although it was nice to see his byline in print, and to know he'd made a bit of a splash and put the cat amongst the pigeons, for once it wasn't the appeasement of his vanity that was giving him cause for satisfaction.

He'd just got off the phone with a somewhat disgruntled Superintendent Maltings, who'd been forced to confirm that the police were indeed taking a deeper look into the Hughes affair.

Which was just what he'd wanted and schemed for all along. Because, although they didn't know it yet, he had one distinct advantage over the police, when it came to the Thomas Hughes affair.

He already knew that there was a killer amongst the Hughes family circle.

And he was determined to see that someone suffer …

With that in mind, he began to write the leader for tomorrow's article, confirming that the police had come around to the *Tribune*'s way of thinking at last and had re-opened the case. The newspaper (and its readers) now awaited their results with bated breath, and were sure that the constabulary – now that they were actually investigating the affair properly – would soon get to the real truth behind Thomas Hughes's death.

The reporter smiled over his trusty black and gold Remington typewriter.

No doubt, when a certain person read of *that* particular development over their morning cup of tea, it would ruin their appetite for breakfast.

And nor would it end there. For the *Tribune*'s bloodhound of a reporter would, naturally, be out and about, asking questions of his own. And the results of his endeavours would be splashed across the front pages of the newspaper for some time to come!

As he re-read his text, Duncan Gillingham smiled wolfishly.

Sooner or later, a nasty little worm that thought it was safely wriggling around unseen and safe in the camouflaging dirt would be dragged out into the cold hard light of day and the full glare of publicity.

And if, in the process, he made a name for himself and forced Sir Basil to at last acknowledge that his soon-to-be son-in-law did actually know his trade, well then, that was just an added bonus, wasn't it?

Chapter 6

'So who do you want to talk to first?' Trudy asked curiously. She'd been in the office for nearly an hour and after reading the case file thoroughly, had found one or two points she wanted cleared up. Which, needless to say, Clement Ryder had been able to accomplish with ease.

She was, in fact, feeling much happier now. In spite of her earlier doubts about meeting up with him again, they had quickly fallen back into their old pattern of working; they had been busily discussing and tossing around the facts and coming up with some items of interest. She had to admit, it did feel good to be slowly getting back to their old, comfortable and familiar ways.

And already their collaboration was giving her some leads to follow.

Both of them, for instance, agreed that it was perhaps a little odd that no member of the dead man's family seemed to have noticed exactly when or how the shed had caught fire.

True, it was dark, and most of the women at least had probably been paying more attention to the children. Even so, it seemed strange, and they would need to talk to everyone there that night – including the children.

It was also of significant interest that the dead man seemed to have a somewhat ambiguous reputation when it came to his business dealings. Although Trudy had pointed out that she couldn't see how that might be relevant. After all, it seemed highly unlikely that any disgruntled shareholder in one of the victim's defunct business enterprises could have sneaked into the family back garden that night and set light to the shed without one of the Hughes family spotting him or her. Even though it had been dark, the bonfire had been lit and surely a stranger would have been quickly spotted?

So it seemed certain that the answer to the conundrum – if indeed there was any conundrum about the man's death in the first place – had to lie within the dead man's family.

Hence Trudy's leading question.

'Well, there's little point in starting with the two family members who gave evidence at the inquest,' Clement mused. 'Not when we can get a fresh perspective from some of the others. If need be, we can always come back to the Wilcoxes later. So, it has to be one of the other Hughes offspring. Do you have any preference?'

Trudy shrugged. 'Why not start with the youngest daughter, Caroline Benham? It's often the youngest girl and baby of the family who's closest to their father, isn't it?'

Clement, who had two children, one boy and one girl who had both long since left the nest, smiled. 'So they say. All right, Caroline it is. I take it you've done some preliminary research on the family already?'

Trudy admitted that she had. They walked outside to his car, and as he drove northwards up the Banbury Road, heading towards the village of Kidlington where Caroline lived and worked, Trudy filled him in on what she'd learned so far.

'Caroline's twenty-one, and recently divorced,' she began, glancing at her notebook, just to refresh her memory.

Clement, steering his 'Auntie' Rover around a rather haphazard cyclist, grunted slightly. He didn't altogether approve of divorce, or the increasing ease with which people could get one, regarding its growing prevalence as a disease of modern society. His generation were the kind that stuck together through thick and thin. Although his own wife had been dead for some years, he had no doubt that they'd still be together, had she still been alive. 'She can't have been married long,' he pointed out a shade testily.

Trudy frowned. 'No. And she married young,' she added, checking the dates in her notebook. 'She was only just eighteen. So they were together for only three years or so.'

Clement sighed. 'Perhaps that was the problem. You can be too young to be married.'

Trudy, who at twenty, hadn't even given marriage a serious thought yet, shrugged. 'She works in a solicitor's office, as a secretary. I think she and her ex-husband must have either sold or vacated the family home, because she's listed as sharing a flat with another woman. I suppose it helps her to be able to split the rent.'

Trudy glanced at her watch thoughtfully. 'At this time of day, she's more likely to be at work than at her flat, isn't she?'

Clement nodded assent, and some fifteen minutes later, he found a parking space at the back of the library, opposite a two-storey building of yellowish brick, where the firm of Brearley, Pierce, Pike and Brearley were located.

But before they got out of the car, Clement said, 'So, how much of the bile and innuendo in the newspaper article is true do you think?'

'Well, the bit about Thomas Hughes's chequered financial history is certainly true,' Trudy said, gazing out of the window at the sodden autumn leaves piled at the roadside. 'It was one of the things that struck me the most about the article. Since it was one of the most easily confirmed or denied aspects of the accusations, I spent some time in the files.'

'Oh? So our captain of industry wasn't all he was cracked up to be?' Clement mused.

'Well, yes he was. But no, he wasn't.'

'Well, that's as clear as mud!' Clement said. He was feeling relieved that whatever doubts his friend had obviously had, they were now quickly settling down into a familiar routine. The atmosphere between them was getting lighter and friendlier by the minute.

'Sorry,' Trudy said. 'Mr Hughes made a lot of money, all right, and was very successful for most of his life, with his own companies. But when he hit sixty, he sold off most of his assets – the mainstay of his fortune – and semi-retired, I suppose you might say. He set up various small ventures, some of which worked and made the investors a lot of money – and one or two that didn't, and lost them a lot of money. But the thing is, he never invested any of his own money very heavily in the more, shall we say, speculative ventures?'

'Hmm. Well, it's something to bear in mind, I suppose,' he said, as they finally made their way towards the solicitor's offices.

The receptionist looked surprised to see a police officer come through the door, and Clement surmised that the firm was one of those that restricted themselves to wills, divorces and other non-criminal specialities.

'Hello, I was wondering if I could have a word with Mrs Benham?' Trudy said with a smile. 'It's nothing to be alarmed about – strictly routine.'

'Oh – is it about her poor father?' The receptionist, a motherly-looking woman in her early fifties, stood up and looked from Clement to Trudy uncertainly. 'It was such a shock when we heard about it. But Caro … Mrs Benham insisted on coming back to work right away. I'll just go and tell her you're here. She's taking dictation from Mr Pike at the moment, but I'm sure he won't mind.'

They waited in the reception room as the older woman disappeared into the back of the building. On the windowsill, a Parma violet flowered with the gusto of a pot-plant that had been well looked after. Wooden filing cabinets lined the cream-painted walls, and one or two hunting prints attempted to give the anteroom a less business-like air.

Outside, Trudy could hear the sing-song voices of some children playing with a skipping rope. *'See saw, Margery Daw, Johnny shall have a new maaaaa-ster, He shall earn but a penny a day, because he can't go any faaaa-ster.'*

She smiled, remembering the song from her own childhood.

There was a stir in the inner doorway and the receptionist and another woman appeared, quickly chasing away Trudy's moment of nostalgia.

The dead man's youngest daughter was a rather plain woman, about five feet nine inches tall, with thick but not very well-cut brown hair. Her large hazel eyes were probably her prettiest feature, but right now they were regarding Trudy and Clement warily.

'Yes, I'm Mrs Benham. Celia tells me you're here about my father?' Her voice sounded doubtful, as if she was half-convinced they were lying to her.

Trudy held out her police identification card, which the other woman took and read doubtfully. 'Is there someplace we could talk privately for a few minutes, Mrs Benham?' she asked gently. 'We just need to ask you a few questions about the night your father … About Bonfire Night.'

Caroline Benham sighed heavily. 'I suppose it must be about this ridiculous newspaper article? It's all so much nonsense … Mind you, I'm not really surprised …' She caught the receptionist's fascinated eyes upon them and drew back her bony shoulders. 'Oh well, we'd better go into the conference room, I suppose – there's nobody booked in there today. Please, step this way.'

She led them abruptly through the inner door, down a gloomy corridor, then stopped about halfway down, thrusting open a door almost as if at random. 'Not exactly as grand as it sounds, is it?' she asked wryly, stepping aside to let them enter. The room, indeed, was unexpectedly small, with an inadequate little square window that let in a meagre amount of daylight. It contained little more than a round table and four hard-back wooden chairs. 'Please, sit down.'

Trudy and Clement did so, and Caroline Benham pulled out a chair opposite them. 'So, how can I help you?' she asked flatly, folding her hands neatly in her lap in a gesture that was obviously habitual. She sounded neither helpful nor obstructive, and Trudy wondered if her show of calculated indifference was a result of mourning. She'd been a police officer for long enough now to know that grief and shock could have many different effects on people.

'You seemed to be about to say something about the *Tribune*'s article just now, Mrs Benham – something to the effect that you weren't particularly surprised by it?' Trudy nudged her gently.

'What? Oh, that. Well, no I don't suppose I was, really,' Caroline agreed with a frown. It had the unhappy effect of pulling her rather prominent eyebrows into a deep V-shape on her forehead, giving her an oddly simian appearance.

Trudy shifted on her seat. 'I find that rather odd, Mrs Benham. Doesn't it make you angry – that the newspapers have been spreading innuendoes about your father's character I mean?'

Caroline gave a grim smile. 'Hardly. If anything, I'm used to it.'

This time it was Clement who stirred slightly on his chair, making Trudy wonder if he wasn't feeling as puzzled as she. She had come to this interview expecting to have to tread gently, maybe even provide a shoulder for the grieving woman to cry on. Instead, she was left feeling as if she was swimming in totally uncharted waters.

'Used to it?' Trudy repeated, letting one eyebrow rise in query.

Caroline sighed heavily. 'What the article said was mostly true, you know,' she said flatly. 'Father was a heartless, ruthless man, and no doubt he cost many people their life savings. Not that

43

that would have worried him much! The man had no heart, you see. No soul. No conscience. So I'm not surprised his chickens came home to roost.'

'Oh,' Trudy said, somewhat at a loss. For some reason, she simply hadn't expected such candour on the part of the victim's daughter. 'Er … forgive me for saying so, but you don't sound … well, very sympathetic towards your father.'

Caroline's square and slightly over-large chin thrust out pugnaciously. 'And why would I be?' she demanded belligerently.

Trudy blinked, trying not to feel shocked. 'You didn't love your father, Mrs Benham?' she mumbled, trying to keep her voice strictly neutral.

Caroline all but snorted. 'I most certainly did not! And I have no objection to making that very clear. In fact, I'd be surprised if anybody *did* love him. He was not at all a loveable man, Constable.'

'Because he was somewhat cavalier with other people's money?' Trudy asked, finding it hard to believe that that alone could be the source of this woman's venom. In her experience it took more than just money to make someone almost vibrate with malice, as this woman was all but doing.

'Oh, that.' Caroline again snorted. 'I couldn't really give a damn about that, if I'm honest. If people were stupid enough to be taken in by Father, then more fool them, I say.'

Trudy took a deep breath. 'So what did your father do to make you hate him so?' she asked.

If she expected her witness to finally back down a little and deny that she actually *hated* her own father, or offer up the excuse that she was fraught and her nerves were at breaking point, or some other such mitigating circumstance, then she was quickly disabused.

Instead, Caroline Benham looked at her with flat, hard eyes that seemed to mirror the dim light in the room. 'I hated him because he murdered my mother,' she said simply.

Chapter 7

Trudy realised her mouth had fallen open, and swiftly closed it. She shot a quick look at Clement, wondering if he wanted to take over, but was gratified to see that he was simply watching their witness with a thoughtful gaze.

If this had been their first case, he might have indicated at this point that he felt that it would be better if he took over, especially if things were becoming crucial. Now though, he was clearly happy to leave it to her to handle things, and she couldn't help but feel a glow of pride that he so obviously trusted her not to mess things up.

'That's quite an accusation, Mrs Benham,' Trudy began cautiously. She didn't want to break the momentum of the interview by consulting her notebook for the facts and was sure enough of her memory to feel confident she didn't need to. 'As I understand it, your mother died in 1957, didn't she?' she asked quietly.

'Yes, that's right,' Caroline confirmed, her rather thin lips pressing into such a tight line that they almost disappeared altogether. 'I was just seventeen.'

Trudy swallowed hard, feeling for a moment that curious sensation of displacement that happened whenever you suddenly felt wrong-footed. 'That must have been awful for you,' she blurted out, and meant it. For a moment, Trudy couldn't help but wonder how she would have felt if her own mother had died three years ago, when *she'd* been just seventeen. She would have been heart-broken.

Suddenly she felt ashamed of herself for judging this woman, as she knew she had been. Although she'd tried to keep up a strictly professional demeanour, she'd been aware that she couldn't help but feel that Caroline Benham's reaction to her father's death had been deeply unnatural and somehow ... well ... just plain *wrong*.

Now she was finally beginning to wonder if there was far more to this than just a daughter's cold, hard-hearted nature.

'I'm so sorry,' she added softly. 'You loved your mother very much, didn't you?'

As if responding to the unexpected – but plainly sincere – sympathy in her voice, Caroline's hazel eyes began to shimmer with unshed tears.

'Yes,' she said, her voice slightly gruff as she glanced down into her clasped hands. 'Yes, I did. My mother was the only one who loved us. When she went ... I just ... well, I knew I couldn't stay living in my father's house for long. So I married Malcolm as soon as I was eighteen, and moved out. Not that *he* cared, naturally. He was glad to see me go.' Caroline sniffed.

'Your father was?' Trudy clarified. 'I find that hard to believe. He'd just lost his wife and—'

'Oh, he didn't just lose her,' Caroline snapped. 'I told you – he *killed* her. We all knew it, but I was the only one who was willing to stand up to him and let him see that I knew. And he didn't like that, oh no, not a bit he didn't,' she carried on, her voice tight and tense with remembered rage and grief. 'He liked people to kow-tow to him and treat him like he was the best thing since the invention of the wheel. Yes sir, no sir, three-bags-full-sir. So he didn't like having me around, knowing that I saw him for what he really was, reminding him always of what he'd done. So no, he was happy to see me go, believe me.'

She was almost panting now, leaning forward in her chair, her eyes a little wild, and Trudy was beginning to feel slightly alarmed. What if the youngest daughter of the dead man had some serious mental issues?

She cast another quick glance at the coroner. She knew he'd been a surgeon before changing his career, and as such, probably wouldn't have had much experience of patients with psychiatric problems; but he was still a *doctor*. And the last thing she wanted to do was cause some sort of mental breakdown in her witness due to her own lack of experience in how to question her properly.

Clement not only caught her worried, questioning glance, but quickly understood the reason for it. He leaned obligingly forward a little in his chair and took up the baton.

'Can you tell me how your mother died, Mrs Benham?' he asked quietly. 'I am a medical doctor, so you can confide in me with some confidence,' he promised, careful to keep his voice calm and matter-of-fact.

Caroline Benham looked at him intensely. 'You're a medical doctor? Then you'd know all about leukaemia? To be specific …' And here she said something totally incomprehensible that Trudy, attempting to surreptitiously take shorthand notes, had no chance of accurately reproducing. There were far too many complicated syllables, and the only word she'd understood was 'syndrome' at the end!

Clement Ryder, though, had no trouble understanding the mouthful that she came out with.

'That's an extremely rare form of blood cancer, Mrs Benham,' he said, looking at her with new eyes. 'Did your mother suffer from this condition?'

'So her doctors said,' Caroline said.

'But that's incurable, I'm afraid. And always fatal,' Clement said softly. 'If your mother died of this disease, then I'm afraid I don't understand how you can hold your father in any way responsible.'

'Oh, but he was,' their witness insisted stubbornly. 'Oh, not for her getting it, or anything like that,' Caroline said disdainfully and rather offhandedly, Trudy thought. 'But he refused to help her when a cure was offered to her.'

'A cure? I can assure you, there's no known cure for your mother's condition. Although they are making great strides in researching various types of leukaemia in the United States, I understand, and have been doing some very promising trials—'

'Exactly! Yes, that's what I'm talking about,' Caroline Benham said, almost leaning across the table now in her eagerness to press her cause. 'When the doctors here gave up hope for her, one of them did tell us about some experimental treatment programmes, one in Seattle and one in California, I think. He said that Mother was a perfect candidate for one of them, and he would recommend her to the doctors over there, if we wanted.'

'But—' Clement was again quickly over-ridden.

'Oh, I know, they didn't make any promises of a total cure or anything like that!' Caroline said, almost as if this vital fact was somehow irrelevant. 'But then, doctors never really commit to *anything*, do they? But the new drugs could have helped give her more time with us, and they certainly would have made her life easier. But would my father, the *miser*, the utter miserable hateful *skinflint*,' Caroline all but spat, 'consent to paying for her flight and clinic and medical fees and the expensive drugs?' She was almost shouting into Clement's face now, her hands clutching the edge of the table, taunt and white-knuckled with strain. 'Would he hell!'

She was glaring first at one, and then the other of them, with such a fixed, almost manic look of hate and despair on her face, that Trudy felt a cold trickle of unease creep up her spine. She knew she was seeing obsession now, stark and entrenched, in the other woman's ugly face, and wondered, for the first time, if it could have led Caroline to actually commit murder.

'His own wife, and he wouldn't lift a finger to help her. And it wasn't as if he couldn't *afford* it,' Caroline panted, slowly sinking back against her chair. 'He didn't even have that excuse! He just didn't want to spend it on a lost cause. A waste of time, he called it. Can you *imagine*?'

For a moment, the room became utterly still and quiet as the horror of the now quietly spoken words permeated both the air and the consciousness of the two listeners.

If all that was true, Trudy thought, appalled, then no, she couldn't really imagine it. The dead man must have been monstrous in his callousness.

But was it true? Their witness didn't seem to be the most unbiased or reliable of people.

Caroline took a deep, unsteady breath, and for the first time gave a slow, but unbearably bitter smile. 'Oh, I can imagine what you're thinking, both of you. That I'm mad and have a twisted mentality, or some sort of mania or something. But I can assure you, it's none of those things. And if you knew my father as I knew him – as we all knew him – you'd know I was telling you the truth. All his life, the only thing my father cared about was money and power and acting like a king with own private empire. My mother provided him with children, and that was all he needed, and when she became ill and useless to him, he wasn't willing to spend his resources on her. It was as simple as that.'

Caroline's smile slowly drained away. 'And so she died. And I left. And now he's dead at last.' Her strength seemed to go as she slumped back in the chair, leaving her voice dull and almost disinterested.

She looked up suddenly at the small inadequate window. 'And I'm not sorry at all,' she told the raindrops that had begun to trickle slowly down the glass.

'Is that why you killed him, Caroline?' Trudy dared to ask, her voice soft and sympathetic.

Caroline Benham laughed then. It was a shocking sound, since it seemed to contain genuine humour in it – ironic and twisted – but there, nonetheless.

'No, I didn't kill him,' she said, sounding ineffably weary now. 'I think Fate did. I believe in Fate, you see. I think it was watching him and waiting to strike, just as it watches all of us. And it finally decided that it was time for Thomas Hughes to pay for his sins. And so the sparks flew, and the shed burned, and the old devil with it.'

Caroline looked away from the window and her eyes, which had had a faraway look, suddenly seemed to focus again. In a shockingly abrupt return to normalcy, she straightened in the chair, placed her hands firmly on the table and stood up. 'I expect you're wondering why I went to any of the family get-togethers at all, feeling like I do.' Her lips twisted into a parody of a smile. 'It's quite simple really – you see, I could tell that it annoyed him whenever I showed my face. Also, I wouldn't give him the satisfaction of letting him think that he had driven me away from the rest of my family! So, if there's nothing further?' she asked coolly.

It was more of a statement or a challenge than an actual question, and Trudy found herself quietly agreeing that there was, indeed, nothing more for now. She was sure in her own mind that pressing their witness now would prove to be futile.

Without another word, Caroline got up and showed them out, passing the curious receptionist without a second look.

Once outside, Clement and Trudy stood under the shelter of the office block's rather inadequate porch and watched the rain.

'Phew,' Clement finally said.

Trudy grinned. She couldn't help it. 'That *was* a bit intense, wasn't it?'

'That's one word for it,' her friend agreed wryly.

'Do you think she's ... you know ... actually mad?'

Clement stirred and thought about it, then shrugged. 'Mental health isn't my area of expertise. But I don't *think* so. I think the loss of her mother was traumatic, and I think she's got a fixed idea that her father's to blame. But she seems rational enough, and she seems to have been able to lead a normal life, for all these past few years.'

Trudy nodded. 'So did you believe her? When she said she didn't kill her father?'

Clement took a long, slow breath. 'Well, if she did, why now? Why didn't she kill him at the time she lost her mother? She'd have been at her most unstable then. Why wait?'

Trudy nodded, but she had her doubts. In her opinion, that young woman was a bit of a powder keg who could explode at any moment. 'Well, if somebody *did* kill Mr Hughes, I think I'm putting Caroline at the top of the list.'

Clement didn't argue. 'It's going to be interesting to see what the rest of the Hughes family has to offer, isn't it?' he said mildly instead. Then he took a long, deep breath of the cold, moist air, put on his Trilby hat and shrugged off the drama of the last ten minutes or so. 'Well, I think I'll go back to the office and see if I can find out who treated Mrs Hughes for her condition. The least I can do is confirm whether or not Caroline's version of her mother's illness is actually true.'

'And I'll report back to DI Jennings and do some more research on the other members of the Hughes family,' Trudy said, a shade ruefully. 'If they're all going to be as interesting as the youngest daughter, I think we need to be better prepared with our facts.'

'Yes, I think you're right,' Clement mused. 'It might even be a good idea to just go back to the Wilcoxes again and get a more detailed view of things from their perspective. There's only so much you can ask someone in open court, after all.'

Trudy wished she'd attended the inquest, but there had been

no reason why she should have, at the time. Now she asked eagerly, 'Did you get the feeling they were holding something back?'

Clement shrugged. 'Not necessarily. But apart from anything else, we need to know how the rest of the dead man's family regarded him, and more specifically if they agree with their youngest sister about his culpability in the death of their mother. I get the feeling there's far more to the Hughes family that we need to learn, and Alice and her husband were the ones closest to him, in that they shared the same home.'

Clement dropped Trudy off near the police station and drove away, but as he did so, his foot began to tremble, making him fumble the clutch and grind the gears noisily. He quickly checked in his rear-view mirror, but Trudy didn't seem to be watching his car depart.

With a sigh of relief, he drove carefully back to his office without further incident. But he couldn't help but wonder. For how much longer would he be able to carry on driving safely?

And that reminded him – he'd promised to teach Trudy how to drive. He'd have to ask her if she'd got her learner's permit yet, and arrange a time to start giving her some lessons.

Whilst he still could.

Chapter 8

The next morning, Godfrey Hughes collected his milk and papers from the communal back door of the converted Edwardian house in Oxford where he maintained his small but comfortable flat. Once back upstairs, and over his usual cup of black coffee and round of toast, he turned reluctantly to the *Oxford Tribune*, and saw with horror that the family were again featured on the front page.

Quickly, and with a growing feeling of nausea, he read how the police had been forced to admit that they were now conducting a more thorough investigation into his father's death, and how they expected to see the results of this activity soon.

A perennial bachelor, Godfrey was tall, as his father had been, standing at nearly six feet, and was rather lean with it. He had a head of thick auburn hair and brown eyes, and was looking rather pale and out of sorts that morning.

With a 'tcha' of distress and dismay, he threw the paper down and checked his watch. As he'd expected, he still had plenty of time before he had to be at St Swithin's College, a non-affiliated college where he taught foreign students English language and culture.

He had planned a lecture that morning about the latest offering of so called 'art' from the world of English cinema, but could drum up little enthusiasm for it.

Instead, his mind went back to his father. Or, more precisely, to his father's last will and testament.

Oh, he knew what was in it. Or rather, he knew what his father had *said* was in it, but as all of Thomas's children knew to their cost, you could never actually trust what the old man said – not 100 per cent anyway. He'd often lie about things, if it were more convenient for him, or if he thought the results of a lie would prove entertaining.

So it was always just *possible* that his father might, in fact, have left his oldest son more than the modest pension that he had claimed had been set up to provide for him. But in his heart of hearts, Godfrey didn't think so.

After all, the old man had made no bones of how he felt about Godfrey's failure to marry and produce grandchildren. What's more, he'd always sneered over Godfrey's one true passion in life, laughing at him for spending nearly all his salary on his 'pathetic little hobby' as he'd termed it, and vowing that the 'Hughes's good money would never be allowed to be wasted on such piffle.' Hence the provision of a mere pension, instead of a lump sum.

Restlessly, Godfrey got up and walked to the window and looked unseeingly out at the city's roads and traffic.

He would like to have more money to spend – and he didn't see why he shouldn't have it. After all, he was the oldest, and traditionally, the older son was *supposed* to inherit, wasn't he?

Of course, Alice deserved her fair share too, he mused, not wanting to think of himself as being ungenerous. She'd been the one forced to live with the old man, being all but blackmailed into looking after him, with the promise of that nice big house in leafy Headington as the ultimate reward.

And Matt, with his three children, there was no doubt he could do with some more money too.

As for Caroline … Well, she'd really all but made sure that she would be written out of the will with her militant attitude and obvious contempt for her father; the old man really did so hate to be thwarted. My, but some of the arguments after Mother died had been really fierce and wonderful to watch, Godfrey mused, his lips twitching with a smile of remembrance. In a way, Godfrey rather admired his little sister for her gumption, even as he disdained her silliness.

Still, with her out of the picture, there was all the more money to go around for the rest of them – well, with any luck.

Godfrey sighed. He'd just have to wait and see what the old family legal eagle had to say for himself when the will was finally read.

But if he really only *did* come in for a modest pension … Well. Something would just have to be done about it, that was all. And Godfrey, who knew himself to be the cleverest of all Thomas Hughes's children, had a very shrewd idea of just what that something might be.

Chapter 9

Kenneth Wilcox worked in Cowley where he owned and ran a large electrical goods store, in a prime spot on a busy main road. Although nowhere near as wealthy as his now deceased father-in-law had been, he was obviously a successful businessman in his own right – but Clement couldn't help but wonder what the dead man had thought about his son-in-law's meagre empire.

He had a feeling that the dead man wouldn't have been that impressed – and had probably not kept his opinions a particular secret from his son-in-law.

On the way through the shop, Trudy paused to admire the new wireless sets and record players, and wondered if she could save up enough money to buy her own record player for her bedroom. The one in the living room tended to be commandeered by her parents, and although she didn't mind their music (a lot of Glen Miller and other war records) she didn't always want to listen to it. Right now, she rather liked Elvis Presley's latest number one hit – 'His Latest Flame'. If she had her own player, she could start collecting her own selection of 45's and 33's.

But once she'd paid for her driver's licence …

'Is there a problem, officer?'

Trudy jumped a little, flushing a little over being caught out daydreaming, and turned to face the salesman who had silently approached them. He was looking warily from her to her companion, and was clearly not quite sure how to treat them.

Clement smiled amiably. 'We were wondering if the owner was in. Mr Wilcox?'

'Oh yes.' The salesman's face cleared with relief. 'Right this way. I hope there's nothing amiss?' He was a tall, slightly worried-looking man in his early thirties. Neatly dressed in a suit and tie, he wore the tight look of someone who constantly feared trouble or disruption. 'They've had one or two break-ins near the motor works recently – mostly newsagents and off-licenses though. Young hooligans wanting cigarettes and booze, I think. Surely they're not targeting other retailers now?'

'Oh no sir, it's nothing like that. It's a private matter with Mr Wilcox,' Trudy said, before adding craftily, 'He's a good boss, I take it?'

'Oh yes. Very. He likes to keep a well-ordered shop,' he said with satisfaction.

'Worked for him long, sir?'

'Since I left school. My word, that must be more than twelve years now.' The shop assistant looked almost bewildered by this.

Trudy nodded. 'And the shop's doing well?'

'Oh yes. Nothing wrong here at Wilcox Electrical,' he said a shade stiffly now – as if she'd just offered some sort of personal insult in questioning the shop's profitability. 'The office is just through here.' So saying, he pushed open a door and led them through a short, narrow corridor to the end door in a series of three. This, he pushed open. Inside was a small anteroom lined with filing cabinets, with space for one small desk and a chair, which was currently unoccupied. 'Oh, it looks as if Mr Wilcox's secretary has just stepped out,' he said, as if such a thing might be a hanging offence.

He crossed the room to a plain wooden door sandwiched tightly between two filing cabinets and tapped on it. He then pushed it open without waiting for a response, and said around the opening, 'Mr Wilcox, a police lady and a gentleman to see you sir.'

He moved back and let them through, then shut the door quickly behind them, no doubt hastening to get back into the shop. Trudy had the feeling that he would be kicking himself for some time to come if he missed a customer or the chance to make a sale.

'Sorry about Albert,' Kenneth Wilcox said, rising from behind his desk. 'He can be a bit abrupt sometimes.' His eyes lingered on Trudy in her smart uniform, and then reluctantly turned to Clement.

He obviously recognised him from the inquest, for a slightly rueful look crossed his face. 'Please, have a seat.'

Trudy noticed that Kenneth Wilcox was looking at her legs as she sat down and crossed them neatly at the ankles. She didn't know whether to feel amused, flattered or annoyed.

He was a good enough looking man, she supposed, maybe fifty years old but looking handsome on it, and was built sturdily – due mainly to muscle rather than to fat. He had probably been a rugby player in his time and with his head of full sandy-coloured hair and bright blue eyes, she could well imagine that most women would find him attractive. From the way his eyes had run over her figure the instant she'd stepped into the room, he clearly found the opposite sex equally as appealing.

She wondered what Alice Wilcox thought about that. She coughed slightly, and had the satisfaction of watching him start a little in his chair, and quickly transfer his gaze from her legs and back to the coroner.

'I take it this is still about my father-in-law?' Kenneth opened the proceedings flatly.

It was, Trudy thought, rather an odd way to put things. It sounded to her almost as if he blamed the dead man for making so much trouble for everyone.

'I've just been reading this piffle in the papers,' he carried on coldly. 'I must say, I think the *Tribune* has gone downmarket in the last few years. Too ready to pander to people's baser instincts, rather than report the actual news, if you ask me.'

'Yes sir,' Trudy said, but not necessarily in agreement. Her dad had always read the *Tribune*. 'And you're quite right, we *have* been tasked with taking a second look into the circumstances of your father-in-law's death. When questions are raised, no matter how, er, nebulous, shall we say, the police are obliged to take an interest. But I'm sure we'll soon have the matter cleared up,' she added with a bright smile.

Her tactics worked, for she sensed the other man relax slightly as he responded both to her smile and to her unspoken promise that they were somehow in this thing together, and that nobody was taking it seriously. People often opened up, Trudy had discovered, when they thought you were on their side.

'Yes, well, I suppose that's only right,' Kenneth conceded with a sigh. 'Not that we, his family, really need this complication, mind you! It was awful enough as it was, without … Well. What exactly can I do for you?'

He looked at Trudy as he spoke, and Clement, well aware that she now had him eating her out of her hand, was happy to take a back seat and simply sit and watch.

'Well sir, let's take these newspaper allegations in order, shall we?' she said, deliberately letting her voice sound weary. As if to say, she knew it was all so much pie-in-the-sky, but she had to be seen to be doing her duty. 'I have to say, I've investigated the business affairs of your late father-in-law and I can't see anything that suggests that something actually criminal may have occurred.'

'I should think not,' Kenneth said shortly.

'Although, I thought I did detect a certain … wariness, shall we say, on the part of Mr Hughes to risk his own money in one or two of his more speculative ventures. But then I daresay that was just sound business sense on his part.' Trudy was careful to keep her voice admiring rather than accusatory, but she wanted to present Kenneth with the opportunity to speak ill of the dead man if he so wished.

'Yes. Well.' Kenneth shifted a little uneasily on his seat. 'Between you and me, the old man could be a bit on the fly side. Oh, I'm not saying he did anything illegal, obviously, but he dedicated his whole life to making money. And he didn't much care how he did it. Er, not that I would say as much in front of my wife, you understand?'

'Naturally not, sir. I'm sure your wife was very fond of her father.'

'Oh yes. Yes, she was,' Kenneth Wilcox said, rather too firmly for Trudy's liking. In her experience, when people said something too vehemently, it usually meant that they weren't too sure of things themselves.

She made a mental note, when they spoke to Alice, to try and draw her out on her true feelings for the dead man.

'So, perhaps the *Tribune* might just have a little something after all,' Trudy continued, 'when they suggest that many people might have had a bone to pick with Mr Hughes? If they invested in some of his latter schemes, and lost their savings, perhaps?'

Kenneth sighed and shrugged. 'Perhaps so. I never really took much notice of his dealings after he sold up his companies and semi-retired.'

'Did *you* invest in any of these later enterprises sir?' she asked guilelessly.

'That I did not,' Kenneth snorted quickly. 'No matter how much he—' He broke off, as if suddenly aware that he was not being very discreet. But Trudy was looking closely at him and she saw him squirm a little under her acute gaze. 'The thing is, I recently came into a small inheritance, and I'm planning on opening another shop in Cornmarket Street with it.' He paused after his mention of Oxford's main shopping street. 'And Thomas … my father-in-law had been trying to get me to hand it over

60

to him. He wanted it as start-up capital for some mad scheme or other. In the end, I had to be quite firm with him.'

'Oh dear. That must have caused certain amount of tension,' Trudy commiserated. 'Especially since you and your wife actually lived in the same house as the man. That must have made it somewhat awkward. Was he very angry with you about it?'

Kenneth blinked, and, watching him, Clement could almost see the exact moment that the man began to finally understand that he was actually being interrogated by the police – and very successfully at that.

Wilcox swallowed hard and sat a little straighter in his chair. 'Well, naturally, it wasn't an ideal situation. But you mustn't get a false impression of our family, er …'

'Constable Loveday, sir,' Trudy said, suddenly realising that she'd failed to identify herself properly earlier.

'Oh, yes, Constable, er, Loveday,' Kenneth said, somehow having difficulty getting out her last, rather distinctive and unusual name. In his seat, Clement (who hadn't failed to notice the man's wandering eye) had to hide the smile that wanted to cross his face.

'You were saying something about your family, sir,' she prompted him helpfully.

'What? Oh, yes. Well, it's no use denying that Thomas could be a hard man to get along with sometimes. But I can assure you, we were all used to his little ways.'

'Yes sir, I'm sure you were,' Trudy said stolidly. For the first time, she allowed her disbelief to show. 'But it's true to say that, at the time of his death, you and Mr Hughes were not on the best of terms?'

Unexpectedly cornered, Kenneth flushed rather painfully. 'Now look here, I hope you're not suggesting that … well, that I had anything to do with that blasted fire?'

'Of course not, sir,' Trudy said neutrally.

'Good. Because let me tell you, I didn't,' Kenneth said, with

61

some heat. 'It had to have been a freak accident, that was all. I didn't even know he was in the shed until we all realised that he was nowhere to be seen around the bonfire. It was dark in the far corners of the garden, and there were so many of us milling about, it was all but impossible to keep track of the comings and goings of any one specific person. The kids were running riot and making a lot of noise! And besides,' he added, a look of crafty relief crossing his face as an idea suddenly occurred to him, 'I wasn't the only one on the outs with the old man at the time. If you really want to talk to someone who had reason to be angry with him, you should go and talk to Mary.'

Trudy blinked, feeling totally wrong-footed. She thought she knew most of the people in the Hughes case, but as good as her memory was, she couldn't think who he meant.

She cast a quick, desperate look at Clement, who said affably, 'Who would that be, Mr Wilcox?' helping her out.

'Mary Everly – Hughes, that was. Thomas's sister,' Kenneth explained impatiently. 'She was there that night too, you know. Alice invited her, I think, since her father "forgot" to do it.' He said the word 'forgot' with heavy emphasis.

'Did your wife's aunt usually attend the family's bonfire night celebrations, sir?' Trudy asked, relieved to be back on track.

'Oh yes. As kids who'd grown up together, Thomas and Mary would have attended the bonfire parties given by their parents, you see, and Thomas was a stickler for keeping up the old traditions. Oh, there might have been a few gaps – during the war and what have you – when the annual party wasn't held, but as a general rule everyone was invited. And this included Mary too, if she wasn't abroad.'

Kenneth paused for breath, but swept on quickly. 'Except, this time, a few weeks ago, I happened to overhear them having a right old ding-dong, and I remember Alice saying something about having to ring up her aunt at the last minute, because she thought her father had forgotten to invite her. You ask me, the old man was still mad at her, and didn't care whether she showed up or not.'

'It sounds as if the argument must have been a serious one sir, if her brother was still being so cold towards her,' Trudy pushed. 'Do you know what it was about, exactly?'

But here Kenneth had to shrug and admit ignorance. 'No, not really. As I said, I just happened to overhear them arguing, that was all. It was at the house, when Mary had come for tea one afternoon. Alice was in the kitchen, and I was just walking past the open door. I heard Thomas shouting. Well, not shouting perhaps,' he modified reluctantly, 'but he *did* have a very loud voice when he was upset.'

He looked, for a moment, rather grim, and Trudy couldn't help but wonder how often this man had felt the lash of his father-in-law's tongue himself.

'But you may have heard *something* significant, sir?' Trudy pressed him.

Kenneth sighed. 'I got the general sense that Thomas was threatening her, or threatening to do something that she wouldn't like. I distinctly heard him say that he was "going to put a stop to it" and that he wasn't happy about what she was set on doing. He went on to call her an old fool who should know better. Which, as you can imagine, didn't go down any too well with the old girl.'

'Nothing more, sir?' Trudy asked hopefully, but her witness gave her a rather shame-faced look.

'Sorry, no. Thomas noticed that the door was open and he walked over and slammed it shut. Naturally, I carried on walking and went to join my wife in the kitchen.'

'Yes, naturally,' Trudy agreed blandly. Obviously, his father-in-law had spied him lurking outside the door and hadn't been any too pleased. She felt almost as chagrined as her witness that the opportunity to learn more about the argument between brother and sister had been cut short.

'Look, if you don't mind, I have an appointment in …' Kenneth made a show of looking at his watch. 'Well, any minute now, in fact. So if that's all …?'

He stood up, an expectant look on his handsome face.

'Of course, sir. Thank you for your time,' Trudy said. Although she had no doubt that his appointment was totally fictitious, she knew that she had got more than enough from the man to be going on with.

Clement nodded at her in silent agreement. They had all but reached the door and Clement was, in fact, reaching out a hand towards the handle in order to open it, when it suddenly opened for him and he jumped back a little. A pretty young blonde woman, around Trudy's age, gave a startled gasp and put a hand up to her chest. Clearly, the coroner had not been the only one to be taken by surprise by the close encounter.

She was wearing a powder blue skirt and cardigan twin set, with a creamy silk blouse and a row of cultured pearls at her throat. She had a small briefcase in her hand, and her big blue eyes went straight to Kenneth.

'I'm so sorry Mr Wilcox, I didn't realise you had visitors. I've dealt with that matter at the bank, sir.'

'Thank you, Susan,' Kenneth said stiffly. 'My secretary, Miss Royal,' he introduced them briefly. Susan backed out into the small little anteroom cum office and took her seat, watching them curiously as her employer ushered them out.

Back on the street, Trudy smiled. 'Well, that was interesting, wasn't it?'

'On many levels,' Clement agreed with satisfaction. 'This case is definitely beginning to have possibilities after all. Did you get the impression that our Mr Wilcox and his father-in-law didn't get on?' he asked dryly.

'I'll say. Dirty old devil. Did you see the way he was looking at me?'

Clement smiled. 'Some women might have found it flattering to be so openly admired.'

Trudy snorted. 'Well, I don't. And I feel sorry for his poor wife. Shall we talk to her next?'

'No. I rather think I'd like to talk to sister Mary, don't you? Find out what the big argument was about. Any idea where she lives?' Clement asked.

'It'll be in my notes.' Trudy reached into her satchel and rummaging through her accoutrements for her notebook. 'Here it is … Oh yes, Mary Everly – her name was mentioned by the other witnesses. She lives in Wolvercote.'

Chapter 10

As Trudy and Clement climbed into his Rover and headed for the attractive village of Wolvercote, which overlooked Oxford's pretty Port Meadow, back in her home on the hill in Headington, Alice Wilcox was blissfully unaware that she had just had her own interview with the police postponed.

She was busy clearing out her father's things. He'd appropriated a study and separate sitting room for himself on the ground floor, and the largest of the bedrooms upstairs. But his clothes now sat in neat piles, ready to be given to a jumble sale, and his books and other assorted, inexpensive items, were quickly finding their way into a series of cardboard boxes, ready to be sent on to Oxfam.

As she worked, she felt a certain sense of satisfaction. *Now* the house was all theirs, they could spread out a bit and have all the space to themselves. No more cooking meals just how *he* liked it either. They could start having things that *they* liked instead. And they'd get to pick which television programmes to watch, and they'd be able to go on proper holidays at last and … oh, all sorts of things, she mused happily. Life was going to be so much better now – for everybody. But for herself especially. No more penny pinching and tip-toeing around him, making sure *he* was happy and comfortable all the time and had nothing to complain about.

Once the family solicitor had been and read the will, confirming that the house was all theirs now, perhaps they might even sell it and move somewhere else? She'd have to discuss it with Kenneth, but she didn't think he'd have any objections.

She hummed a happy song as she worked. Her brothers and sister would be glad to see the will read as well. Matthew would be the happiest of them all to finally get his hands on his share of their father's fortune, of course. And Godfrey could indulge in his own weird little hobby to his heart's content. And Caroline … Alice sighed. Well, if Caroline *had* been written out of the will, she was sure that she could persuade Kenneth to agree that she must have *something*. After all, they also had his nice little inheritance on top of everything else, so they would be on easy street.

Alice paused in the act of dusting down an old hunting-scene painting that her father had always admired (and she'd always hated) and frowned slightly.

Yes. The inheritance – that was safe enough now too. She'd been a bit worried about that, ever since she'd discovered that father had been badgering Kenneth to hand it over so he could play with it.

But Kenneth had held firm.

Alice smiled, then happily thrust the hideous painting into the box due to go to charity and nodded in satisfaction. Yes, she really admired Kenneth for standing up to her father. Not many people had the gumption.

With not a care in the world, Alice began to sweep up her father's eyeglasses and shaving kit and other personal bits and pieces, busily and competently erasing her father's presence from her home.

Rupert Burrows drove his Austin Healey into Wolvercote and tooted the horn as he crossed the very high, humped back bridge

67

on the far side of the village. It was almost impossible to see any other car coming up the other side, so everyone knew you had to sound a warning, but hearing no answering toot, he motored over and a few yards on, automatically indicated left, down a narrow, rather over-grown lane.

He was no stranger to Mary Everly's delightful cottage, that stood back from this lane in large grounds, surrounded by weeping willows and more often than not, wild rabbits, that trespassed regularly into her garden from the surrounding fields.

But as he drove closer, he saw that an unknown Rover was already pulling up in front of the small garden gate, and he instinctively drove past without stopping.

Although there was nothing *wrong* in him visiting Mary, after all the fuss her brother had kicked up, he knew she was still rather sensitive about their recent engagement, and probably wouldn't want him to put in an appearance if she had unexpected callers.

A tall man with fair hair and moustache and large, pale blue eyes, he met his own reflection in the driving mirror and frowned. He could see her point of view, of course, and he was in no position, really, to object to it, but damn it all, it came to something when you had to pussyfoot around when visiting your own fiancée. It wasn't as if they were youngsters, needing Daddy's permission!

And yet, with a sigh, he carried on driving. He'd park up somewhere and have a stroll along the river, now that the rain had finally stopped. Not the ideal weather for it, perhaps, but he consoled himself with the knowledge that whoever was calling on her probably wouldn't be staying long. Mary knew that he was coming, so she'd be sure to get rid of them as quickly as possible.

Anyway, he couldn't feel annoyed for long. After all, now that Thomas Hughes was dead, all their troubles were over.

Chapter 11

Trudy heard a car drive past behind them in the narrow lane but didn't bother to look around as she walked up the somewhat unevenly paved front path of Mary Everly's garden.

She could tell by the neatly trimmed rose bushes, box hedging and a now leafless wisteria vine that was growing rampant up the cottage walls, that the owner must be a keen gardener – or employed someone who was. No doubt in spring and summer, she mused, this would be a wonderful spot to behold.

Beyond the cottage, a water meadow that was now looking grey and damp lay flat and forlorn, but between the bare willow trees in the distance she could just see a flat glimmer of silver grey – which was probably the river Cherwell or possibly the Thames. For a lifelong native of Oxford, Trudy could be remarkably vague on its geographical features!

The cottage was a classic example of its type, with a front door set firmly in the middle complete with an upside-down V-shaped porch, and with a window on each side. Above, two bedroom windows mirrored the arrangement below, and at one side, a chimney stack climbed up, and was currently emitting a steady grey plume of smoke from the fire.

'Pretty place, and a pretty spot,' Clement said, unerringly

echoing her own sentiments. In one sheltered spot beside the coal shed, a stand of Michaelmas daises still bloomed, their shade so pale a tint of lilac that they almost looked grey. Trudy was still admiring them as Clement lifted up a polished brass doorknocker and rapped it briskly.

There was a short moment of silence and then the door opened quickly. The woman who stood in front of them looked to be in her late fifties or early sixties, and was tall, thin and somewhat regal-looking. The eager look of welcome that had been on her face subsided abruptly as she realised that they were strangers to her.

'Oh, good morning. I'm so sorry, I was expecting someone else. Can I help you?' she added politely. Her pale blue eyes flickered slightly as they swept over Trudy's uniform.

'Hello, Mrs Everly. I'm WPC Loveday, and this is Dr Clement Ryder, city coroner.' Trudy showed her credentials, which the older woman studied briefly.

'This is about my brother, I take it?' she said with a long-suffering sigh. 'You'd best come in then.' And so saying, she stood aside to let them pass.

She was dressed in a pair of warm, tailored wool trousers in a deep navy tone, and with it wore a Fair-Isle-style jumper in shades of blue, white and grey, set in a geometric pattern. Her hair was the colour of old gold, and fashioned in the latest style. Discreet make-up made her look younger than her probable years, and apart from a gold watch, her only other jewellery was a pair of neat, pearl earrings.

She gave the air, Trudy thought, of somebody who was used to living well and always putting up a good front.

'Please, come into the lounge,' Mary Everly said, leading the way from the small hall, where a grandmother clock ticked ponderously in a shadowy corner, and into a small but pleasant room that overlooked the front garden. Done out in tones of apricot and apple green, it did a lot to brighten up the gloomy, grey November day that was trying to press in from outside.

'Is Mr Everly not at home?' Trudy asked curiously. It was possible that the interview might prove upsetting, and sometimes the steadying support of a spouse could be an advantage.

'My husband has been dead for some years now,' Mary Everly said, with a slightly wry smile, and Trudy felt herself flush.

'Oh, I'm sorry. I didn't realise!'

'No reason why you should. Please, take a seat.' Mary indicated the two armchairs and a small sofa that were grouped around a low walnut coffee table. 'He died abroad. He was a diplomat you see, and we were often in the tropics. In the end, he got one of those vague fevers that sometimes see us Europeans off. Now—' she dismissed her widowhood with a wave of one bony hand '—what exactly can I do for you?'

Trudy reached for her notebook and opened it at a fresh page. 'I take it that you *are* aware of the articles that have been written about your brother's, er, fatality, that have been showing up recently in the *Oxford Tribune*?' she began cautiously.

Her witness, seated in one of the armchairs, folded her hands neatly in her lap. 'Yes, Godfrey telephoned me about it, all hot under the collar as usual. Of all my nephews and nieces, he tends to be the most vocal,' she added sardonically.

'Well, as a result of the questions raised, my superior, DI Jennings, has asked me to just check up on a few details. You *were* there at the bonfire party the night the shed caught fire, I take it?'

'Yes, I was. I got to the house in Headington around … let me see. It must have been, oh, six-ish, I would say. I helped Alice in the kitchen for a while – preparing the food and things. Then we all went outside to see the bonfire lit. But it was such an atrocious night – wet and windy, as I'm sure you know. And they had trouble getting it lit.'

She paused for breath, and Trudy nodded. 'Can you remember who recommended they try paraffin?' she asked quietly.

'I think it was Kenneth,' Mary said after a moment of thought.

71

'But I didn't really take much notice,' she added punctiliously. 'Anyway, they got it lit and going eventually, and then the children started clamouring for the fireworks to start. So my brother went into the shed to collect them.'

'Did you see him actually go into the shed, Mrs Everly?'

'Now that you mention it, no, I don't think so. I saw him set off and presumed that's where he was heading. I wasn't really paying much attention, to be honest. I'm long past the age when fireworks are a cause for excitement. Besides, the shed was in the back of the garden somewhere, where it was darkest. And I was watching the bonfire, trying to make sure it didn't run out of control. It was a bit silly to have lit it in such a strong wind, even if it was set up in the most sheltered part of the garden. I said as much to … who was it now … Matthew, I think, at the time. But my brother insisted things go ahead as planned. Thomas never did like to have his plans thwarted – even by Mother Nature,' she added. She sounded both grim and amused, and Trudy looked at her thoughtfully.

'He sounds like he was something of a character. Was he always so stubborn, even as a child?'

'Oh yes, always,' Mary said at once. 'More often than not our parents despaired of him. He was one of those people who always think they know it all – and will move heaven and earth to prove they're right, even when they're wrong. Most especially, I suspect, when they *are* wrong and secretly know it!' The older woman shrugged and spread her hands in a 'what-can-you-do' gesture. 'But then, they forgave him when he became so successful.'

'Yes. He inherited the family business, didn't he?' Trudy nudged her.

'Not quite. Our parents owned a couple of shops, and when he was twenty-one, Thomas badgered them into letting him have one of them to run as *he* wanted to. He always maintained times were changing and new business practices needed to be followed in order to make "proper" money as he always called it. Dad was cautious at first, being both old-fashioned himself and wary of Thomas's eager enthusiasm for change, but within a year my brother's shop was making more than twice the amount that Dad's was.' She gave a brief shrug. 'After Dad retired, Thomas naturally took over the second shop, sold them both, diversified, and within a decade, had built up Hughes Enterprises. The rest, as they say, was history.'

'Were you surprised by any of this?' Trudy asked. Having a witness who was obviously so willing to talk – and so honestly – was always a bonus, and she intended to make the best of it before putting the woman on her guard with more personal questions.

'Not at all,' Mary said. 'I was younger than Thomas by some years, but even back then I could see how driven he was. He was clever, willing to take risks and, to give him his due credit, work like a dog, for years and years, in order to make something of himself.'

'He sounds like an ambitious man.'

'Oh yes.'

'Money meant a lot to him, would you say?' Trudy pressed.

'Oh, good grief, yes. It was his be-all-and-end-all if you ask me. I never thought it was particularly healthy – but of course, his cronies and other men of business thought him the bees' knees.'

'What did his wife make of all this?' Trudy slipped in.

'Mildred? Oh, she didn't mind. Why should she? She got a grand home and furs and holidays abroad. Plus her children went to the best schools and what have you.' Mary shrugged one elegant shoulder.

'You don't think she minded her husband working such long hours?'

Mary gave another of her sardonic smiles. 'I very much doubt it, Constable. I imagine that she was relieved to have the house to herself most of the time. My brother tended to … shall we say, fill the space, wherever he was.'

'We've spoken to your niece, Caroline,' Trudy pressed on. 'She was rather, er, emphatic, when it came to her mother. And about her final illness in particular.'

Mary Everly's thin face tightened perceptibly. 'Yes. I imagine she was,' she conceded.

'She said, in fact, that her father refused to pay for treatment that might well have helped prolong her life.'

'Yes,' Mary said shortly.

'Yes, that's what Caroline believes, or yes, you think it's true?' Trudy asked frankly.

'Both.'

Trudy blinked at this rather flat, terse statement. She shifted a little on her seat, not quite sure how to take this witness. She was not exactly hostile (well, not yet!) but she wasn't being all sweetness and light either.

Beside her, she noticed Clement was also watching the widow with keen interest. She cast him a quick glance, tacitly offering him the opportunity of taking over if he felt like it, and he accepted the silent invitation by leaning forward slightly on the sofa.

'Did you get on with your sister-in-law, Mrs Everly?' he asked quietly.

'Mildred? Yes, in so far as it went. You have to remember, I was a diplomat's wife and spent many years away from England, so I never saw a great deal of my relatives. So I can't claim to be any expert on my brother's family life. But whenever we met up, I always got on all right with her.'

'Were you here when she was in the final stages of her illness?'

'No – well, not when she actually died,' Mary admitted. 'We were over here for a few months between our Singapore posting and the Malay posting, when she'd just been diagnosed and was beginning to go downhill fast, the poor old girl. It was quite sudden and the change in her was shocking. She went like a skeleton almost.' Mary sighed heavily. 'Of course, Caroline, as the youngest one, and the only one still left at home, felt it all the most.'

'And she'd have been the one in the best position to know what attitude her father had taken to his wife's illness?' Clement mused, almost to himself, then nodded. Yes, that would explain why, of all the Hughes siblings, she was the one who hated her father with the greatest degree of intensity.

'I agree,' Caroline's aunt said sadly. 'I've no doubt she saw and heard a lot that upset her. And seventeen is such a hard age to learn one of life's more harsher lessons, isn't it? Not still a child, exactly, but hardly grown-up either. I felt sorry for her, to be frank. But being abroad so much ...' She shrugged helplessly. 'There was little of use that I could actually do for her.'

'Did you believe her when she claimed that her father wouldn't finance her mother's medical treatment in America?' Clement asked, watching her closely.

'Oh yes,' Mary said, without hesitation. 'I'm afraid it would be just the sort of thing that Thomas *would* do, you see. Refuse to spend money on a lost cause, I mean. I can almost hear him saying it. "Just throwing away good money after bad."'

She paused, aware of the simultaneous looks of shock that had crossed the faces of both of her visitors. 'Sorry, but I've never believed in shirking the hard facts,' Mary Everly stated. 'My brother, you see, always enjoyed rude good health himself, and like so many people who've never had to experience and deal with illness, he tended to pooh-pooh the extent and awfulness of it. Which would only have made matters even worse. When Milly became all but bed-bound, he simply refused to acknowledge what was happening and retreated into his own world – and his world was, and always had been, about making money.'

'I pity his poor wife,' Clement said heavily, which was a sentiment that Trudy heartily shared.

'So did I,' Mary responded. 'So did we all – not just Caroline. But my brother had a calculator where his heart should be, and his children – *all his children* – knew this better than most. And it wasn't just that he had to succeed in business – he needed to succeed more than anybody else.' Mary sighed. 'There was a sort of ... of ... *glee* about him whenever he pulled off a really big coup. Do you know what I mean?'

'I think so,' Clement said. 'He was the sort of man who enjoyed power.'

'Yes. Money, acquisitions, power, influence, being seen as the big man ... all of these things were meat and drink to him.'

'And he wouldn't have had much patience to spare for a suddenly ill, needy and ailing wife. Or with a frightened and grieving daughter.' Clement nodded. 'No wonder Caroline married so young and left home the moment she could.'

Mary again made her what-can-you-do gesture of helplessly spread hands. 'I have to say, I was rather relieved when I heard she'd married so young and left the family home,' the older woman said. 'I think it was almost certainly the best thing that could have happened – for both of them. I can only imagine the horrible atmosphere which must have existed in that house after Mildred died!'

'Such a man must have fallen out with almost every member of his family at some point or other I imagine,' Clement mused craftily, and Trudy, busily scribbling down her notes, was careful to hide her smile of approval at this neat little bit of fishing.

'Oh yes. He was especially scornful of Godfrey, of course.' Mary sighed, then seeing Clement's questioningly raised eyebrow, hastened to explain. 'He was the oldest son, you see. Alice was the first-born, but as a girl, didn't really count with Thomas, I'm afraid. But he never married, for a start, and so failed to produce the much longed-for offspring. As well as that, Godfrey I'm afraid ... well, let's just say that he's not the most forceful of men. He's an academic and a bookworm – the sort of person just suited to life in Oxford. Not at all the get-up-and-go chip off the old block that Thomas had always wanted in a son. So I suppose it was inevitable that he and my brother never saw eye to eye. Matthew was probably his favourite – if you could say he had a favourite.' Mary paused to give another of her bitter, amused, smiles. 'Mind you, after Caroline turned on him – which is no doubt how he saw it – I rather think I saw signs that Alice became more of a favoured child, as a result.'

'But he quarrelled with her too?' Clement asked.

'Oh yes. As you said, he fell out with everyone eventually.'

'And with you too, I imagine?' the coroner slipped in deftly. But if he expected her to get suddenly defensive or disconcerted, he was disappointed, for yet again Mary Everly merely flashed another of her wry smiles.

'Oh yes, me too,' she admitted.

'In fact, you and your brother had quarrelled fairly recently I gather,' Clement said, careful to keep his voice as matter-of-fact as her own had been.

'My, my, you *have* been poking your noses into the Hughes family business, haven't you?' the older woman said, her tone understandably a little more waspish now. 'Who have you been talking to, I wonder? Not that it matters unduly, I suppose. But yes, we had words recently.'

'May I ask what about?'

'You may ask,' Mary said, 'but I have no intention of answering you. It was of a strictly personal nature and had nothing whatsoever to do with my brother's tragic accident, of that I can assure you.'

'I see.' Clement made no move to press her and Trudy reluctantly agreed that it would serve no purpose for her to try to either. Mary Everly was clearly a lady who meant what she said, and once she'd said it, wouldn't be moved.

'Can you tell me where you were when you first became aware that the shed was on fire?' Trudy asked, taking control of the interview once again.

'I was … Yes, I was talking to one of Matthew's children, I

77

think. The eldest, Benny. I was being pestered to provide him with some sparklers, which of course, I didn't have. I heard someone shout something like, "look out – the shed's going up in flames" or something along those lines. I turned to look, and sure enough, I saw the shed was on fire. I just remember feeling very annoyed, more than anything else,' Mary shrugged. 'I had remarked earlier on how unwise it was to have a big bonfire alight when there was such a high wind. And to be proved right so quickly … but of course, at that point I had no idea that Thomas was inside.' Her voice became a little hushed now with remembered horror. 'It wasn't until we realised that he didn't seem to be present amongst us, and we couldn't find him that we began to wonder … and by then, of course, it was too late. Somebody – not Godfrey, but either Matthew or Kenneth I think – tried to get closer to the shed door, but the heat was too much.'

Her voice subsided with a harsh sigh. 'In spite of all his faults, I'm rather sorry my brother's dead,' Mary Everly said then.

She sounded, Trudy thought, slightly surprised by her own words.

Chapter 12

'Where to next?' Trudy asked a few minutes later, as, after taking their leave from Mary Everly, they walked back down the garden path and towards the Rover.

Clement thought about it. 'I think we need to speak to the family solicitor, don't we? When a rich man dies, it always pays to know who benefits from his last will and testament.'

Trudy nodded. It had been on her to-do list as well, and she already had all the particulars to hand. 'They're an outfit called Bowen, Bough and Bowen. They have offices in Summertown. I checked on the map, and I think the address puts them on the same street as the library.'

On the way back into town, Clement stopped at a telephone box to put a call through to a colleague of his and arrange to meet him for lunch the following day. He'd already been asking around, and knew that this colleague had been on the team that had treated Mildred Hughes in her terminal illness.

As he'd expected, Dr Raymond Willoughby had no objections to having his brains picked in return for being treated to lunch at The Mitre – especially if Clement was willing to throw in a bottle of fine claret.

Back in the car, it took Clement and Trudy only ten minutes to make their way to the leafy and gentrified suburb of Summertown. There they found the Hughes family solicitor's office, midway down an avenue lined with cherry trees and tucked discreetly amongst a nest of Victorian and Edwardian terraced houses.

Just as they were getting out, Clement remembered his mental note to ask her about the driving lessons, and looking across the roof of his Rover, said, 'By the way, have you applied for a driving licence yet?'

Trudy shook her head. 'No, but I've almost got the money saved. I could have one by the new year.' Hope clearly flared in her eyes, and he smiled wryly.

'Did you think I'd forgotten my offer to teach you? Shall we begin in January then?'

Trudy caught her breath and grinned from ear to ear. But then she tensed. Would she really be able to learn to drive? Anxiety nibbled at her, and she glanced down at the Rover thoughtfully. It was such a responsibility, to be in charge of a vehicle. What if she was no good at it? It would be so embarrassing. But then her backbone stiffened. If PC Rodney Broadstairs could learn how to do it, she was damned sure she could as well! It would be such a massive achievement, and would give her a huge amount of freedom and independence. Well, if she could ever afford to buy a car of her own, at any rate.

'All right then,' she said boldly, before she could change her mind. Clement grinned at her.

'That's the spirit,' he said. As they walked across the small car park, she was almost skipping beside him with anticipation.

The middle-aged lady seated in the small foyer did not look impressed by casual callers who came in without a proper appointment, and not even Trudy's uniform seemed to mollify her.

After a sniff or two, she deigned to see if 'one of the younger partners' was free to see them, disappeared somewhere for quite some time, then finally returned and stiffly informed them that young Mr Bough could fit them in for a few minutes.

Trudy bit back the urge to giggle as the stiff-backed woman escorted them up a set of narrow stairs and showed them through to an office. She announced them abruptly and snapped the door closed behind her.

The room bore a large sash window, numerous rows of filing cabinets, an almighty aspidistra in a large blue-glazed pot, and an intrigued-looking young man, just rising to his feet behind a desk overflowing with 'briefs'.

Behind a sea of beige folders, peppered with the red and pink ribbon bindings peculiar to his calling, young Mr Bough regarded them with interest. At around thirty years of age, Trudy wouldn't have thought of him as being particularly young – but then, with another suppressed giggle, she supposed that all the other partners might well be in their dotage, which would make him the baby of the firm.

'Thank you for seeing us, Mr Bough,' Trudy said, introducing herself and Clement. 'It's concerning the last will and testament of Mr Thomas Hughes. We were hoping that you could help us.'

'Please, take a seat,' the solicitor said. He had an ugly but pleasant face, surrounded by abundant dark brown hair that had been ruthlessly tamed by a rather fierce haircut. Large, round, horn-rimmed glasses covered deeply set dark brown eyes. 'Mr Hughes … oh yes,' he began, with a vague air that instilled little confidence in either of his callers. 'The er … unfortunate gentlemen who died in a fire on Bonfire Night, is that right? As a matter of fact, I'm due to read the will to the family first thing tomorrow morning.' He paused and regarded them thoughtfully, a frown beginning to pull down his bushy dark eyebrows. 'Er … it's not quite the done thing to … er, jump the gun, as it were.'

He looked curiously from one to the other, as if seeking reassurance of some kind.

'I take it you don't read the *Tribune* sir?' Trudy said.

'That rag! Not on your life! An *Oxford Times* man, that's me,' he said firmly.

Trudy nodded, and then briefly explained the situation, her remit and her request. 'So, you see, if you could just give us the main points on the distribution of Mr Hughes's fortune, it would help the police enormously in our inquiries,' she finished.

'Hmm. I'm not so sure that the partners would agree to it,' he said, making her heart sink a little. But then he seemed to rally. 'But I can't see that there would be much harm done. So long as I have your word that you'll be discreet,' he added. 'No blabbing to the family that you got first dibs, so to speak?'

'I can promise you, nobody will know that you've been so helpful, Mr Bough,' Trudy said, watching with both satisfaction and a touch of impatience as the rather mercurial solicitor got up and began to hunt feverishly through the filing cabinets for the document he wanted.

It took him a long two or three minutes to find it, accompanied by much muttering under his breath. Trudy supposed that it would usually be his secretary's job to accomplish such a simple but vital task.

With his prize eventually in hand, he returned to his chair and perused the document.

'Ah yes, here we are. Hughes, Mr Thomas. Hmmm, a fairly hefty document, but then Mr Hughes was a man of some means. I believe it was Mr Reginald Bowen who drew up the original document, and he'd have been most particular … let me see, nearly five years ago now, was it? Hmm. All right, let me just have a quick look through …'

He broke off his muttering to suddenly look up at her, and gave her an unexpectedly sweet smile. 'As luck would have it, I was going to look it out and spend some time acquainting myself with the basic provisions and contents anyway. As I said, I'm seeing the family tomorrow and I like to know the major points

'… Unfortunately, Mr Reginald is no longer with us, so he can't …' He looked back down at the document. 'Hmm. Yes, it doesn't seem to be that complicated for such a wealthy man, not when it comes right down to it. Oh dear me, no charitable bequests at all,' he muttered under his breath, sucking in a shocked whistle as he did so. 'The partners would find that most upsetting. One expects men of means to be charitable, don't you? Noblesse oblige and all that. But then, Mr Hughes seems to have been a rather … Hmm.' He peered closer at the pages, making Trudy wonder if he needed a stronger prescription in his eyeglasses.

Eventually he looked up at them and blinked, as if in surprise to find them still there. 'Oh, yes. Right. What did you want to know exactly? I can't read out the whole thing, naturally – that would be much too irregular. But I don't see that answering one or two really pertinent questions would be that unforgivable.'

Trudy kept her – by now rather fixed – smile firmly in place. 'Thank you, Mr Bough. I really just want to know who the main beneficiaries are, and to what extent. I know, for instance, Mr Hughes had four children – Godfrey, Matthew, Alice and Caroline.'

'Ah yes. Right, let's see …' He pursed his lips, turned a few pages, nodded, muttered some more, then suddenly fixed her with a surprisingly keen eye.

'Well, unfortunately, his youngest child, Caroline, is not mentioned at all.'

Trudy shot Clement a quick look then turned her attention back to the man of law. 'I see.' It shouldn't really surprise her, but it did. She'd have thought that, no matter what the family troubles, a father would, at the very end, want to make some sort of provision for all his offspring.

'The eldest daughter Alice, gets the house in Headington, but again, does not inherit any of the deceased's capital or other assets.'

'No money at all?' Trudy asked, surprised, and scribbling down the details hastily in her notebook.

'Afraid not. He does … er … make some comment about how women have husbands to take care of them, and that includes financially. But I couldn't possibly read out such a … er … private message, not here or now. Naturally, tomorrow, at the official reading and with the family present, it's my duty to relay all of the deceased's er … comments. But some of them are quite extraordinarily … well, blunt.'

He shook his head over one particular page, shuddered and quickly turned it over. 'The things some people do say …' He shook his head regretfully. 'Let me see … His sons … Yes, the eldest, Godfrey gets an adequate pension for his lifetime, but not access to the lump sum. Oh dear … Yes, the deceased has made some particularly disparaging comments about the likelihood of his spending it on … Good grief.'

The 'young' Mr Bough's eyes widened a little behind his glasses. 'How extraordinary. Can't say as I fancy that myself but then …' He broke off, turned a shade of red and once more turned the page abruptly. 'Let's see, the bulk of the estate goes to … ah yes, here it is, Matthew Hughes.'

Trudy shot Clement another quick glance. 'The youngest son gets the most money, sir? Is that what you're saying?'

'Hmm? Oh yes, that's so.' The loquacious solicitor dragged his eyes from the pages and regarded her once more. 'The bulk of the estate consists mostly of investments, savings and a significant amount of stocks and shares. There are other beneficiaries within the family …' He read these out, then fell silent.

'Can you give me an idea of how much money we're talking about, Mr Bough?' Trudy appealed.

'Oh well, that's not so easy to say. It depends on the price of gold at the time of selling for a start. Mr Hughes kept around twenty per cent of his savings in the form of gold. And of course, stocks and shares rise and fall every day on the open market. But when they're sold … er … and the sales of some real estate … but then there's tax and … Oh my, my mental calculations never were … I should say Mr Matthew Hughes would inherit getting on for three quarters of a million pounds, to perhaps, just over a million.' He shot out the last sentence abruptly.

Trudy sat there, stunned. She couldn't imagine having that much money. 'Oh,' she heard herself say blankly.

Once more out on the street, Trudy watched as Clement unlocked the car, aware of a growing sense of excitement. Once she'd slipped into the passenger seat, she waited impatiently for her friend to start the car. As he did so, he nudged the little lever that worked the indicator and with a 'tcha!' of annoyance, he quickly flicked it back into place. His hands, Trudy noticed, shook a little as he reached into his jacket pocket for a packet of mints. He popped one in his mouth and sucked thoughtfully.

Sometimes Trudy worried about Dr Ryder when he showed these occasional signs of stress or tiredness. She knew that if something were ever to happen to her mentor, she'd be stuck doing nothing more than routine office duties back at the station – the only way she could ever hope to continue to investigate proper, interesting cases was with this man by her side. And yet, how selfish was that? Guiltily, she wondered if it was possible that she kept telling herself that everything was all right purely because she didn't *want* anything to be wrong? And yet, Dr Ryder was an experienced medical doctor – he'd spent years working as a world-class surgeon for heaven's sake! Surely, if he were really ill, he'd know about it? And she'd never seen anything that really worried her, had she? He'd never seemed to be in pain, or even look ill, for that matter. No, she had to be right in thinking that he just sometimes got tired, that was all.

'This has to put Mr Matthew Hughes at the top of our suspect list, doesn't it?' she said, eager to start discussing possibilities with him.

'It certainly makes him a person of interest,' Clement agreed, a little more calmly. 'But don't forget, everyone but Caroline benefited in some way. Even his sister Mary got a twenty-thousand-pound inheritance. And a pension for life is nothing for Godfrey to sneeze at, nor are the deeds outright to a large house in Headington for Alice. As well as trust funds for all his male grandchildren.'

'Yes, but a million pounds,' Trudy breathed.

'Would you kill your father for a million pounds?' Clement asked, and suddenly Trudy felt herself come down to earth with a bump.

'No, of course I wouldn't,' she said with a sigh. 'You're right. I mustn't jump to conclusions.'

But even as her mentor drove through the darkening afternoon and dropped her off outside the police station, she couldn't help but feel a sense of real excitement.

For the first time since being given the assignment, she was beginning to really feel as if there might be something in the newspaper's muckraking after all. Perhaps there *was* more to Thomas Hughes's death than a bizarre accident. And if he *had* been killed, then his murderer must, by now, be quite confident that they'd got away with it.

But he or she hadn't counted on herself and Dr Ryder, she thought with inner satisfaction. They simply wouldn't stop until they'd tracked the killer down.

What's more, she realised with a rush of happiness and pride, she wasn't scared or worried at that prospect at all!

Chapter 13

The next morning, Duncan Gillingham walked slowly down Broad Street, always keeping his quarry in sight, but taking care to mingle and blend in with the usual mix of shoppers, students and tourists that perpetually clogged the city streets. It simply wouldn't do for him to be spotted and challenged. Not now that the game and the stakes were getting so interesting.

Ever since the police had reluctantly confirmed that they were now 'looking into' the Thomas Hughes affair, his stock was riding (temporarily at least) high at the paper, and he was determined to make the most of it whilst it lasted.

Especially when it gave him such a heaven-sent opportunity to earn both brownie points at work, whilst at the same time giving him the perfect excuse to pursue his own, private vendetta.

Of course, Sir Basil Fletcher wasn't his greatest fan, but at least he could console himself with the fact that that had nothing whatsoever to do with his writing ability. As he walked, Duncan couldn't help but grin. Sometimes, watching the old man try to hide his chagrin could be really entertaining – especially when he was forced to accept Duncan into his home as a guest. Of course, all he really wanted to do was throw him out on his ear and keep him firmly in his place. Which was very low down on the totem pole.

At least the actual editor of the *Tribune*, Bill Niven, was a newspaperman through and through, and the paper's owner had enough confidence in Bill to let him have his head. Bill knew a good story when he saw it – and was willing to back both his hunches, and (to a certain extent) those of his reporters. Especially when they promised him even bigger headlines to come.

Of course, Bill might not be quite so happy with Duncan if he knew that he was skiving off his latest assignment to cover a story at City Hall in order to pursue his own goals instead. But he was confident that he didn't actually need to attend the council meeting where a contentious proposal was struggling to get through in order to write a good piece. Besides, if he missed anything juicy he could always pick up on it at the pub later, where his fellow journalists always retired for a bevy and a gossip.

Right now, he had far better things to do with his time than actually do his job. Like keeping his eye on one particular member of the Hughes family.

Of course, Duncan couldn't be totally *sure* that Thomas Hughes's death hadn't been accidental, in spite of the promises he'd made to Bill that he was on to something there. But knowing what he did about the personality of one of the people at the centre of the mystery, it seemed extremely likely to him that the man's death was suspicious. But he could hardly rely on the police finding the evidence and securing a conviction with so little to go on. No, it was up to him to find that proof, and right now, he was the only one who knew where to look for it.

The person he was following suddenly paused and started to turn around. Without breaking stride, Duncan quickly side-stepped into the shop nearest to him – a newsagent's, as it happened. Instantly he was enveloped in slightly warmer air and the smell of tobacco and humbugs. His quarry had clearly thought of something they urgently needed in the post office next door to the shop, so whilst he was waiting to resume his surveillance, Duncan sauntered to the counter and ordered some cigarettes. He favoured the unfiltered woodbines over Players No6 or Benson & Hedges. Whilst he was there, he also bought a tin of pipe tobacco for his father, and a box of chocolates for his girlfriend, then remembered to neatly fold away the green shield stamps that came with his change. His mother was saving up for a set of cutlery she had her eye on for Christmas, and was constantly pestering her offspring for the damned things.

Not that he would have to worry about such penny-pinching himself for much longer. Not once he married Sir Basil Fletcher's only child, Glenda.

Lingering in the shop doorway until his quarry re-emerged form the post office, Duncan lit a cigarette and smoked thoughtfully.

Glenda was a nice enough looking girl, not too bright but with a good heart, and he had an engagement ring all picked out. He needed only a few more months of saving his salary before he could afford to buy it, and was confident that she would accept his proposal when he popped the question. It was clear to everyone that she was mad about him. Just as it was equally plain that her father was not.

Oh well, Duncan thought, with another grin. Too bad the old man thought his precious only child could do much better for herself than marry one of his junior reporters. Mind you, Duncan could sort of see Sir Basil's point of view. It wasn't even as if he was even lower middle-class. His father had worked on the Morris Minor production line for years– something that no doubt gave Sir Basil nightmares.

But Glenda, bless her heart, didn't care. From the moment they'd met at the *Tribune*'s Christmas party last year, the writing had been on the wall. Glenda had noticed the young, handsome and well-built man with thick black hair and intriguing green eyes at once. And Duncan had made sure that he was introduced to the *Tribune* heiress.

And he hadn't looked back since. The courtship had been straightforward enough in spite of the obvious pitfalls presented by her father's mostly silent but palpable disapproval. But as if to make up for that, Glenda and his own parents – slightly to everyone's surprise – had got on like a house on fire. Although the daughter of the peer had attended Cheltenham Ladies' College and then a Swiss finishing school, Glenda was no snob. She didn't care that he had grown up in a council house in Cowley, or that he now resided on a narrowboat on the Oxford canal in the less than reputable area of Jericho. In fact, Duncan suspected she found the whole thing rather 'romantic'.

Of course, having grown up with no money, Duncan saw nothing 'romantic' at all about living on a cramped boat, and couldn't wait for the time when he was able to move into some nice flat somewhere. Perhaps in the prestigious north of the city – in one of those whitewashed mansions on Woodstock Road maybe. For he had no doubt that Sir Basil wouldn't be able to bear it to see his princess slumming it, and would cough up with a desirable residence of some description once marriage had made Duncan officially his son-in-law. Perhaps he'd even stretch to a cottage in Osney Mead?

His pleasant daydreaming was quickly cut off as a familiar figure stepped out of the post office and back into the dark, damp, cold November morning.

Duncan, his green eyes narrowing in enmity, doggedly took up his pursuit. He had no real hopes that anything would come of his surveillance, but you simply never knew. All he needed was one small thread to pull on, one juicy secret to uncover, one sniff of corruption or scandal, and he wouldn't hesitate to spread the news of it across the banner of the *Tribune*.

Duncan knew that he couldn't rely solely on his ploy of setting the plod into looking into Thomas Hughes's hideous death to pay the dividends that he craved. Especially if, despite his personal belief that it was murder, the incident turned out to have been a freak accident after all. But that didn't mean it couldn't be turned to his advantage, if he was careful and played his cards right.

He'd have to find out which flatfoot was handling the investigation, instigate a meeting and then make sure that he nudged him in the right direction. A few helpful hints, a bit of friendly manipulation over a pint or two at the Eagle & Child, and who knew what might be achieved? He'd discovered early on in his childhood that he had the knack of making people like him; winning friends and influencing people had never been a problem for him.

But whilst it was sweet to think of a certain someone actually being arrested for the murder of Hughes (and all the shock, pain, and fear that would generate) Duncan was a realist, and knew that the odds of it happening were low at best. No, ensuring that his quarry became a 'person of interest' to the police had always been just one more step in his war of attrition – just one more way of piling on the pressure, and making life in general difficult and miserable.

But if he was to get the revenge he craved, he needed a back-up plan. Any plan would do. So long as he could get his payback, he wasn't fussy. Which meant watching and waiting for his opportunity. Sooner or later something would crop up and then he wouldn't hesitate to go straight for the jugular.

Chapter 14

Whilst the reporter pursued his vendetta downtown, Alice Wilcox anxiously set about making the lounge in her Headington home as welcoming as possible. Mrs Greaves had come in an hour earlier than her usual time and had 'obliged' by vacuuming and dusting everywhere, and now Alice set about arranging the bronze chrysanthemums she'd bought that morning into a large glass vase, and setting it in the centre of the coffee table.

In another hour, the solicitor, that nice Mr Bough, would be coming over to read the will, and she felt a shiver of excitement lance through her. No doubt Godfrey, Matthew and his family, and Auntie Mary would all start to arrive within the next half an hour or so, and she wanted the place to look nice. Caroline had refused to come.

She paced a little, walking to the window every now and then, anxiously looking out to see if Kenneth had come back from the shop. She wished he hadn't insisted on going in. It hardly seemed worth it, when the solicitor was due to arrive at ten-thirty.

She paced, straightened up an undistinguished landscape painting that hung on one wall and made sure that all the anti-macassars were straight on the backs of the chairs and sofa.

She felt unbearably nervous. It was one thing to know what her father had *said* was in his will. But her father was a born liar.

At the police station, Trudy got on with her usual duties, but was also impatiently watching the clock. Dr Ryder was meeting his old colleague for lunch in order to learn the facts about Mildred Hughes's final illness, but after that, they were going to interview Godfrey and perhaps Matthew Hughes, time permitting. The minutes seemed to be dragging. More than once she felt the sharp edge of Sergeant O'Grady's tongue for not paying attention to the ringing telephone.

But she found it hard to concentrate on typing up shoplifting reports. Round about now, for instance, the Hughes family would be learning about the terms of their father's will and she couldn't wait to find out how the two men especially had taken the news. One, that he was now worth a fortune free and clear, with money to spend whenever and however he wished; the other that, although he could rely on a pension, it would be meted out to him in a set amount for the rest of his life by executors bound to follow his father's strict orders.

Catching PC Rodney Broadstairs grinning at her cheekily, she reluctantly dragged her mind back to her typewriter, and her witness statement from a woman who'd had her handbag snatched by a young hooligan in New Inn Hall Street.

Then her mind was back in Headington again. How would Alice feel about only inheriting the house? Would Caroline really not care that she hadn't even been mentioned …?

An hour and a half later, Dr Ryder signed the last of the letters in his 'In' tray, and sat back with a sigh. His fingers and wrist hurt slightly and he rubbed them impatiently, looking down at his digits with a scowl. It was probably just the usual writer's cramp – or maybe even a touch of arthritis.

But any weakness in his hands and feet worried him.

He reached into the bottom right-hand side drawer of his desk and withdrew a tube of strong mints. He popped one into his mouth and began to suck it, the gesture all but automatic now. Halitosis was one of the symptoms of Parkinson's disease and it had become second nature to him to consume a breath mint whenever he was due to socialise.

He was looking forward to seeing his old friend, and was interested in learning more about Mildred Hughes's case. Like all doctors, he found rare conditions fascinating.

But he was very much aware that his old friend was still a practising physician, and would have a doctor's sharp eye, so he knew he would have to be careful during lunch. It was one thing to keep his condition a secret from laymen. Hiding his symptoms from someone who had no medical knowledge or experience was relatively easy. But it would be a different story when it came to his former colleagues.

With a grim smile, he reached for his favourite Trilby hat, shuffled into his raincoat, cheerfully informed his secretary that he would be out for most of the rest of the day and stepped outside to walk the short way to the pub in the High Street.

Fortunately it wasn't raining, but the streets were still damp from an earlier downpour and once or twice he felt his feet slide on the sleek pavement.

He told himself it meant nothing, yet he had to concentrate on making sure he lifted his feet with every step. Shuffling was another dead giveaway of his condition.

Chapter 15

'So Caroline was right,' Trudy said in disgust, a few hours later, as she and the coroner made their way to Godfrey Hughes's flat in Clement's trusty Rover.

'Basically,' the coroner confirmed. 'According to James, Mildred Hughes might well have had a longer life expectancy had she gone to the United States for the experimental treatment. Mind you, it couldn't have been *guaranteed*,' Clement warned her, changing gear to pass a coal lorry that was trundling along well below the speed limit. 'The thing about experimental trials is that nobody can predict them. What's more, some patients will always respond better to treatments than others.'

'But if she'd been *your* patient, would you have recommended the treatment?' Trudy asked curiously.

'Oh yes. The potential benefits far outweighed any negatives, as far as I could tell. Mind you, I was a surgeon, not a blood specialist,' Clement temporised.

'And her doctors did explain all this to the family?' Trudy pressed.

'Yes, according to James.'

'But she didn't go? To America, I mean?'

'No,' Clement said.

Trudy shifted a little in the seat to look at him more closely. 'Did your friend seem surprised by that? I mean, given the circumstances, and knowing that the family could afford the treatment and travel, he must have *expected* that they'd opt to go to America.'

Clement sighed heavily. 'I know. And once I'd got a few glasses of claret down him, James did become rather more communicative. Basically, he confirmed Caroline's account of things. Over time, it became clear to him that Thomas Hughes was the driving force in the family, and that what he said was law. And his opinion of Mrs Hughes was that she was a placid, rather worn-down lady, who was used to going along with her husband's wishes.'

'Yes, but surely not to the extent that she wouldn't put up a fight to have the best medical care!' Trudy protested hotly.

Clement smiled sadly. In his many years of medical experience, he'd treated patients with all sorts of problems – both physical and mental. So it wasn't hard for him to picture a woman too browbeaten to stick up for herself.

'Don't forget, she was ill, Trudy,' he tried to explain gently. 'Seriously ill people often get tired. Too tired to cope with added pressure. They lose concentration. They become depressed and uncaring. And yes, even too uncaring, sometimes, to care whether or not they live or die.'

He indicated into the road where Godfrey Hughes kept his modest flat, and started looking for a parking space. 'James got the impression that, towards the end of her illness, Mrs Hughes had simply had enough. That she didn't want any more treatments, any more needles, any more medicines that made her feel sick and giddy and even more ill. She just wanted to stay at home quietly and to die in peace. At least, that was what she told him.'

Trudy heard the underlying question in the final sentence and stared at him. 'You think that's what she *really* thought and wanted? Or is that just what *he* said she thought and wanted. And said it so often that he made her believe it?'

Clement shrugged helplessly. He understood her anger, of

course, and the fact that her youth allowed her to feel so outraged by such injustice made him want to applaud her. In stark contrast, he himself felt jaded and every one of his fifty-eight years. When he'd listened to his friend describing his patient's hopelessness, it made him almost glad that he was no longer in medical practice.

'Did Thomas Hughes ever say outright that he wouldn't fund the treatment for his wife?' Trudy demanded.

'Not in front of James or the hearing of the other doctors, no. But then, he wouldn't, would he?' Clement said.

Trudy shook her head, and for a moment stared out of the windscreen, as Clement concentrated on parking the car. 'You know,' she finally said, shoulders slumping slightly, 'I simply can't understand someone like that. I mean … if he'd been a poor man, someone like my dad, who just didn't have the money available, you could understand it. But to be that rich and still say "no". What an absolute *bastard!*'

Trudy heard herself say the swear word, and inwardly flinched. Had she been at home, she'd never have dared use it. But here, in the car with the coroner, she felt she could express her anger without restraint.

And, as if to confirm her belief, she heard Clement Ryder say mildly, and without a touch of rebuke or censure, 'Yes. Wasn't he just?'

Trudy slumped back in her seat. 'It's becoming clearer and clearer the more we learn about him, that Thomas Hughes wasn't a very nice man at all, isn't it? He let his wife die when he could have helped her. He didn't care a fig that people lost their savings in some of his get-rich-quick schemes, so long as he was all right and his money was never at risk. He treated his family like … well, I don't know what. It almost seems as if that fire …' She trailed off, not quite able to say what she was thinking.

Clement, who had no such scruples, smiled sardonically. 'Was Nemesis catching up with him?'

'Who?' she asked, puzzled.

'The Greek goddess of retribution,' Clement supplied. 'You're thinking that he deserved what he got, are you?'

Trudy nodded. Not that she'd ever wish anybody dead, of course. But still.

'Do you think that if someone *did* knock him on the head and deliberately set fire to the shed, leaving him to burn to death, that that someone should get away with it? Because the man who died wasn't a nice man?' Clement asked quietly.

Trudy flushed. 'No. Of course I don't.'

'All right then,' Clement said. 'So let's go and talk to another one who was present at that bonfire. And one, moreover, who's just learned that he's not getting his fair share of his father's fortune either. He should have something interesting to say, don't you think?'

Trudy didn't need asking twice!

Chapter 16

Godfrey Hughes was a tall, lean man, with brownish hair fast going grey at the temples and light brown eyes. Trudy took in his smart dark blue suit and blood-red tie as he opened the door in answer to their knocking, and wondered if he wore the suit in honour of the reading of his father's will or if he intended to go back to work in the afternoon.

She knew that he was a teacher at St Swithin's from the preliminary research she'd done on him, and also remembered several members of the Hughes family commenting on the fact that he had never married.

He had the air of a well-groomed, slightly fussy cat, and Trudy could well imagine her old gran calling him one of life's perennial bachelors.

'Mr Hughes? I'm WPC Loveday, and this is Dr Clement Ryder. He held the inquest into your father's … er … passing. Could we have just a few minutes of your time please?' she began pleasantly.

She saw the man's eyes widen slightly at this, and he visibly hesitated. For a second he looked from her, to Clement, then back to her again, and for a moment Trudy thought that he was actually going to saying 'no' and bar them from his residence. Then he gave a slight shrug and took a step backwards.

'Very well, but I'm due back in school at three o'clock, so I don't have much time. I was about to make myself a sandwich for a late lunch.' He sounded both slightly petulant and rather weary, and she gave him a sympathetic smile.

'I'm sorry sir, we won't be long,' she promised – not altogether truthfully. 'As you may be aware, a local newspaper has made certain innuendoes about your father's death, and it behoves us to investigate the case a little further.' She found herself slipping into a more formal way of speaking, probably influenced by the fact that the man was a teacher.

'That rag!' Godfrey sniffed. 'My study is through here.' They were standing in a tiny hallway, with just enough room for a hat and coat stand and a tiny console table, upon which rested a telephone.

He opened a door to his immediate left and Trudy went inside, then stopped so suddenly that Clement, following on behind her, actually walked into her back. He muttered an apology and then his eyes too, widened, as they took in the contents of the room.

Trudy, with the words 'my study' still echoing in her mind, had stepped into the room with the preconceived idea that a room lined with books would await her. Maybe a gentleman's desk, and a set of those green-leather button-backed armchairs that seemed to find their natural habitat in libraries and snugs the length and breadth of the land.

Instead, she found herself in a square shaped room painted pure white, with pale wooden floors and not a book in sight. There *were* many shelves, however, all of them lined with …

Her eyes, which had swivelled to her left, focused on the closest object to her. It was a small wooden statue, maybe twenty inches in height. It had an almost abstract shaped head, all planes and angular facets for cheekbones, but with an oddly contrasting, smoothly rounded belly. And jutting out beneath it, stretching out horizontally almost as much as the statue was tall, was a huge … well … man's *thing*.

Trudy blinked, her eyes not quite believing that she was seeing what she thought she was seeing. Obviously, it was a piece of art, and looked tribal. Hastily she tore her eyes away from it. But there was not much respite wherever she looked.

On another shelf, behind a small, very pedestrian-looking desk, was a vase, depicting two figures moulded in plaster of Paris. The origin of this one seemed classical Greek to her, with probably mythological figures dancing in a very odd way. Their position was …

No. Not dancing. Trudy gulped. Definitely not dancing.

She was aware of heat flooding into her face, and she tried desperately to assume a casual expression.

Seemingly totally unaware of her predicament, Godfrey Hughes walked to the desk, pulled out an old wooden chair that looked as if he'd stolen it from one of his own classrooms, and sat down.

'Please, won't you be seated?' He indicated two further, mismatched chairs that were placed in front of the desk. 'I was just catching up on some marking.' He looked towards a pile of blue schoolbooks that were set in a pile on one corner of the desk.

Clement sat down, careful not to meet Trudy's eye. His own gaze met those of a wooden, extremely pregnant female, with long pendulous breasts, and guessed that she came from some-where in the Congo – or maybe from one of the Polynesian islands. Trudy finally managed to meet his amused gaze with one of superb indifference, and he slowly transferred his gaze once more to the man in front of him.

Trudy, without a word, took out her notebook. This interview, she decided generously, could be all Clement's.

Her silence left the coroner groping for an icebreaker. 'Do you enjoy being a teacher, Mr Hughes?' he asked eventually, producing a somewhat bland smile.

Godfrey sighed softly. 'Education is a noble cause, of course.

And I was always an industrious child and enjoyed school myself. Naturally, too, I needed a profession, but failed to inherit my father's habit – or love – of acquiring wealth. So teaching seemed as good a profession as any.'

He spoke carefully and precisely, as if he was in a schoolroom right now. But Trudy, refusing to look up from her notebook, didn't care to think what the subject might be in a classroom that was littered with objects such as these.

'Was your father disappointed by your choice of academia?' Clement asked, thinking that Mary Everly had probably been right on the button when describing her late brother's attitude to his eldest son. 'I imagine he'd have preferred that you followed in his footsteps?' he mused, careful to keep his voice non-judgemental.

'Oh yes, and he never got tired of telling me so,' Godfrey said, his voice cool but perfectly controlled. He watched Clement without any obvious signs of curiosity or impatience, which Trudy noted, but didn't quite understand. Most of the other members of his family had at least shown signs of being made indignant at having to answer their questions. Some, she suspected, had been angry whilst others had been worried. But none had shown this utter lack of animation.

'Of course, Matthew made up, somewhat, for his disappointment in me,' Godfrey Hughes swept on. 'But even then, having risen only so far as to become a manager of a department store – and not even his own – meant that he was not always the golden boy.'

Although his tone of voice didn't alter by a fraction, Trudy and Clement were left with the distinct sense that this fact was a source of much satisfaction to the other man.

'I see. Yes, we've heard a lot about the … er, eagerness with which your father amassed his fortune, Mr Hughes,' Clement said, deciding it was time to get down to business. 'I hope you don't mind my being so blunt?'

102

'Oh, not at all,' Godfrey said with aplomb. 'I'm well aware that my father, to be just as blunt, was as rapacious as a herd of Visigoths when it came to business, Dr Ryder. He dedicated his whole life to the accumulation of money and power. He certainly had no time to indulge in any of the finer things in life, such as art.'

So saying, he waved a hand in the air indicating the objects around them, and Trudy, unable to help herself, took another quick look at the shelves, her eyes falling on a piece of jade. It was a beautiful green colour, and for a moment, it looked like little more than a mound of weirdly sculpted bumps and lumps. It took her puzzled brain a few seconds to realise that what she was seeing was at least four separate human bodies, all male, all naked, and all doing things that must surely be physically impossible.

She turned her eyes once more to her notebook.

'Yes. It's a quite remarkable collection of erotica that you have here,' Clement agreed. 'You're obviously a dedicated collector. Is that a pre-Colombian piece of pottery you have over there?'

Trudy, by now, was wise enough not to look.

'Yes. I know a man in Panama,' Godfrey said, with false modesty. Clement, who thought the quote sounded as if it belonged in a third-rate spy thriller, bit back the smile that wanted to leap to his face.

'Such a collection must take up a lot of your time. And funds?' he added casually.

'Oh yes. All my spare time – school holidays and what have you, I spend abroad, searching for my treasures,' Godfrey admitted, again with patently false modesty.

Clement nodded. 'I take it your father had no time for your collection?'

'Not him! Philistine,' Godfrey said. But again, without any obvious sign of heat. It was as if his father's indifference had long since ceased to register with him. 'I regularly have people from the Ashmolean come to look at one or other of my Babylonian pieces. And I have a very rare carving of obsidian, for instance, that brings professors from all over the world to my door.'

'That must be gratifying. And now that your father's gone, I take it you'll have no trouble in acquiring more pieces? They can't come cheap, I'm sure,' Clement added craftily.

For a moment, a flash of genuine emotion seemed to cross Godfrey Hughes's face. But whether it was hate, anger or even twisted humour, it came and went too fast for either Trudy or Clement to identify it.

'I've never used my father's money to acquire my collection,' he merely said, then added, 'and I never shall.'

Of course, both Trudy and Clement knew that he would now never have the chance. It was now perfectly obvious to them why the dead man had made sure that his eldest son wasn't given any lump sum in his will, but rather a pension, to be meted out in dribs and drabs. Thomas Hughes had wanted to make sure that his son didn't spend good money on pornographic art.

'If we could just go over a few points on the night your father died, Mr Hughes,' Clement said quietly. 'Did you see your father actually go into the shed?'

'I don't believe so, no.'

'But it was you and your brother-in-law Kenneth, your sister Alice's husband, who started the bonfire?'

'Yes. It was wet and we had to use some paraffin from the shed to get it alight.'

'Did you fetch the paraffin?'

'No. I believe it was Kenneth. Or maybe he sent Matthew to get it. I wasn't really paying much attention.'

At this, Trudy sighed over her notebook. Wasn't it remarkable that, with all those people at the bonfire party, not one of them seemed to have noticed anything useful? For a moment, she allowed herself to mull over the delicious idea of a family conspiracy. What if they were *all* in on it? What if, at some point, all of the dead man's children had got together and decided to kill their father, and in such a way as the evidence would all go up in smoke, and they could be each other's alibi?

It was fast becoming clear that the victim was not the sort of man who had been universally loved, not even by his nearest and dearest.

But she knew what DI Jennings would say to her if she foolish enough to present him with such a theory! *Evidence, WPC Loveday*, she could hear him thundering. *Bring me evidence!*

Clement carried on doggedly talking over the events of that night, from the first sign of fire in the shed, to the time the fireman left, when the shed was no more than a mound of smoking ruins. But if Godfrey Hughes had seen or heard anything suspicious, he was not about to tell them.

Finally, when his voice, which had been eerily emotionless throughout, tapered off, Trudy thanked him for his time and rose from her chair with alacrity. Careful to keep her eyes on her feet, she left the study, with all its artfully copulating humans behind her, and once she was safely out in the hallway, gave an obvious sigh of relief.

Godfrey Hughes closed the door firmly behind them.

As she walked down the set of wooden stairs into the communal foyer, Trudy paused on the threshold of the front door to observe the cold, wet and near-dark afternoon outside, struggling to find something to say to her companion.

Clement, once again sensing her predicament, said sotto voce, 'Well, that was interesting.'

Trudy burst out laughing.

Chapter 17

Since the weather was so grim, and it was nearly fully dark already, they decided to wait until Monday to talk to Matthew Hughes.

It was still rather dim and grey, as mid-morning, Clement drove them along the High Street, parking in one of the city's many winding, narrow, medieval lanes that lead off it.

On a prime spot not far from the bridge over the river, Blewitt & Sons (established 1821) sold any number of items to its discerning customers. Spread over three storeys, it could offer diverse items ranging from toys to ladies' underwear, confectionery to bathroom taps and carpets to lawnmowers – thankfully, not all in the same department.

It didn't take them long to learn that Mr Hughes managed the ironmonger's department on the top floor. There was an antiquated lift, but neither Clement nor Trudy quite trusted the ill-fitting contraption, and both opted to take the stairs instead.

They found the newly created millionaire in a section of gardening equipment, checking that a shipment of rakes and spades were being displayed properly. As Trudy approached him, she wondered if the man had already written out his notice, for she couldn't imagine anyone worth nearly a million pounds, remaining in his humble job at a department store.

'Mr Hughes?' Trudy recognised him from his likeness to his father, whose photograph adorned Clement Ryder's case file. Like his father, Matthew was tall and thin, with the same brown hair and rather square chin. The only thing he hadn't inherited was his father's rather big nose. Eyes that were hazel, like those of his sister Alice, turned to look at them, and then narrowed slightly as Trudy introduced herself and Clement.

With a muttered word or two to the shop assistant who was working on the display he turned and led them towards the back of the long, open-plan floor, where a series of offices overlooked an uninspired view of air vents, garages, and rubbish bins.

He smiled vaguely as he offered them a seat – of which there were only three in the room, taking the one behind the small desk for himself.

'Yes, both Alice and Godfrey have told me about this, er, further investigation into Father's accident,' Matthew said, 'and that I should expect a visit.'

Trudy knew from her notes that Matthew was thirty-seven years old, but he looked older to her. There was a bluish-grey smudging beneath his eyes that gave mute testimony to the fact that he hadn't been sleeping well lately, and his suit, respectable thought it was, seemed to hang on him oddly, as if he'd lost weight recently.

Was it possible that they'd finally found someone who actually mourned the loss of his parent?

'I'm sorry to bother you at a time like this, Mr Hughes,' Trudy heard herself saying sympathetically. 'We'll try not to be long. But as I'm sure you can appreciate, whenever allegations are made of a serious nature, we have to follow them up.'

Matthew listened patiently, and at the end of her set speech, smiled briefly. 'Even if these allegations come from some muck-raking reporter out to make a name for himself at our expense, and sell a few more copies of his awful rag?'

'You don't think there's any truth in his innuendoes then, sir?'

107

Trudy said, deciding on the spur of the moment to take the bull by the horns. So far they'd been going about this case all softly-softly, and she was curious what would happen if she put a little bite into things. 'There does seem to be some truth in the *Tribune*'s claims that your father was not universally liked, sir,' she pointed out. 'I've done some research on some of your father's less … shall we say, conventional businesses, and it does seem to me that he caused many people to lose considerable amounts of money.'

Matthew winced a little at this, but made no move to come to his late father's defence. Which didn't surprise either Trudy or Clement, for surely his family could have had no illusions about him.

As if to confirm that, the dead man's youngest son shifted slightly on his seat, and said quietly, 'I was never in business with my father. As a consequence, I can't really comment, can I?' He spread his hands wearily, in a gesture that reminded Trudy of someone.

'Why was that, sir?' she asked. 'I've just spoken to your older brother Godfrey, and I can see why *he* preferred not to join the family concern—' she saw Matthew smile slightly at this '—but you yourself are in retail.' She indicated the office around them. 'So why not join Hughes Enterprises?'

Trudy was really interested in his answer, because if this man had been more estranged from his father – and for a long period of time before his death – then they needed to know about it.

Matthew drew in a long, slow, breath. He seemed to hesitate for a moment, and Clement was sure he was contemplating what lie to tell them. Then he seemed to change his mind and he deflated slightly, letting out a heavy sigh. 'Let's just say, even as an eighteen-year-old, I knew that working for my father would be hellish, and leave it at that. And no, before you ask, I never regretted that decision. My position here may not be as spectacular as one I could have expected if I'd joined my father's firm, but it pays well enough for our needs.'

'He must have been disappointed, though?' Trudy pressed him. 'With Alice married, and Caroline estranged from him, and Godfrey … well, going into the scholastic profession,' she said diplomatically, 'he must have been relying on you to toe the family line?'

Matthew shrugged. 'Father got used to his children disappointing him, Constable. We know, because he often told us so. He said, for instance, that I had no gumption working my way up the hierarchy here, whereas if I'd joined him, I could be a top-flight executive by now. But he totally failed to understand why I didn't want the sort of high-pressure job that working at Hughes Enterprises would have entailed. Nor could he ever appreciate why spending time with my wife and children instead of working day and night making money, appealed to me. It was certainly not a factor that had ever concerned *him*,' Matthew added.

Trudy nodded. 'I don't mean to sound offensive, Mr Hughes, but I've spoken to most members of your immediate family now, and it seems to me that none of them were, well, close to your father. Would you say that's fair?'

'Very,' Matthew said with another brief smile.

'Caroline blames him for your mother's death. Did you?' Trudy tried next.

'Without doubt,' Matthew said. 'Father treated her abominably.'

'Did she want to go to America for the specialist treatment?' Trudy asked. 'Only there's been some conflicting testimony about that. Her doctors seemed to think that she wasn't that keen.'

Matthew turned to look out the window, clearly not seeing the grey and dull view, but something else entirely. 'My mother lost heart,' he finally said. 'And died. In the end, I think it was a relief for her. Does that answer your question?' he asked harshly.

Now it was Trudy's turn to wince. She'd obviously caused him pain, which instinctively made her want to cringe. On the other hand, she knew she couldn't let things rest.

'I understand from Mr Bough that the family has just heard your father's will being read?'

'Yes,' he said, a shade warily, and shifted his gaze to her once more.

Trudy wasn't surprised by his sudden interest. After all, his inheritance and what it would mean to become a wealthy man must have been pushed to the forefront of his mind. But that was only human and didn't necessarily mean that he was any more money-grubbing or avaricious than anyone else. But it would be interesting to find out, Trudy mused cannily, just how *much* he coveted his father's fortune.

'And I understand that you were the main beneficiary?' she asked, careful to keep her tone neutral.

'Yes.'

'Were you surprised?' Trudy asked, expecting another short, one-syllable answer. Instead, the youngest son of the dead man shifted a little on his seat again then gave another of his slightly ironic smiles.

'Yes and no. Yes, I supposed I was the obvious one he'd choose. The girls were both out – Alice because she was married, and the old man expected her husband to provide for her, and Caroline because she'd had the nerve to stand up to him and show her contempt. And Godfrey … well, let's face it, I'm sure we can all understand why Father would never have let Godfrey get his hands on the family money. Which only left me. And yet …'

He paused, sighed and turned again to stare out of the window. 'I wouldn't have been at all surprised, when the will was read, if he'd left me nothing at all, either.'

He was quiet for so long, a small frown tugging at his brows, that Trudy was forced to prompt him once more. 'Why was that, sir?'

'Hmmm?' He turned to face them, then spread his hands in a gesture that once more reminded Trudy of someone else. 'It's just that I don't want you running away with the feeling that I was his favourite. I can assure you that I wasn't. I argued with him as much as any other of my brothers and sisters. Well, Caroline excepted of course. Once or twice … Oh, never mind.'

Trudy wanted to push him further, since she could guess what he'd been about to say. Namely that once or twice, Caroline Hughes's intense hatred for her father had probably boiled over into a real shouting match. Maybe even became physically violent? But she sensed that this man wasn't the sort to 'rat' on his siblings.

'Can you tell me what you argued about?' Trudy asked instead.

But Matthew only drew in another deep breath. 'Oh, what couldn't we argue about? You have to understand, Constable, my father could make a saint want to spit. He could argue about "art" with Godfrey until they were both red in the face. He could interfere with Alice's running of the household, or the way she was raising her children, or the price of her grocery bill or any damned thing you'd care to mention, and practically reduce her to tears. And it was the same with me. Why hadn't I been promoted for over two years? Why did I go on holiday instead of buckling down, why did I wear a black suit instead of a grey one, or a blue one? He could find fault with anything and everything.' Matthew broke off and laughed. 'Father expected the world to shape itself to accommodate him, rather than the other way around. There was really no dealing with the man in any sensible way.'

Trudy nodded. 'It must have been very trying for you sir. Did you see your father go into the shed on November the 5th?' She abruptly changed tactics.

And for a moment it worked, because her witness looked taken aback and clearly had to mentally readjust his attitude. Unfortunately, his version of events that night matched pretty much with what everyone else had already told them.

When he'd finished he smiled, and said, 'Is there anything else?'

To which, Trudy of course, could only say, 'No thank you, sir, I think that will be all for the present. Thank you for your time.'

Matthew watched them rise and leave. His eyes were thoughtful. He thought it odd that the coroner, who had overseen his father's inquest, had not so much as uttered a word throughout the interview.

Chapter 18

Outside, Trudy glanced at her watch, saw that it was nearly lunch-time, and that she had some time yet before she had to get back to the station and do some 'proper police work' as DI Jennings sarcastically called it.

'So what did you make of him?' she asked, as they made their way down the narrow lane back to the car. 'You were very quiet in there.'

'Hmmm. I was busy watching him – besides, you were doing fine without any input from me,' he told her truthfully.

'And what did you observe?' Trudy asked curiously.

'I thought he looked tired. And it was not just that he was pale and had bags under his eyes. His whole manner seemed ineffably weary somehow,' Clement said. 'As if everything was too much of an effort. He couldn't even get angry, could he?'

'I know what you mean,' Trudy mused. 'I did wonder, at first, if he might be the only one of the family to actually care that his father was dead.' Trudy paused. 'But the more we talked, the more it became obvious that he wasn't. So what did you think about his story?'

Clement shrugged. 'It's hard to say. He seemed honest and straightforward enough.

'I agree. I think, if it wasn't an accident, then we definitely have to look at the family. So shall we go and see Alice now? She's the only one we haven't interviewed.'

They had arrived back at the car, and Trudy waited whilst Clement searched his pockets for his car keys. He found them, then in trying to isolate the ignition key from the door key, fumbled with the set and dropped them. He gave a mild curse before bending down and picking them up from the pavement.

Trudy, as always whenever she noticed his unusual clumsiness, pretended not to notice. If she believed that drinking caused his lack of co-ordination, she'd probably have been more concerned – not least because he was nearly always driving. But she'd never smelled alcohol on him, and she was confident that, by now, she could tell when a man was stone-cold sober and when he wasn't. Far more likely, his occasional frailties were due to his increasing age. And it didn't seem very polite or politic (not to mention nice) to make any comment on what was bound to be a touchy subject. Like most men 'of a certain age' she was sure that, in his own mind, Dr Clement Ryder was still as fit and active as he'd been twenty years ago!

No, turning a blind eye and pretending ignorance seemed by far the best option.

'There are others that I think we should interview first,' he said quickly as he opened the door. 'Witnesses who are usually more sharp-eyed and intelligent than most people think, but are often overlooked,' he added, slipping in behind the steering wheel.

He reached across to open the passenger door, hoping Trudy wouldn't think anything of the dropped keys. But he was aware of a slight tremor in his hand as he pressed down on the door lever.

For a moment Trudy didn't know what he was talking about, but by the time she had climbed in and shut the door, she'd worked it out. 'You mean the children who were at the bonfire party?'

114

'Yes. I think we should talk to some of them. Gently, mind, and with their mothers present. But kids are often more resilient than we give them credit for, and as I've said, can be quite observant.'

He didn't want to start the car just yet, not until he'd felt the momentary weakness in his hands fade, so he needed to keep his companion talking. 'Have you noticed how vague everyone has been about who did what?'

'Oh yes,' Trudy said at once. 'Perhaps it was Kenneth who suggested the paraffin, or maybe it was Godfrey? It might have been Aunt Mary who did this, or perhaps it was Alice.' Trudy mimicked the way her witnesses had answered her questions, her exasperation obvious. 'It would be nice to get some straightforward, no-nonsense answers to questions, wouldn't it? So do we start with Alice and Kenneth Wilcox's children?'

Clement unobtrusively rubbed his hands against his thigh. 'Well, we can talk to them when we go and see her. First, let's call around on Matthew's children. They'll be coming home from school around now.'

'All right,' Trudy agreed.

Cautiously, Clement raised the keys to the ignition, and was relieved when he managed to slide the right key home without any further ineptitude.

The rain having begun again, he switched on both his headlights and his windscreen wipers, and carefully pulled away.

Chapter 19

Matthew and his wife Joan lived in a nice but modest semi-detached house on the outskirts of Osney Mead. Like his Aunt Mary, the house where he lived had a view of water meadows, but there any similarity ended. The house had been built just after the war, and had none of the olde-worlde charm of Mary Everly's nineteenth-century country cottage in Wolvercote.

Grey, pebble-dashed, with a modern garage and shed built on, it looked like what it was: a functional, well-built but unspectacular house, built in a cul-de-sac of fourteen similarly semi-detached houses.

'Number twelve, I think it is,' Trudy muttered, taking a quick peek into her notebook to be sure. 'No, number nine,' she corrected herself, then looked around and pointed. 'That one.'

Trudy and Clement dashed through the rain together up the short garden path, and were glad to take shelter under the generous porch roof.

Joan Hughes answered the doorbell's summons quickly. She was a short, pretty woman, with a lot of curly fair hair and pale blue eyes. She looked flustered at the sight of Trudy's uniform, and listened with a distracted air as Trudy introduced herself and Clement and explained their mission.

'You've just spoken to my husband, you say?' she asked, looking up and down the street nervously, as if expecting her neighbours to be watching, and wondering about a visit from the police. In spite of that, she made no immediate move to invite them in.

'That's right. We just wanted to get your version of what happened the night your father-in-law died,' Trudy said, with a gentle smile.

'Well, I'm not sure,' Joan said, shifting uneasily from foot to foot.

'We won't take much time, Mrs Hughes,' Trudy pressed. Of course, if the woman refused to admit them to her house or speak to them, they'd have no choice but to walk away. But this was the first time she'd encountered any real resistance from the dead man's family, and it made her feel curious.

Beside her, she could sense Clement was intrigued too.

'Oh, all right then, you'd better come in,' Joan reluctantly agreed, moving back to allow them into the hall. 'Please, go into the lounge, second on the left. I just have to pop upstairs to see to Helen, my littlest. She's not well.'

'Oh, I'm sorry,' Trudy said, beginning to feel a little foolish. Here she'd been, imagining all sorts of suspicious reasons why the woman didn't want to talk to them, and all the time she was worried only about her sick child. 'Nothing serious, I hope?'

'My other two are already in the lounge, playing, I'm afraid. I'm about to give them their lunch before they go back to school. If they start to get a bit boisterous, or if they make a nuisance of themselves, just tell them to be quiet. I'll be back down in a jiffy,' the harried blonde woman said, and quickly began to climb the staircase.

Once she was out of sight, Clement whispered, 'This couldn't be better. We get to chat to the children without "Mum" there to make them mind their manners.'

Trudy grinned. She knew from her research that the youngest child was only four years old, and therefore no use as a potential witness, but that the eldest, a boy called Benjamin was nine years old, and his middle sister, Clarissa, was seven.

When they walked into the lounge, both children were lying on the floor, doing a jigsaw puzzle. The boy was going to be tall and thin like his father, and the girl, who had mass of honey-gold ringlets, was just as obviously going to be as pretty as her mother.

Both of them looked up at the unexpected entrance of strangers, and stared at Trudy in particular in amazement. 'Gosh, are you a policeman?' the little girl asked shyly.

'Yes,' Trudy said, knowing what she meant, and not taking offence at her implied change in gender. 'And you must be Clarissa? And this is your brother, Benjamin?'

'Benny,' the boy corrected her at once, sitting up and forward so that he was resting on his bent knees. 'Who are you? Have you come to arrest me?' he demanded self-importantly.

'Why, what have you been up to?' Trudy shot back, but with such a wide grin that the lad promptly relaxed.

'Hah, nothing! So you can't then!' The boy then looked at Clement, and clearly felt impressed by what he saw. 'Who are you then, sir?' he asked much more politely, but clearly intent on discovering this stranger's bona fides. In the absence of his father, his manner clearly said, he was the man of the house and should be taken seriously.

'I'm Dr Ryder. I'm a city coroner. Do you know what that means?' Clement looked around the pleasant, beige-coloured room, his eyes settling on some chairs upholstered in a nubby-textured, taupe three-piece suite. 'Do you mind if we sit down?'

'Of course you can,' Benny said magnanimously. Clement smiled his thanks, selecting one of the armchairs for himself, whilst Trudy opted for the other. On a pine coffee table in front of them was a scattered selection of women's magazines and an open biscuit tin with a picture of the Queen on it.

'That's a grand picture of a dragon,' Trudy said, seeing that

118

the picture on the puzzle the children were working on represented St George fighting a dragon.

'Not bad,' Benjamin agreed, whilst his sister, still lying supine on the floor, seemed content to simply watch and listen with a slightly open mouth and say nothing. But Trudy suspected this might change once her shyness abated.

Wanting to get some answers before Joan Hughes returned, she turned to Benny and said gently, 'We're here to talk about your grandfather and what happened to him. Would it frighten you to talk about that?'

Benny shot a quick glance at his sister, whose big blue eyes rounded slightly, but showed no signs of filling with tears. 'Nah, we don't mind that. Gramps died in the shed when it caught fire. But it never hurt him, because Daddy said he fell and hit his head and so he was asleep when it happened.'

'Yes, that's right,' Clement said. 'I'm a doctor, and I promise your Gramps didn't feel a thing.'

'Did you see Gramps go into the shed to get the fireworks, Benny?' Trudy asked, and felt her heart leap a little when the little boy nodded solemnly.

'Yes, I did. Lukey said that he was really looking forward to seeing the rockets being let off, and Gramps said he'd better go and get them then.'

Trudy nodded. Lukey, she suspected, was Lucas Wilcox, Alice's twelve-year old son.

'Did you watch him go all the way to the shed?' she asked next.

'Yes – me and Lukey did. We were looking forward to the fireworks beginning, see,' Benny said earnestly. 'We were getting bored with just the bonfire, although it was rather fun watching Uncle Godfrey and Uncle Kenny try and get it started.'

'Did you see anyone else go into the shed? After your Gramps, I mean,' Trudy said quickly, as her young ears had caught the sound of Joan coming back down the stairs.

'Nah, cause Auntie Alice went in and brought out the hot chocolate, and we wanted to make sure we got first dibs.'

Trudy's heart fell a little, but she knew she shouldn't have expected miracles. Quickly, just as the door to the lounge began to open, she said, 'Can you remember who it was who said that the bonfire needed paraffin to get it started?'

'What's that?' Joan asked sharply, a puzzled look shooting from Trudy to her son and to Trudy again. She was obviously unhappy that they had been talking to the children about that night without her, and Trudy, knowing she was technically in the wrong, bit her lip guiltily.

'Nah, sorry,' Benny said, his eyes dropping quickly to the floor. He stretched out with elaborate casualness once more to help his sister build up the snort of fire that was coming from the dragon's nose. 'Here's a bit with flames on it, Clarrie,' he said helpfully, handing it over. But his gaze, Trudy noticed, slid from his mother to her visitors and then back to his mother again.

Joan, hearing the mention of fire, shuddered visibly, then sat down abruptly on the sofa. 'This whole thing has been a nightmare,' she muttered. 'I'll be glad when it's all over and done with.'

Trudy looked at the other woman thoughtfully. Not long ago, Joan had learned that her husband had just inherited a fortune. Yet she didn't look at all happy. There was no ... joy at all in her. Which was odd, surely? All right, Trudy mused, nobody liked to come into money by having a family member die. But from all that she'd learned about Thomas Hughes, she couldn't imagine that he'd got on any better with his daughter-in-law than he had with anyone else. So it wasn't as if she was actually grief-stricken. And wasn't it only human to want to celebrate a life-changing event, such as inheriting a huge amount of money?

For a moment, Trudy tried to imagine what she would do if she came into a million pounds. Images of holidays abroad, the latest Paris fashions, bright sparkly jewellery, and a big shiny motor car, all flittered in and out of her mind.

'So, how can I help you?' Joan asked helpfully, interrupting Trudy's fantasies.

But, as it quickly transpired, the other woman couldn't help them at all. She thought it might have been Godfrey who suggested the paraffin, and her husband who had called the fire brigade. And she hadn't taken any particular notice of her father-in-law's movements at all, preferring to stay in the kitchen and help Alice with the food. Twice during the interview, she left to pop upstairs to see to her little one, but whilst, each time, Trudy asked Benny about the night of the tragedy, the lad had nothing useful to contribute.

'Well, that was more or less a waste of time,' Trudy said grumpily as they made their way back into the city. She would have to put in an afternoon's work at the station, but it wouldn't be that long – especially on such a cloudy and overcast day – before it was dark again. With the winter nights drawing ever closer, soon, she knew, the shops would start to display their Christmas wares. Not that she minded – she rather liked Christmas-time, with all the pretty lights and decorations.

'Was it?' Clement asked. He thought he'd detected a certain reticence in the lad Benny, when his mother had come into the room. He'd certainly stopped being so talkative. But that might simply be because he'd been raised to understand that children were meant to be seen and not heard.

On the other hand, it wouldn't surprise him if the lad had remembered something about that night, and, for reasons of his own, hadn't want to talk about it.

He made a mental note, if all else failed, to see if he could talk to young Benjamin Hughes alone.

'Shall we talk to Alice tomorrow?' Trudy said as they approached the remains of Oxford Castle, and Clement agreed. So he dropped her off at the police station and drove back to his office.

As he did so, he felt the tremor return to his right hand.

That night, in his pleasant terraced Victorian house near Keble College, and with a nice view overlooking the park, Clement ate the supper that his charlady had left for him, then went through to the cosy front room, where he soon got the fire merrily crackling away.

With a sigh, he poured the merest splash of his favourite brandy into a bulbous glass, and leaving it to warm and settle, sank into his chair. Following his nightly ritual, he reached for his regular paper, found a pencil and turned to the crossword page. Picking up the notebook that was kept on a sideboard within easy reach, he checked the time on the grandfather clock that was ticking away contentedly in one corner, made a note of it in one column and then proceeded to do the crossword.

When he'd worked out the final clue – an anagram – and jotted it down with a distinct sense of satisfaction, he noted the time and wrote that down in a second column. This procedure was one of several that he'd thought up to try and keep a measure of his mental acuity.

After casting his eyes over three months' worth of crossword completions, he was reassured that he wasn't slowing down in any significant manner. So far, his damned disease seemed to be content to cause him only minor symptoms.

Though it was only a matter of time before they got worse, and he knew it.

But that was a bridge to be crossed only when he came to it. Ruthlessly squashing any feelings of depression or anxiety that tried to nibble at the edge of his consciousness, he swallowed his meagre mouthful of brandy, and walked over to the wireless to search for a concert to listen to before going to bed.

Beethoven, Bach, Haydn or (at a pinch) Chopin, he'd found, could usually be relied upon to restore a man's spirit.

Chapter 20

The next morning, bright and early, Duncan stepped under the shelter of a shop doorway opposite the Police Station and cursed the weather. It wasn't actually raining, as such, but it wasn't dry either. It was, as his dad would have said, 'damping'. A dull grey miasma, not as thick as fog, but not as thin as mist, seemed to drape over the city, coating everything with a slick, cold dampness. It made the pavements slippery and slowly soaked through your clothes, making you feel uncomfortable. Luckily, there was no cold wind to speak of, otherwise he might have put off his surveillance for another day.

But now that he'd managed to track down the name of the police officer tasked with investigating the Thomas Hughes case, he was eager to start work. It had cost him a few pints down at the Dog and Duck, but PC Rodney Broadstairs had been easy enough to pump gently for information. Especially since the poor lad was feeling a bit put out that his more junior colleague – and a woman at that – had been given the job instead of himself.

It had surprised Duncan too – and annoyed him considerably. It just went to show, as he'd suspected, that Oxford's finest weren't taking the *Tribune*'s campaign seriously. He'd done a quick trawl through the archives on the intriguingly named WPC Loveday, and although she'd had a few unexpected successes since joining the force, the truth was that she'd barely finished her probationary period. And at just twenty years old, she was hardly a seasoned and experienced investigator.

No doubt her remit had been to just to cross the 'T's' and dot the 'I's' and be seen to be paying lip-service to the investigation, and then after a few days, a week at most, file it away as case closed.

Well, they'd see about that!

He grinned then perked up considerably, as, through the police station doors, a gaggle of uniformed constables came out, and set about their daily routines. They nearly all set off on foot, though some, he was sure, would collect bicycles so that they could ride to wherever their beats began. There was only one woman in the bunch, and luckily for him, she didn't seem to be in need of two-wheeled transport.

Keeping back, he slowly followed her, relieved when all of her male companions gradually fell away, scattering across the city with various degrees of enthusiasm or ennui. He knew his luck was really in when she stopped by an otherwise deserted bus stop and stood patiently waiting.

As he approached her, Duncan's eyes widened appreciatively. It had been hard to tell what she looked like from a distance, and the rather dull uniform hadn't done her any favours, but as he moved to stand beside her, he could clearly see what a stunner she was. Her complexion was clear and flawless, her figure full and curvaceous without being dumpy. And even though the bulk of it had been hidden under her cap, he could now see that she had beautiful, long, curly dark hair.

When she turned, sensing his presence beside her, and looked up at him, he was just a little taken aback by the heart-shaped face and the stunning, big, dark brown velvet eyes. His heart gave that little flutter it always gave when he found himself near a really beautiful young woman, and his appreciative smile was automatic.

Trudy, on her way to interview the witness to a purse-grab last evening, sensed the nearness of a fellow passenger, and turned to see who it was. She expected to see a middle-aged housewife, perhaps, on her way to the shops further down the street, or maybe a car factory worker on his way to the early shift, since the bus terminated in Cowley, where Morris and the other motoring companies had their manufacturing lines.

Instead, she found herself looking into a pair of cat-green eyes, set in a very good-looking, triangular shaped face. A few inches taller than herself, the man had a mass of near-black hair, and was dressed in a smart suit, underneath a damp black-wool overcoat. He was, Trudy guessed, not quite thirty. His smile showed a set of near-perfect white teeth, and she felt herself stiffen in response to the look in his eye.

She knew he was going to try and chat her up, and for some reason this threw her into a bit of a panic. It puzzled her, even as she took a step back and turned to face him more fully, feeling her face tighten into the look she reserved for strangers who had the potential to cause her trouble. She couldn't understand why she felt so defensive about something that she would normally dismiss without a thought.

It wasn't as if lads trying to get her attention was anything new to her. Often they teased her about her uniform, and she'd josh them along, threatening to arrest them for being cheeky, and no harm was done. So seeing a look of speculation in a man's eyes wasn't something that normally ruffled her feathers this way.

She'd only had one boyfriend, Brian, and she'd known him all her life. In fact, she wasn't even sure that he could properly have been called a boyfriend at all, since their 'courtship' had mostly consisted of her watching him play rugby, interspersed by the odd trip to the cinema. That, and a few meals at the local café that invariably consisted of fish and chips.

But since she'd become 'available' again, she'd not wanted for potential suitors to take his place. So far, though, she hadn't really been interested. She'd been too caught up in her work and coming to grips with her feelings after her near-death experience.

But now, looking at this very attractive, older man, her heart was doing a little pitter-patter in her chest that made her breath literally catch. And it felt both good and worrying at the same time.

'Hello. It's WPC Loveday, isn't it?' Duncan said.

Trudy's look turned ever more wary. 'Yes. I don't know you, do I?'

Duncan, reading her body language, felt alternatively amused, intrigued and annoyed. Annoyed, because the last thing he wanted was for her to get her back up, since he was going to need her co-operation. Getting on her good side and buttering her up necessitated earning her trust, and dealing with a suspicious little madam was the last thing he needed.

On the other hand, she was so obviously young and inexperienced, and yet very much attracted to him, that he couldn't help but feel amused by it. It had such entertaining possibilities.

It was not that he was *so* full of himself that he thought every woman would fall at his feet, but he wasn't unaware that the opposite sex usually found him attractive. He'd had enough dalliances with a variety of women, starting at the age of sixteen, not to recognise the signs when a woman had been smitten.

Although Glenda liked to think he was monogamous, he'd made no such promise. Which made for intriguing possibilities in a situation like this.

In that initial moment of meeting and mutual awareness, Duncan had to admit that had WPC Loveday been anyone other than who she was, right now, his thoughts would be running in a very different direction.

In fact, they still might, if he didn't keep a strong hold on himself. But, he reminded himself grimly, he had other priorities right now.

So he smiled again, making it a totally sexless effort this time, and held out his hand. 'No, you don't know me yet, but I think it might be a good idea if you remedied that. My name's Duncan Gillingham.'

For a moment, Trudy thought only how unusual his first name was. She'd never met a Duncan before, and it suited him. It was slightly exotic, but manly at the same time.

Then her brain seemed to give her a mental kick, and she remembered where she'd heard it before. 'You're the reporter for the *Tribune*,' she said, her tone of voice now definitely accusatory.

Again, Duncan felt a little thrill kick his insides, a purely instinctive male response to an attractive woman's disapproval.

'Guilty m'Lud,' he shot back, with another grin. 'But please don't hold that against me. Somebody has to go around asking questions and being a nosy parker. And we don't all have the luxury of a police officer's badge to help us out.'

Trudy blinked. She wasn't sure, but she thought she was being teased – and maybe put in her place. And maybe put on notice of something – something that she didn't quite understand. Annoyingly, her heartrate accelerated a little further.

'Is there something I can do for you, Mr …' For a horrific moment she couldn't think of the damned man's name. Then, thankfully, it came to her. 'Gillingham?'

'Well, as a matter of fact, I rather thought there might be something I could do for you, Constable,' Duncan said, with a far softer smile. She really was a prickly little cat. And at the moment, all he was getting from her were claws and the odd hiss or two. That wouldn't do. 'I have some information that might be pertinent to your investigation into the Thomas Hughes case and thought that you might be interested.'

It was, he knew, an irresistible piece of bait to dangle in front of the police, and he saw her eyes flash with curiosity. He might, under other circumstances, have warned her just what curiosity was alleged to have done to felines, but he couldn't afford to be that generous right now.

'I see. Well, I can't stop just this minute,' Trudy stunned him by saying casually, her eyes going over his shoulder towards the bus she could see approaching them. For a moment, she wished that it was her father driving, but as it got nearer, she could see that it wasn't him behind the wheel. And then, inexplicably, she was suddenly glad that it wasn't him.

'What are you doing later on this afternoon?' she asked abruptly.

Duncan – whose experience of being given the brush-off by women was practically zero, felt a flash of anger, followed by a flash of appreciation, shoot through him. So she wanted to play a game of one-upmanship did she? Well, that was all right by him. He could eat young girls like her for breakfast. Then he reminded himself that he needed this particular young girl and smiled amiably. 'For you, I'll make time, Constable Loveday,' he said with mock suggestiveness. 'Just say when and where.'

Trudy, who'd been pleased with the way she'd gained the upper hand after such a slightly rocky start, gave a small shrug. 'Do you know the coffee shop opposite Christ Church college? The one with the green and white awning?'

'Yes. What time?'

The bus pulled in, and Trudy turned to face the opening doors. 'Sometime around three o'clock. I can't be more precise. I may be late.'

'For you, I'll wait until the end of time,' Duncan promised with a theatrical sigh, and gave her back another grin as she stepped on board the bus.

He stood and watched her, totally confident that she would turn around and look at him over her shoulder. He knew she just wouldn't be able to resist it.

Trudy dug into her purse for pennies as the bus conductor watched her board. It took more of an effort of will than she would have liked to walk to the nearest seat and sit down, and not glance out of the window at the handsome, sure-of-himself reporter.

But she managed it.

Just.

Chapter 21

Sir Basil Fletcher glanced at his watch when Dr Clement Ryder walked into the hotel dining room where they'd arranged to meet, and saw that it was just gone noon. It was rather early to be thinking of eating lunch, but Sir Basil had another appointment at two o'clock, and he wasn't the kind of man who liked to rush his meals. At fifty-six, his digestion wasn't as good as it once was.

But when one of the city's coroners called him and asked to meet for a friendly chat, his newspaperman's nose for a story had twitched irresistibly. Although he now owned several regional papers, and his days as a cub reporter working for someone else were long gone, he still felt excitement run through his veins whenever the possibility of a good story loomed on the horizon.

True, he had perfectly good editors overseeing the day-to-day running of each of his papers, and they in turn had a whole flock of reporters and stringers to call upon to gather in the hot stories and report the latest scandals, but still. Every now and then he liked to dip his toe in the water, so to speak.

He recognised Dr Ryder the moment he appeared in the doorway, of course, for his lunch guest was a man of some significance. First as a surgeon, and now as a coroner, he was a man of influence with powerful friends in high places in both town and gown. In a city like Oxford, Dr Ryder often dined at High Tables in various colleges. He also had the ear (reluctantly, or so it was rumoured) of the police.

Naturally, over the last few years especially, the *Tribune* had reported on some of the inquests where this man had held sway. Known to be someone of high principles and with no tolerance whatsoever for suffering fools gladly – or suffering them in any other way, come to that – he was what Sir Basil recognised as definitely being a 'character'. And thus he was someone that it didn't pay to ignore.

Tall, handsome, with a shock of white hair and impeccably dressed in a suit that screamed of the attentions of a tailor in Savile Row, Sir Basil wasn't at all surprised when the head waiter himself deigned to leave his reservation podium and offer his services in person.

Sir Basil was under no illusions that he himself could so effortlessly command a room. He had neither the looks nor that certain air that made head waiters notice him. Only the fact that he was well known here in his home city (and that he had acquired a title for services to journalism in the Honours List a decade ago) ensured that he could get the best table and the best efforts of the waiters.

He watched in slightly disgruntled amusement as the head waiter (a terrible snob who went by the unlikely name of Cedric) escorted Clement to his table, and smiled a friendly acknowledgement as the coroner reached him.

'Clement, nice to see you again,' he said amiably. Oxford was too small a city for its prominent men not to cross paths fairly regularly. Especially when you were fellow Masons and members of the same golf club.

'Basil, you're looking well,' Clement responded, just as amiably. For a while they were taken up with the usual ritual of choosing the wine (for help with which Cedric imperiously summoned over the wine waiter) and then perusing the menu and ordering

131

the food, but eventually they were left alone to get down to business.

Clement began cautiously. 'So, how's life treating you, Basil?' he asked briskly.

'Fine, can't really complain,' his companion said. A rather overweight man, with the florid complexion of someone who had either high blood pressure, or who was perhaps a little too appreciative of the finer things in life, Sir Basil's small dark eyes twinkled with mischief as he watched his old acquaintance.

Clement, perhaps sensing the other man's amusement, let his own lips twist into a smile. So much for pleasantries, he thought ruefully. He should have known there was no point in employing subtlety when engaged with a man who had made his fortune selling newspapers.

'I wanted to talk to you about this Thomas Hughes story that you and your atrocious rag are busy pushing,' he said jovially.

Sir Basil, not one whit insulted (even he conceded the *Oxford Tribune was* rather a rag – but a very *profitable* rag), grinned widely. 'I rather thought it might be. The inquest was one of yours, wasn't it?'

He knew that it was, of course, because the moment Dr Ryder had rung to ask him to meet up for lunch, he'd been racking his brains as to what the coroner might possibly want with him. And for a man as wily as Sir Basil, (who moreover flattered himself that he always had his finger firmly on the pulse of what was happening in society) that hadn't taken long to figure out.

'Yes – as I'm sure you're aware,' Clement said, with a matching grin. 'Look here, Basil, let's stop fencing about, shall we? You're a man who makes his living out of knowing what's what. Do you know – or does this reporter of yours, Gillingham – actually *know* something about the Thomas Hughes affair that the police don't? Or is it just so much pie-in-the-sky made up to sell more papers to the gullible public?'

Sir Basil sighed wearily.

'I don't personally know anything at all about it,' the newspaper owner admitted cautiously. 'But then, it's been many a year since I sat down at a typewriter to personally knock out a story. So I don't have the contacts I once had. I'm more of an overseer nowadays, than anything else. But I don't think it's much of a secret that, as a financier, our Mr Hughes sailed rather close to the wind a couple of times. I knew people – and I'm sure you did too – who got their fingers burned once or twice by unwisely investing in some of his more … shall we say, imaginative, schemes?'

Clement nodded. He paused as the waiter bought their first course – farmhouse pâté for Sir Basil, and mulligatawny soup for himself. When they were once more alone, he said, 'Yes, but the *Tribune* seems to be pointing the finger more at the immediate family. This reporter, Gillingham – I'm beginning to get the feeling that he's on a bit of a crusade of some kind. One or two of his follow-up articles seem to have been written with the express purpose of upsetting the Hughes family.'

Sir Basil ripped apart a slice of thick farmhouse loaf and set about studiously buttering it. Finally, smearing a large portion of pâté onto it, he eyed the comestible with vague disfavour, and put the piece down, uneaten, on his side-plate.

Clement, who knew his companion usually had a very hearty appetite indeed, watched this procedure with some interest.

'All right, just between you and me, Clement,' Sir Basil said, glancing around uneasily at the still almost-deserted dining room, 'can you assure me this will go no further?'

Clement smiled, not at all missing the irony of having one of the county's biggest purveyors of gossip asking him for secrecy and discretion. 'I can assure you I won't go spreading whatever you say across the front pages of your rivals,' he promised dryly.

'Touché!' Sir Basil said with a grin. 'Right. Well, the thing is, I don't know what Gillingham's up to, but I'm willing to let him have his head.'

Clement nodded. 'You trust his instincts then?'

Sir Basil snorted inelegantly. 'In a pig's eye!' he said, his already roseate face turning an even rosier shade of puce. 'The little blister is a pain in my … proverbial. He's cocky, clever and just riding to be taken down a peg or too. And I, for one, will be on the sidelines cheering.'

Seeing Clement's look of surprise at such vehemence, he gave a long sigh. 'Sorry, sorry. But just the thought of that … that … mongrel makes my blood boil.' The newspaperman reached for his glass and took a long gulp of wine, quaffing it like water. No doubt, such cavalier treatment of such a fine vintage would have made the wine waiter (and Cedric) cry, if they had witnessed it.

'If you feel like that about it, I'm surprised you're letting him have so much headline space,' Clement said, patently fishing for more information.

'Oh, of course, he's a good reporter,' Sir Basil reluctantly admitted. 'Maybe one of our best, I suppose. And Bill Niven, my chief editor at the *Tribune* thinks so too, worse luck, and he's a good man. I'd back his judgement any day of the week.' Sir Basil paused to sigh heavily. 'But just between the two of us, I'm hoping against hope that Mr Duncan Gillingham comes a cropper sooner or later. And preferably sooner. I suppose that's why I'm willing to give him so much rope over this Hughes affair. With any luck, he'll hang himself with it.'

Clement absently swirled his soup with his spoon, whilst eyeing his companion thoughtfully. Poor old Basil certainly was in a funk about something, he mused. 'Mind telling me why you want to see your own reporter make such a hash of things?'

'Because the bugger's all but engaged to my Glenda, that's why!' Sir Basil said grimly.

'Ah,' Clement said. Glenda, he knew, was Sir Basil's only child and the apple of his eye. And as a father himself, he now understood completely what was troubling the other man. 'I take it you don't approve? His family not out of the top drawer, is that it? He picks his nose and doesn't know his fish fork from his pickle spoon?'

Sir Basil was forced to laugh. 'I wish. No, snobbery's got nothing to do with it,' he admitted. 'I just don't *trust* the man, Clement, and that's a fact. He's too damned smooth, too damned good-looking, too damned *clever*. You know the sort?'

Clement did. 'Ambitious, is he?' he asked succinctly.

'Yes. And using my Glenda to climb the ladder,' Sir Basil growled. 'The trouble is, right now, she just can't see it. She's too caught up in first love – and you know how that can be,' he added darkly.

Clement smiled with real sympathy now. 'Oh yes. I dare say he can do no wrong in her eyes.'

'Exactly!' Sir Basil huffed. 'But I know the little toad doesn't really love her. He just sees her as a way of getting his hands on what will one day be all hers. I'm just hoping and praying that she'll see him in his true light before she goes and marries him. At least I'm going to insist on a long engagement.'

So saying, Sir Basil drained his wine, then stared morosely into the empty glass.

Clement sighed. Although he could sympathise with the man, listening to his woes wasn't really what he was here for. 'So, you don't know if Gillingham has any real basis for his innuendo that Hughes's accident might not have been so accidental?' he pressed.

'Hmm? Sorry, I've no idea what Gillingham knows, might have guessed or otherwise surmises,' Sir Basil said, raising his eyes from his glass and reaching for the wine bottle to pour another.

Clement, watching him, wondered if he'd started drinking earlier in the day.

'But surely he's told his editor what he's working on?' Clement wasn't about to give up.

Sir Basil again sighed as he poured his second glass of wine. 'No, I'm afraid not. Like a lot of his kind, he's a bit paranoid that if he gives too much away, he might get scooped. And how well

I understand *that!* As a junior reporter myself once, I liked to play my cards close to my chest as well. Trust no one, that's our motto! It gets to be a habit. But like I said, Bill rates him, so he's willing to let him have his head for a while, and see what comes of it.'

Sir Basil eyed his wine thoughtfully. 'He's certainly got his nose to the grindstone on this one, I'll give him that. He's obviously hot on digging up the dirt in that family. And much as I might like to think that he'll over-reach himself one day and fall spectacularly flat on his face, thus giving Glenda second thoughts, I'm not exactly holding my breath. For all that I can't stand the little swine, I have to admit he does have the nasty habit of being right. So he's probably onto *something* about this Hughes affair. But what …?' Sir Basil shrugged graphically.

And with that, Clement had, perforce, to be content.

Chapter 22

'So we're finally visiting the scene of the crime,' Trudy said thoughtfully, as Clement's 'Auntie' Rover laboriously climbed Headington Hill on their way towards the address where it had all begun. 'If this had been a straightforward investigation, any police officer in charge would probably have visited the Wilcoxes' home before doing anything else.'

Not that looking at a pile of ashes could probably tell them much, she mused philosophically. And she *had* seen the photographs taken of the shed and the surrounding gardens just after the incident, when she'd gone through the coroner's files at the outset of the case.

Still, there was nothing better than seeing something with your own eyes.

As they pulled up outside the nice, large, detached house, Trudy wondered at how ordinary it all looked. Both the Wilcox house and the neighbouring houses were set in a wide, tree-lined avenue. You'd hardly have believed that just a short while ago, the area would have been bathed in the flashing lights from police cars, an ambulance, and a fire engine.

Now, fallen autumnal leaves blew around in little eddies as a cold and rising wind played with them, but on Bonfire Night, the wind had been much stronger.

As she got out of the car, Trudy found herself automatically sniffing the air, but of course now – and given the damp weather they'd had – there was no residual scent of charred wood left in the air. In fact, because the fire's location had been retained in the back garden, there were no visible scars of the tragedy at all.

She'd only ever been at the scene of a house fire once so far in her career – a case of suspected arson, which had subsequently proved to be a case of faulty wiring. But she could still picture the blackened, charred shell of the family home where, luckily, no one had died, and the smell of acrid burning was something she'd never forget.

Now she looked around the pleasant leafy avenue with interest. They were right on the outskirts of the Headington area here, which, due to its elevated position, boasted fine views of the surrounding countryside and of Oxford itself, laid out in all its splendour below. She wondered, idly, just how many spires there were (dreaming or not) but didn't fancy actually counting them.

'Nice area,' Clement commented, as if reading her mind. He wouldn't have minded living here himself.

'Well, he was a rich man wasn't he, our Mr Hughes?' Trudy said pragmatically. 'How do you think Mrs Wilcox took it when the will was read? Getting only the house, I mean, and a trust fund for her son, but no actual money herself?'

'Let's find out, shall we?' Clement said with a smile. 'But remember, we need to speak to the children too. They'll both be home from school for their lunch, I take it?'

Trudy nodded. After meeting Clement outside the hotel where he'd had lunch with Sir Basil Fletcher, she'd made a quick check of her research on the family in her notebook. 'Yes, their daughter Olivia has just turned fifteen, and she goes to the local girls' grammar more or less at the end of the road. And their boy, Lucas, is ten, and attends the local primary school, which is about hundred yards or so that way.' She pointed vaguely behind her.

After walking up the crazy-paving path set in a large and well-maintained front garden, by mutual consent, instead of knocking at the door, they skirted around the side of the house, which led them into a large, slightly overgrown back garden. Large and mature shrubs, lilac trees and one or two scraggly examples of topiary gave it a rather romantic, semi-gothic look, especially in the dim, grey, November afternoon.

Clement supposed that the family only engaged a gardener during the summer months, and that the grounds were allowed to let themselves go a bit from autumn until the springtime brought a new burst of growing activity.

The plot, he saw at once, backed onto a large field, where farmland took over from suburbia. He looked across the pleasant scenery to where a large and majestic elm tree, host at the moment to a pair of noisy rooks, stood leafless and magnificent against the skyline. He was not a photographer, but if he were, he thought he might have taken a photograph of that lone, skeletal image. He'd always liked elms – they were his favourite tree, and he couldn't imagine the English landscape without them.

'It seems a bit lonely,' Trudy said, looking out over the furrowed, bare earth, which had clearly been recently ploughed by the local farmer. 'And not many places where a stray spark might have blown in from. Apart from their immediate neighbours on either side,' she said, glancing to her left and right.

In each instance, a six-foot tall, wooden-panelled fence provided privacy. 'Still, on a windy night, I suppose the embers that caught on the shed might not have come from the Wilcoxes' own bonfire. I expect that's some comfort to them,' she added.

'If the fire was accidental, yes,' Clement reminded her sombrely.

Trudy glanced at him sharply. 'You're more inclined to think it was deliberate then?'

Thus challenged, Clement was forced to shrug helplessly. 'How can we possibly tell? There's no forensic or medical evidence to tell us one way or another, is there?'

Trudy agreed glumly. 'You think we're just wasting our time then?'

'I wouldn't say that – not yet anyway. Let's go and hear what the lady of the house has to say about things. And let's hope either Olivia or Lucas had sharper eyes than those of the adults present that night.'

Alice Wilcox looked much as Clement remembered her from the witness stand in his courtroom. Slightly plump and pretty, and with her auburn-tinged hair a little unkempt, she looked at them blankly from big hazel eyes as she stood in the doorway. At their knocking, she'd answered the door promptly, and her momentary confusion fled as she suddenly recognised Clement.

'Oh, Dr Ryder. Please, do come in. Oh yes, Godfrey said you'd called round to speak to him, and might do the same for me. And you've talked to my husband too, of course,' she added belatedly. 'Would you like to come into the parlour? The children are in the kitchen at the moment eating their lunch.'

'Well, actually Mrs Wilcox, it was both you and the children we wanted to talk to,' Trudy said, deliberately inserting herself into the older woman's notice. In Alice Wilcox, she recognised a woman who would automatically defer to a man, and she needed to establish her own presence and authority quickly. 'And I'm sure you'd prefer to be present when we talk to them, yes?'

'Oh yes, of course,' Alice said, glancing at her uncertainly and clearly feeling a little flustered. 'Well, please do come in. We have a dining room, of course, but when it's just lunch and for the children, we tend to eat at the little table in the kitchen.'

As if aware that she was babbling inanities, she abruptly stopped talking.

The kitchen was much larger than Trudy had expected, with a door to a larder in the far wall. The room boasted one of those new big white washing machines, along with a chest freezer, two items that her mother could only dream of. Pushed against another wall was a long rectangular table, at which were seated two children, both dressed in their respective school uniforms. Empty plates boasting a few breadcrumbs had been pushed into the centre of the table.

'Mum, can we have cake now?' the boy asked, although his eyes were fixed firmly on Trudy. Lucas Wilcox was a handsome chap, with his mother's colouring and looks. Beside him, his older sister seemed to take after her father. It should, Trudy thought inconsequentially, have been the other way around.

'Of course you can. This is Dr Ryder, and …' For a moment Alice was stumped, since she hadn't asked for, or received, Trudy's name.

'I'm WPC Loveday,' Trudy said with a smile. 'We're here to talk about your granddad. Is that all right?'

Olivia's glance went straight to her mother. Her brother merely frowned slightly and said nothing.

'I'm not sure what we can possibly tell you that you don't already know,' Alice began a shade nervously. 'Oh, please take a seat, where are my manners? Would you like a cup of tea and some cake? It's a cherry cake – I made it yesterday.'

'Tea would be nice, thank you,' Clement said, 'but I've just had lunch, much as I'm sure the cake would be delicious.'

His smile was meant to help settle her nerves, and apparently did so, for in very short order they were all sitting amicably around the kitchen table, with Lucas tucking heartily into his slice of cake. Olivia cut her slice carefully into quarters, but made no move to eat it, Trudy noticed.

'So, what do you remember about Bonfire Night?' Trudy asked brightly, talking first to the little boy, who seemed fascinated by her uniform.

'Oh, it was great at first,' Lucas said earnestly through a mouthful of cake, earning him a telling off by his mother, who reprimanded him about speaking with his mouth full.

He carefully swallowed the cake, then beamed unrepentantly at Trudy. 'Uncle Godfrey and Daddy had to use paraffin to get the bonfire started but when it did, it really went up with a "whump" didn't it, Ollie?'

'Don't call your sister Ollie, Lucas,' Alice corrected her son automatically.

'Sorry,' Lucas said, just as automatically. 'Me and Benny were waiting for the rockets – we like those best – oh, and the bangers as well – to come out. So Granddad went off to the shed to go and get them.'

'Did you see him go in?' Trudy interrupted, sensing the boy was about to go galloping on with his account.

'Yeah, 'course I did,' Lucas said, sounding surprised she should ask.

'Can you remember, was the shed door already open, or did your granddad have to open it?' Trudy asked, to test his powers of observation – and veracity.

'It was open,' the boy said firmly. 'Mummy had just come out and was carrying something, and she didn't shut the door behind her.' He sounded very sure of his facts, but Trudy knew that sometimes children had a hard time telling remembered truth from imagined fantasy.

'All right. What happened then?' she asked, willing to give him the benefit of the doubt.

'Mummy went into the kitchen for a bit and then came out with the food and so Daddy went off to fetch a shovel or something so that he could push the potatoes in at the bottom.'

'A shovel? Was that kept in the shed?' Trudy inserted quickly, wondering if Kenneth Wilcox had been in the shed at the same time as his father-in-law – and if so, why he hadn't mentioned it.

But at the same time as Lucas began emphatically shaking his head, Alice spoke.

'No, as I said at the inquest, I'd just gone into the shed to find something to use for pushing the food into the bottom of the fire, and found the old rake. We use the same one each year you see – an old thing that's not much use for gardening now. I left it outside the back door – the one that leads off the kitchen. Kenneth would have retrieved it from there.'

'I see, well that's clear enough,' Trudy said. She looked deliberately at the Olivia now. 'Did *you* see your granddad go into the shed?'

'No. I was talking to Aunt Caroline,' Olivia spoke for the first time. She picked up a piece of cake and bit into it.

'Your Aunt Caroline didn't get on with her father much, did she?' Trudy said casually.

She felt the girl's mother shuffle uneasily on her chair at this, but Alice didn't actually intervene.

Olivia, after swallowing her cake, shook her head. 'No. She always said he killed Granny.'

This stark pronouncement made her mother go a trifle pale. 'I really don't think …' Alice began weakly and Trudy quickly backed off.

'Did you notice anyone else go into or near the shed that night, Olivia?' she asked instead.

'Not really. We were all watching the bonfire, you see. Sometimes, a gust of wind would blow a bit off newspaper or wood off, and one of the grown-ups would chase it and kick it back onto the fire. Except for Uncle Godfrey. He said his shoes were patent leather and he couldn't risk it.'

'What's patent leather?' Lucas piped up, but nobody rushed to tell him.

'Did you see your Aunt Mary talking to your granddad at any time?' Trudy asked generally, but both children shook their heads.

Clement, listening closely, thought this rang true. If brother and sister had had a falling out recently, they had probably taken pains to avoid one another.

'Did any of you see how the shed actually caught fire?' Trudy asked next, but wasn't surprised when both children shook their heads.

'What about your cousins who were there, Benny and Clarissa?' Trudy tried craftily. 'Did they tell you any secrets about that night?' She knew that often children who'd seen something might confide in someone else of their own age, rather than in an adult. 'Because if they did tell you something about Bonfire Night and made you swear not to tell, it's all right to tell a police lady.'

Lucas looked impressed by this, then disappointed. 'Nah. Benny didn't say anything. Lucky dog.'

Trudy looked at him thoughtfully. 'Why is he a lucky dog?' she asked casually.

'Because him and Clarry and Helen are all going on a super holiday. I heard Mummy and Uncle Matthew talking about it yesterday.'

'Lucas! What have I told you about eavesdropping?' his mother flashed, her face flushing in embarrassment.

'I wasn't listening at the door or anything! Promise! I was just sitting here eating my biscuits,' her son said indignantly. 'I can't help it if your voices are too loud can I?' he added, looking in appeal at Clement, who smiled and shook his head, indicating his support.

'This was after the reading of your father's will, I take it,' Clement said mildly, turning to smile at the flustered Alice.

'Yes. I didn't realise our voices were carrying to the kitchen. Not that there's any secret about it. Matthew told me that, given the circumstances, he's taking his family to the United States.'

'Lucky dog,' Lucas said again. 'I wish *I* had been given a lot of money and could go off on holiday any time I wanted. I'll bet they get to see the Grand Canyon,' Lucas sighed enviously. 'But Daddy says I have to wait for my money until I'm older. I don't think that's fair, do you?'

Once again, Clement was appealed to, but this time, wisely, Clement pretended not to notice.

'I think that's enough of that,' Alice said firmly, rising to her feet. She was obviously uncomfortable talking about the family's financial business in front of strangers. 'Lucas, finish your cake.' And to Trudy and Clement she said, 'I'll show you out, shall I?'

With no graceful way of continuing to question the children, Trudy reluctantly let herself be shepherded out into the front hall.

But Clement wasn't quite finished yet. As they approached the front door, he said quietly, 'I understand that your father wanted your husband to invest in one of his business deals, Mrs Wilcox?'

'How did … Oh, yes, I think he did mention it. Kenneth came into a family legacy a little while ago, you see. But he wasn't interested in going into something with Father. He has his own plans to open another shop instead in the city centre,' Alice said, recovering quickly.

'I can't imagine that made your father very happy,' Clement said sympathetically. 'From what we've learned about him from others, he seems to have been a man who liked to get his own way.'

Alice flushed. 'Yes, well, father could be rather difficult sometimes,' she admitted.

'It must have made life a little uncomfortable for your husband, especially, I imagine?' Clement carried on, careful to keep his tone sympathetic. 'Living in what amounted to his father-in-law's house, whilst not being on the best of terms with him.'

'Oh, Kenneth gets on with everybody,' Alice said miserably, and pointedly opened the front door.

'Well, thank you for your time, Mrs Wilcox,' Clement said. Trudy murmured her own thanks, and as she brushed past her, Alice gave her a smiling nod. But then she closed the door so quickly behind her, Trudy almost fancied she could feel the wood of the door catch the heel.

As they walked thoughtfully back to the car, Trudy said wryly, 'Well, so much for children being more observant than adults.'

But her mind wasn't really on their latest, abortive interview. Instead, her heart was beginning to race a little, because soon she would be meeting Duncan Gillingham at the café.

Of course, it was strictly business – just to talk about what he knew or had discovered that had made him so suspicious about the fire, she reminded herself. But even so, it was a bit of a treat to have a break at a nice café in the middle of her working day – especially with a good-looking young man.

Beside her, Clement shook his head. 'Did you notice how quiet the girl was?' he asked.

'Olivia? Yes, she wasn't very forthcoming was she,' Trudy acknowledged vaguely. 'But perhaps she's just used to her little brother being the chatterbox of the family.'

She wondered if she'd have time to pop home and put on a little lipstick before going to the café. Then realised how silly that idea was. Even though DI Jennings was very unlikely to find out that she'd nipped back home whilst on duty, her mother would certainly wonder why she had done so.

And besides, what did she really need lipstick for anyway? It might swell Duncan Gillingham's head if he thought she was making the effort for his sake. Which she most certainly was not!

'Trudy?' Clement's voice, raised a decibel above its usual level, not only made her jump, but indicated that it wasn't the first time he'd called her name.

'Sorry, I was just thinking,' she said. Which was true – she *had* been thinking, just not about the matter in hand. She was grateful to duck her head in order to get into the passenger seat of the Rover so that Clement wouldn't notice any tell-tale hint of guilt that might have given her away.

Clement started the engine and glanced up at the nice house on the hill. No doubt about it, the Wilcoxes had fallen on their feet, inheriting that house. But at what cost? He was sure Thomas Hughes had led his long-suffering daughter a merry dance for years. And how must Kenneth Wilcox have felt about not being the true master in his home?

He frowned thoughtfully as he checked his rear mirror and pulled away from the kerb. Unless he was mistaken, the children in this case knew something that he did not. Reticence was not usually high in the average child's repertoire, but he'd come across it twice recently. Just now in the case of Olivia Wilcox, and not long before, in the case of young Benjamin Hughes.

He would have been prepared to bet a significant amount that both of them had seem *something* significant that night, but were obviously not going to say so. Perhaps they'd made one of those solemn pacts, with dire consequences for anyone who dared tell, that children were so fond of. If so, it might be impossible to get them to open up.

'So, where do you want to go next?' he asked, and was startled to see a look of something close to panic cross his companion's face.

Trudy looked hastily down at her satchel and quickly searched through it for her notebook. 'I think I need to do some more research – perhaps at the library. You can drop me off at your office, that'll be easiest,' she mumbled.

The coroner's office wasn't far from the café where she would have to meet Duncan, so if it should start raining again, at least she wouldn't have to arrive looking like a drowned rat.

Whilst she was well aware that if Clement knew that she was meeting the reporter he'd want to come, especially after his meeting with the owner of the newspaper, she was very reluctant to have her mentor tag along this time. She just had a strong feeling that Dr Ryder and the reporter would not hit it off, and she didn't want any antagonism getting in the way of a successful interview. After all, it was just possible that what Duncan had to tell her might bust the case wide open. At the very least, she hoped to solve the riddle of why he had started the campaign for a proper investigation into the Hughes fatality in the first place.

147

And that reminded her. 'By the way, what did Sir Basil have to say? About the *Tribune*'s storylines, I mean?'

Clement, wondering what was bothering her, sighed. 'Hmm? Oh, Sir Basil is just the owner. He might have been a reporter himself in days of yore, but these days he doesn't have much to do with the daily running of the papers, let alone the stories they print. He has full confidence in his editors to do all that.'

'Oh. So he has no idea what's behind it at all?' she asked, disappointed. 'Surely he must have some idea what Dun … Mr Gillingham is up to?' she asked casually.

Clement shot her a narrow-eyed glance, and noticed she was staring fixedly out of the passenger window.

'I'm afraid not,' he said slowly. 'Sir Basil's is not that young man's greatest fan, I think it's fair to say,' he added, with a smile of remembrance at the newspaper owner's distaste for his prospective son-in-law.

'He's probably a bit jealous, I suppose,' Trudy predicted. The old man probably wished he was still young and chasing down scoops, rather than sitting behind a desk.

They drove the rest of the way into the city in silence, and Trudy gave a sigh of relief when she finally climbed out of the car. She didn't like playing her cards close to her chest and keeping the coroner in the dark, so to ease her conscience, she did actually go into the library and look up some things, but she didn't stay long.

She wanted to be at the café in good time. But only because it was bad manners to keep people waiting, she told herself firmly.

Chapter 23

As WPC Loveday passed a few minutes in the library, Rupert Burrows turned down the familiar road to Wolvercote, and was soon parking up under a weeping willow tree beside Mary Everly's pretty cottage.

Luckily this time there was no sign that her unwanted visitors of a few days ago had come back for another interview. She'd told him all about them, of course, when he'd returned to the cottage once the coast was clear, and they'd both agreed that it was unfortunate to have the authorities sniffing around the family's private business.

He retrieved a bunch of last-of-the-season asters from the back seat, knowing how much Mary loved flowers, and checked that his tie was straight before knocking on the door.

It wouldn't do to turn up looking down-at-heel.

As always, Mary looked smart and calm, and he smiled with relief as she thanked him with genuine happiness for the flowers and ushered him into the cottage's front room. She quickly arranged the asters in a vase, and within five minutes, she was reaching for the tea-strainer and was pouring them a fragrant cup of Earl Grey in front of a smouldering log fire.

It was all very pleasant, and Rupert was looking forward to the time he could live here too. His little flat in Kidlington was all very well, but it was a bit bijou and really rather drab. Alas, what with the upkeep of the car, his club fees and all the other things that laid claim on his beleaguered purse, it had had to suffice for many a barren and lonely year. What's more, the prospect of a lonely old age without any relief in sight had been staring him in the face, until he'd met up with Mary again a year or so ago.

He'd first run into her when he'd come up to Oxford to study, and they had run around in the same large circle of friends for years. He'd even played golf with her late husband once or twice, before he'd joined the Foreign Office. But of course, once he'd been made an ambassador, they had then spent many years abroad, and inevitably they had lost touch with one another.

But he'd recognised Mary the instant they'd met outside the theatre one night and the rest, as the saying went, was history.

'Poor old Alice is in a bit of a state,' Mary said absently, pulling Rupert from his reminiscences as he sighed contentedly over his teacup. 'She rang me up a little while ago. Apparently, you-know-who were back at the house, talking to the children this time! Can you imagine?' Her voice rose slightly in reproof. 'Honestly, I don't know who the police think they are nowadays. Well, I say police, but it's only a slip of a girl really. So I suppose it's not too bad.'

Rupert frowned. 'I'll be happy when all this business about Thomas has blown over,' he said fretfully.

'So will I,' Mary said, her tone taking on a little bite. 'The last thing we need is for strangers to go around stirring things up. Who knows what damage they will do?'

She cast her suitor a slightly fond, slightly exasperated look, knowing full well that he was hardly the knight on a white steed that foolish girls dreamed of. But then she gave a mental shrug. She was hardly a foolish girl any more. Besides, she'd known Rupert on and off for ages now, and had no real regrets about her choice of companion.

After her husband had died, she'd assumed that she'd settle down into widowhood without too many regrets, and such had been the case for the first year or two. After that, however, she began to find that silence and aloneness began to chafe. It was not, after all, as if she was truly *old* yet. She still had plenty of good years left in her, but she found it more and more difficult to contemplate them alone. There were just so many instances when having a man around made life so much easier.

Going on holiday, for instance, was not so much fun when one travelled alone, she'd discovered. The old biddies who frequented holiday hotels on the coast did tend to be so sympathetic! And there were plenty of times, say, when the electricity went off during a winter storm, when it would have been nice to have someone else there, just to share a candle with, and groan or laugh about the absurdities of coping in the dark. Someone to make you a hot drink when you had a raging cold, or deal with taps that dripped, or clear gutters when they began to overflow.

And so, gradually, the idea of remarrying began to seem more and more attractive. Of course, the problem with that was one which had plagued ladies of a certain age since the time Jane Austen began penning her witty novels and probably long before that too – namely, the dearth of suitable, available men.

And therein lay the rub, Mary thought with a touch of wry impatience.

But after running into Rupert Burrows again, and finding him to be the answer to all her problems, it was annoying (to say the least) to discover that execrable older brother of hers resolutely refused to consider his old army colleague to be suitable for her in any way.

Of course, he *was* a few years younger than herself, Mary acknowledged, watching Rupert fondly as he sipped his tea. But only by six years, so it was not as if she could be accused of robbing the cradle! But his undoubted good looks (whilst attracting Mary in the first place) had also been something else that her brother had held against him. Tall, handsome, blond men with blue eyes and a full moustache, according to Thomas Hughes, were nearly always up to no good. Especially if they were reduced to living on an inadequate army pension!

As if she needed the warning! Of course, Mary had always known that part of her attraction for Rupert was her financial security. She was, after all, no silly dreamy-eyed or innocent girl, unaware of the world and the way it worked. But Rupert was hardly a full-fledged gold digger, just as she was no great heiress. And if *she* had no objection to acquiring a handsome husband to see her through her old age, at the cost of keeping him in the small but necessary luxuries in life, then what business was it of Thomas's?

She looked at her fiancé fondly once more, wondering what he was thinking. Dressed in his best Harris tweed suit, with his old regimental tie impeccably knotted, he looked the epitome of a respectable if unremarkable man at ease, and it was hard to understand why her brother had been so pig-headed and determined to prevent their marriage.

He certainly couldn't have objected to poor Rupert's background. Born in Sussex to a perfectly respectable land-owning 'gentleman' farmer and the daughter of a Bishop, he'd gone to good (if not top-notch) schools, and earned a place at Oxford, where they'd first met. He'd trained as an architect, and had never married. Perhaps because the war had intervened just when he had probably been considering settling down.

Here Mary Everly let out a gentle sigh. Yes, that was where the true trouble lay, of course – in that regrettable incident during the war.

She could still recall the glee in her brother's face when he told her all about it, fully expecting her to be shocked to the core, and disavow Rupert on the spot. And she could still (with much more satisfaction) remember how the look on his face had changed when she'd rounded on him in no uncertain terms.

After all, she'd pointed out with equal glee and cold fury, Thomas could hardly claim to have had a 'spectacular war' himself, could he? Working at the War Office, *he'd* never seen the battlefield, or had to put his own life on the line. And why should she give Rupert up over things that had happened years ago? Mistakes were being made all the time. Besides, everyone knew that bad things happened in the war. It was a *war*, for Pete's sake!

The resulting row had been furious and loud, with Thomas insisting that his sister would only be allowed to marry Rupert over his dead body, and the fallout had resulted in an estrangement between them that had never been breached. And now that her brother was dead, Mary mused pragmatically, it never could be.

'Would you like a biscuit, Rupert?' Mary asked mildly. 'I baked some shortbread yesterday – your favourite.'

'Lovely idea, old girl,' Rupert beamed. But his smile faltered as soon as she'd left the room, and when she returned with the biscuit tin, she found him staring pensively into the fire.

'It will all blow over, won't it Mary?' he asked her anxiously. 'I mean, this newspaper Johnny will eventually start picking on someone else, and you and I will be all right, won't we?'

Mary looked at his worried big blue eyes and smiled softly. 'Of course it will, Rupert. These things have a way of working themselves out, you'll see. Now, how do you feel about a spring wedding?'

Chapter 24

Trudy saw him the moment she walked into the café. He had changed his suit since she'd met him at the bus stop that morning, and she couldn't help but wonder if he'd gone back to his home to change into a nicer suit in order to impress her.

Then, more pragmatically, she told herself he'd probably had to interview someone prominent earlier that afternoon and his editor had told him to make himself look very smart and presentable.

As she approached, she saw the moment he noticed her, and watched his face light up. She wouldn't have been human if she hadn't felt pleased at the unspoken compliment, and for a moment, her breath fluttered in her throat. Then she was smiling politely at him, and heard herself say coolly, 'Mr Gillingham, thank you for waiting.'

'You're not late,' Duncan said at once, half-rising politely from his seat, as she drew out one of the chairs in front of her.

The café was almost empty, with the lunch hour crowd long departed, and the afternoon tea brigade not yet in evidence, but the few customers who were there, Duncan noticed with a hidden smile, were covertly watching her. He didn't find it in the least surprising – the combination of an attractive young woman, wearing a police officer's uniform, was bound to bring her attention, no matter where she went.

To his intense gratification, Trudy swept off her cap, revealing a mass of curly near-black hair, which had been twisted into a becoming chignon atop her head. A few strands had escaped their confines during the day, and now lay curling over her forehead, and creeping out to caress her cheek. He had to resist the urge to reach out and push one back from just below her ear.

She did not, however, take off her jacket. Perhaps too much informality wasn't to be expected on their first meeting.

And Duncan was going to do everything he could to make damned sure that this was only their *first* meeting.

'So, thanks for meeting me,' he began, glancing up as the waitress approached. She was slightly older than Trudy, a pretty girl with blonde hair and big brown eyes, and Trudy noticed the way that she smiled at him as she came up to his side.

'Let me treat you to afternoon tea,' Duncan said to Trudy, who smiled briefly but shook her head.

'Just a cup of tea for me please,' she said firmly to the waitress, who barely glanced at her. Even though she didn't think finger sandwiches and dainty cakes counted as offering a bribe, it had been drummed into her at training college that a police officer always had to be careful about accepting any kind of 'gift' from the public, witnesses and especially suspects. Although, of course, the reporter could hardly be said to fall into the latter category, Trudy thought gratefully.

'And for the gentleman?' the waitress prompted, her smile widening ever further as Duncan looked up at her.

'Oh, the same for me too, thanks.' He gave her a determinedly vague smile. He had noticed that the WPC hadn't failed to register the blonde girl's obvious interest in him, and he wanted to make sure that Trudy Loveday knew that it wasn't reciprocal.

The waitress left with obvious reluctance, and Trudy was careful to keep her face bland as she glanced across the table.

His black hair gleamed in the light from the streetlamp outside the window, and she thought again how attractive he was. A bit like Cary Grant, but darker, and with a hint of danger about him. Perhaps it was his unusual green eyes.

'So, Mr Gillingham …' she began crisply, telling herself that she was going to keep this all strictly professional, but before she could even begin, he grinned at her and interrupted.

'Oh please, call me Duncan,' he said. 'I hope we're going to get to know one another a bit over this Hughes story, and it seems so formal to go on calling each other Mr this and Constable that, don't you think?'

His smile was so winning, and he was so obviously sure of his charm, that Trudy couldn't stop herself from shooting back coolly, 'No, I *don't* think, Mr Gillingham.' She reached into her satchel for her notebook and ostentatiously turned to a fresh page.

When she looked at him again, he was grinning, trying to look abashed, and failing. 'Sorry, but I do I really have to keep calling you Constable Loveday?'

'Yes, Mr Gillingham, you do,' Trudy said, resisting the urge to grin back at him. 'This is official police business.'

'And what if it wasn't? Could I call you by your first name then? By the way, what is it?' he cajoled cheekily.

Trudy, who never used her full name, (what her parents were thinking of, naming her after her Aunt Gertrude she had no idea!) sighed patiently. 'This morning you said you had some information about the death of Mr Thomas Hughes.' She tapped her notebook tellingly with a biro pen.

When she'd been at school, she, like all her classmates, had learned to write with an old-fashioned nib and a bottle of ink, and she was forever thankful to Mr Biro for his wonderful invention. Even so, some of her older colleagues still only used pencils whenever they could, and regarded the 'new-fangled' biro pens with suspicion.

'From the stories you've been writing for your newspaper in

the last few days, you've been hinting about Mr Hughes's death not being an accident,' Trudy swept on. 'Do you care to tell me why you think that there was something untoward happening at the bonfire party that night? I take it you attended the coroner's inquest?'

'I did,' he assured her. 'And duly listened and made note of the man's nearest and dearest trotting out the family line,' Duncan added, eyes twinkling. She really did look lovely when she was being all severe and constabulary. But a slight flush on her cheeks and the quickness of her breathing told him that WPC Loveday was not as coolly indifferent to him as she would have him believe.

'You think they were lying?' she asked sharply, and all at once she really was all business. Which told him that, pretty as a picture though she might be, this lady also had ambition – and would be no pushover.

Duncan sighed a little, and hastily reminded himself where his true priorities lay. It was all very well flirting with the unexpectedly delightful police officer in charge of the case, but he had to remember that he needed to lead this particular horse to water – and make her drink it.

'Oh, maybe not lying, exactly,' he said casually, preparing the ground carefully, 'but let's just say, they were not exactly falling over themselves to be perfectly truthful either.'

Trudy continued to tap her notebook with her pen. 'In what way, exactly, Mr Gillingham?' she asked with exaggerated patience.

'You know, by now of course, about the old man's dodgy business ventures?' he began cautiously. He needed to lay the groundwork before he started to steer her in the right direction, and it wouldn't do to let her know that she was being manipulated.

'I've done my research, Mr Gillingham. None of Mr Hughes's financial affairs were illegal,' she shot back crisply, confirming his opinion that WPC Loveday had her wits about her.

'No, but a lot of people lost a lot of money because of him.

And you'll have noticed that he never invested any of his own pennies when it came to the more risky schemes? It's no wonder he made a fortune.'

'If that's all you have …' Trudy began to make getting-ready-to-leave gestures, and Duncan laughed, holding his hands out in an appeasing gesture.

'All right, all right, obviously that's not all.'

Trudy sighed elaborately and leaned back in her chair, looking cross and bored, but the truth was she was enjoying herself enormously.

Just then, the waitress returned with the tray and took her time setting out the teapot, milk jug, sugar bowl, and cups and saucers. 'Are you sure there's nothing else you'd like, sir?' she asked coyly.

Duncan again smiled vaguely at her but shook his head, and with a small sigh, she slipped away.

'So what else do you have to go on?' Trudy pressed.

'You know the man's youngest daughter hated him, don't you? Caroline Hughes. She blamed him for her mother's death.'

Trudy gave nothing away, but it was obvious this man had done a lot of digging and had unearthed a lot of the Hughes family secrets in the process. Was it possible he'd discovered something that she and Clement had, so far, missed?

'And that he made his older daughter, Alice's life, hardly worth living?' Duncan went on. 'I've spoken to the Wilcoxes' daily woman and the old part-time gardener who both say the old man treated her like a slave. Even reduced her to tears sometimes.'

Duncan took a sip of his tea, watching her closely for any reaction. Annoyingly, though, he couldn't tell if she was impressed or not.

Trudy continued to say nothing. She hadn't known about the latter, but when she took a moment to think about it, it didn't exactly surprise her. From all that she'd learned about the dead man, he'd been selfish and uncaring about his treatment of those supposedly nearest and dearest to him for all his life.

'And did you know that his eldest son only received a measly pension in the old man's will?' Duncan pressed on, his twinkling green eyes daring her to deny any of it.

Trudy, who in spite of herself, was becoming more and more impressed by the depth of the man's knowledge, wondered grimly who he had charmed in the solicitor's office to get such information. Probably one of the partners' secretaries no doubt, she thought sourly.

'So it's not as if there weren't a lot of people glad to see the back of him, Constable,' Duncan insisted. 'Surely, by now, you've gathered some evidence that the blow he took to his head wasn't the result of any exploding firework? I mean, you have to ask yourself, how likely is it that one of them knocked him out? Would a rocket really have the heft behind it to knock a man clean out? Wasn't it mentioned at the inquest that he might have hit his head on a wooden shelf? It's not such a leap, is it, to say that he was hit over the head by something wooden? Otherwise, any grown man should have been able to crawl out of that shed when it caught fire unless he'd already been seriously incapacitated, surely?'

Trudy blinked. 'Mr Gillingham, I do hope you haven't asked me here to try and pump me for information?' she said indignantly. 'Because if you have, I can tell you now that you're wasting your time. If, or when, the police force has any information it wants to share with the press, our—'

'All right, all right, pax,' Duncan grinned. 'And as if I'd *dare* try and grill you, WPC Loveday!'

Trudy reached for the sugar bowl and added two lumps to her steaming cup of tea and slowly stirred it in. 'Do you actually have *anything* relevant to tell me, Mr Gillingham, or are you just wasting my time? You do know it's an offence to waste police time, I take it?' she added with a slight smile.

'Are you going to arrest me, Officer?'

'Don't tempt me!' Trudy shot back, and for a moment Duncan

159

felt a distinct stirring in his loins at the thought of this woman slipping the handcuffs on him. Then he laughed and dragged his mind back to the matter in hand.

'All right – straight up this time,' he said, leaning forward a little in his chair, and casting a quick glance around. 'Have you cottoned on yet to what a truly nasty piece of work Mr Kenneth Wilcox is?' he asked, his voice deadly serious now.

Trudy felt her chest tighten slightly. 'Go on,' she said cautiously.

She wasn't a fool, and she knew that when a journalist invited you to a café, you could bet all the doughnuts on the menu that they would try and get something from you that they could quote in one of their stories. And she'd made a promise to herself that she would give this handsome young man not even a crumb that he could put in print and attribute to a 'source within the police force'.

But she was now very aware that if Duncan *had* discovered something of real importance, then she needed to get that information out of him – and to do so without resorting to quid pro quo.

She felt herself tensing as she realised that she was going to have to be very careful now – not by so much as by a look or a gesture must she give away that she had no idea what he was getting at.

'Mr Kenneth Wilcox – husband of Alice, and prime mover and shaker around the bonfire that night,' Duncan said drolly, careful to keep his voice light and neutral. 'Of all the people there that night, who would have known the contents of the shed better than him? What's more, he would have had ample time before the family members started to arrive to make a good reconnaissance of that garden shed. And who knows what he might have done whilst he was in there?'

Trudy allowed herself to smile sceptically. 'Like what? Set up a booby trap for his father-in-law?'

Duncan shrugged. 'You may scoff, but how do you know that

he didn't?' he challenged. 'The whole shed went up in flames very quickly, didn't it? He might have scattered some of that paraffin around in order to help it. And say he *had* set up some kind of contraption – a heavy garden implement hanging by a rope, all set to swing at head-height when someone snagged a trip wire or what-have-you … well, all evidence of it would have gone up in flames, wouldn't it? And if the fire investigators found bits of burnt rope and the remains of a sledgehammer or what have you – well, it was a garden shed. What would have been surprising about that?'

He watched her to see her reaction as he took a sip of tea. Of course, he had no idea if what he'd said was feasible. But then, so long as it got her thinking seriously about Kenneth Wilcox as a suspect, what did it really matter?

For a moment, Trudy thought it over. Of course, it all sounded a bit 'Boy's Own' and Heath Robinson-ish to her. But *could* it have happened that way? She and Clement had always assumed that if Thomas Hughes *had* been murdered, then it had been very simple and straightforward. Namely, that someone had simply followed the man inside the shed when he or she was sure that nobody was looking and hit him over the head, then set fire to the shed.

But what if some kind of booby trap had already been set in place? It was just possible, wasn't it? Everyone who'd attended the last few bonfire parties at the Headington house would have known that it would be Thomas who always 'did' the firework display. And a booby trap would give the killer an alibi – and might account for the fact that nobody was admitting to seeing anyone go into the shed, other than the dead man.

Then she remembered that Alice Wilcox had been in the shed shortly before her father. So if there was a trap, surely she'd have set it off? Unless she was the one who'd set it? But would a woman have the know-how to do something like that?

Then she frowned. 'I don't know. It all sounds a bit complicated and far-fetched to me,' she grumbled.

Duncan shrugged casually. 'Oh, I'm not saying that it did happen that way for sure. Only that's it's a possibility, and that Kenneth Wilcox would have been in an ideal position to do it. What's more, everyone I've spoken to says that he couldn't stand his father-in-law.'

Trudy made a few notes, then glanced up at him quickly. 'Of course, any one in that family could have done the same. His sons visited the house – and garden – regularly. They must have been inside the shed at some point.'

'Even the awful Godfrey?' Duncan grinned. 'Yes, I know. But none of the others are quite as nasty a bit of work as our Kenneth.'

Trudy nodded slowly. 'That's the second time you've said something along those lines. Care to elaborate, Mr Gillingham?'

'Duncan!'

'Mr Gillingham,' Trudy said implacably. 'What do you have against Mr Wilcox exactly?'

But Duncan was too wily to lay it all out for her. She might start to look the gift horse in the mouth. Besides, unless he was much mistaken, Trudy Loveday was the kind of girl who liked to make her own mind up about things.

So instead he smiled widely. 'Ah, now *that* you'll have to wait to read all about in some future edition of the *Tribune*, WPC Loveday,' he teased. And, as she was about to open her mouth to protest, cajoled charmingly, 'Oh come on, you can't be so hard-hearted as to deny a reporter his scoop, can you?'

'Withholding evidence in a police investigation is a crime, need I remind you?' Trudy said, feeling genuinely angry for the first time. As if sensing this, Duncan quickly backed off.

'All right, all right. It's just that I've learned some very nasty facts about Kenneth that would turn your stomach. Unfortunately, they don't relate – directly anyway – to his father-in-law's death. On that subject, I swear that I don't have any *evidence* per se,' he said hastily. 'And you can hardly say I'm withholding anything from you, can you?' he added with another smile. 'Look, here I

162

am with you, telling you everything,' he said, holding his arms out in a generous gesture.

'Hardly everything,' Trudy corrected him, trying not to grin back at him. 'What exactly do you have against Mr Wilcox?' she persisted.

'Nothing that I can take to a court of law. Well, not yet,' he added wryly. 'But let's just say, from what I've been finding out about him, he's definitely a wrong 'un. And I'm just saying – you won't be disappointed if you dig into his background a bit more. And Thomas Hughes, say what you like about him, was nobody's fool, and since the two of them lived in the same house, you can be pretty sure that the old man must have had a fair idea of what kind of a man his son-in-law was. And I doubt he was the kind of man to put up with it for long. Who knows – perhaps he'd threatened to toss him out of the family on his ear and Kenneth took exception.'

'And that's it?' Trudy said in disgust. 'That's all you dragged me here to say?'

Duncan grinned. 'Is that what I did? Dragged you here?' He glanced around the pleasant and warm café and grimaced. 'Well, what an utter rotter I am. Let me buy you a cake to make up for it.'

Trudy felt her lips twitch and quickly looked away. But Duncan had noticed it, and now that he'd planted the seed of Kenneth's villainy successfully in her head, felt that he could afford to relax and play a bit.

'If you're really nice to me, I might even stretch so far as to make that a cream cake?' he said with a mock-leer.

163

Chapter 25

'I think we should talk to Kenneth Wilcox again,' Trudy said casually the next morning. She was in the coroner's office, waiting for him to finish writing up some notes. For once it wasn't raining, and as she stared out of the window, she wondered what she could get her mother for Christmas.

Her father was always easy to buy for – a pot of his favourite Brylcreem and some warm socks.

Perhaps she could find some of her mother's favourite Pears soap …

'Why Wilcox?' Clement's voice interrupted her mental shopping, and she shrugged nonchalantly.

Taking a deep breath, she finally told him about meeting Duncan – making no mention of the tea and cream cake – and was off-hand and casual as she relayed the gist of their talk.

'He seemed sure that Kenneth was someone of interest, so I thought we might as well do a follow-up interview and see if anything comes of it,' she concluded. 'Why, did you have something else in mind?'

Clement, not sure that he liked her casual tone of voice, looked at her over his paperwork, but merely smiled and shrugged when she finally looked at him. 'Sure, why not?' he said.

But as they collected their coats and headed outside, he wondered why she hadn't told him about meeting up with this reporter chap before. And more especially, why she'd hadn't asked for his company at their cosy teatime chat.

Always before, they'd discussed every aspect of their cases, and had mutually agreed on how to proceed, and he was not sure that he liked being kept out of the loop in this way. He was going to have to make it clear, as tactfully as possible, that it wasn't a good idea for her to keep things from him.

As they drove towards Kenneth Wilcox's shop, Clement's mind went back uneasily to his talk with Sir Basil. Obviously, the man had been biased and prejudiced against his least favourite reporter, but then Clement wasn't sure that any man would be deemed good enough for Sir Basil's only child. And as a father himself, he knew how protective he was when it came to his own daughter's wellbeing and happiness. So, when the newspaper owner had been going on about Duncan Gillingham's many faults, he'd listened, but had tended to take it all with a pinch of salt.

Now, though, he began to wonder. Sir Basil had been convinced that the man didn't care tuppence for his fiancée, and was only marrying her in order to gain all the advantages that came with being the boss's son-in-law. By his account, Gillingham had not only deliberately set out to seduce his daughter, but was both smarmy and manipulative and generally an underhanded, sly, untrustworthy dog.

When he'd finally walked away from his lunch with the still fuming newspaper man, Clement had felt both sympathetic and amused in equal measure. He'd felt genuinely sorry that the man was so unhappy, but he also couldn't help but feel as if Sir Basil's woes were more imagined than real.

Now though, he was beginning to feel uncomfortably as if his cavalier reaction to Sir Basil's troubles might be coming back to bite him. It seemed possible that Trudy too might have fallen for

Gillingham's dubious but charming ways, and he wasn't feeling anything like so sanguine.

Of course, it was possible that he was worrying for nothing. As he negotiated Cowley's streets, he cast her a quick but comprehensive glance. She was looking innocently out at the streets, but hadn't yet said a word.

'So, how did you come to meet up with the reporter?' he asked. 'Did he phone the station?'

Trudy, taken by surprise by the question, found herself blurting out 'Yes, that's right,' before she'd even stopped to think. And the moment the lie was out of her mouth, she found herself regretting it.

What made her even angrier with herself was the fact that she couldn't understand why she'd done it. After all, what was wrong with simply telling Clement the truth? That Duncan had met her at the bus stop …

Suddenly, her thoughts came to a crashing halt, as for the first time, she began to think, really *think*, about that first meeting. She knew what *she'd* been doing at the bus stop … but why had *he* been there? It seemed too much of a coincidence to suppose he'd just run into her. Besides, he'd already known who she was.

At this realisation, she gave a little internal grimace at this evidence of her naivety. Of *course* he'd known who she was – he was hot on the trail of investigating a story, after all. Probably one of the first things he'd have made a priority was to find out which police officer was looking into Hughes's case, and then … what … staked out the police station? Lain in wait for her …

She let her breath out slowly, feeling more and more of a fool.

Of *course* he'd waited for her to appear and then followed her, and when she'd stopped at the bus stop, he'd made his move. And she, gullible twit that she was, hadn't questioned any of it, even agreeing to meet him at a café later to talk some more.

'I'm surprised that he got past the switchboard, or the officer on duty,' Clement said mildly, jarring her already jolted equilibrium even further. 'Surely DI Jennings doesn't approve of his officers fraternising with the press. Well, at least without his approval?'

Trudy felt herself go cold as she realised that Dr Ryder, as quick and intelligent as he was, already suspected that she had been lying to him. The thought made her feel slightly sick.

And now how was she supposed to get herself out of this mess? Because he was right – normally, reporters on the scrounge for news were given short shrift by the police station's personnel.

So did she compound the lie by saying that he'd just got lucky, and been put through to her? Or did she come clean?

As the silence lengthened, she felt more and more awkward. How could she confess to Dr Clement Ryder of all people, that she had wanted to meet a witness on her own because … well, admit it, she told herself grimly, because she rather fancied him!

It was pathetic. And it would make her sound so … silly. And Dr Ryder was always so competent and able and superior.

She shifted in her seat and wriggled internally, but in the end she knew she'd just have to bite the bullet. 'He didn't ring the station, you're right. He came up to me whilst I was waiting at a bus stop and told me he had some information on the Hughes case. So I agreed to meet him to discuss it.'

Her voice came out clipped and cool, but she knew her face was flaming with shame and anger. Just wait until she saw Mr Duncan Gillingham again. She was going to give him what for! Making a fool of her, tricking her …

'Sounds as if he wants to be able to quote you as his police source,' Clement said mildly. But although he was careful to keep his voice light, inside he felt a hard knot of anger forming in his stomach. 'You need to be careful about that,' he added the warning even more emotionlessly.

She was obviously hiding something, and her high colour was a tell-tale sign of strong emotion. He thought she was mostly embarrassed and angry, and hoped that was all. But clearly Sir

Basil had been right to suspect his soon-to-be son-in-law's character, if he could persuade Trudy Loveday to forget her police training.

'Oh, don't worry,' Trudy said grimly. 'I made it clear that I wasn't going to be giving him any information about an on-going investigation. And I didn't,' she added truthfully and with intense satisfaction. It felt wonderful to be able to say *something* in mitigation.

'Good for you,' Clement said genially. But his lips were grim as he began to look around for a parking space. From now on, he was going to be keeping a weather eye out for Mr Duncan Gillingham.

Because if that young man thought he could take advantage of his young friend, he was soon going to learn differently – and in no uncertain terms.

Chapter 26

If it was true that your ears burned whenever someone was talking about you, then that morning, Duncan Gillingham's ears should have been on fire. Instead, he awoke late, had a late breakfast, and then drove his Moggy Minor leisurely to his parent's house at the back end of Holywell, all without feeling any discomfort whatsoever.

Being a reporter meant that he didn't always have to show up at the office on the dot of nine, or put in a regular working day and leave on the dot of five. Right now, if his editor should ask, he was following up a lead to his story. And in a way, he thought grimly, as he pulled up outside his parent's little pre-fab, that *was* what he was doing. More or less.

He sighed as he got out of his rather rusty and down-at-heel car and looked down the narrow little road of look-a-like prefabs where he'd grown up. Erected in the building boom just after the war, when the soldiers returning from the battlefields needed somewhere to live – and fast – he could just about remember his mum and dad being so excited to get their new house. Everyone had been so pleased with their little terraces and rows of semi-detached constructions, and the neighbourhood had always basked in working-class pride.

Even now, brass door furniture sparkled with well-polished buffing, front steps were scrupulously scrubbed, and the front gardens were all neatly clipped and scrupulously maintained. No paint was allowed to peel here on window frames, or weeds to grow up through the pavements.

But it still depressed him every time he came 'home'. And in the glowering November cold, the sight of the cramped, unlovely street made him shiver all the more.

As a young man, he couldn't wait to move out and get away from here. When he'd landed his first job he'd scrimped and saved every penny, finally saving enough to buy the narrowboat where he now lived. His parents were so proud of it because it was his outright, making him the first of the family not to live in rented accommodation.

Now his life felt a million miles from here. True, Jericho, the part of the Oxford canal where he was moored, was hardly a salubrious area itself, but then it was only the first stepping stone in his life plan.

He saw the lace curtain twitch in the front room of his parents' house, and knew that his arrival had been noted. It was not surprising – he was still one of only a handful of people who came from here who could afford to own and run a car.

He quickly walked up the neat garden path, guarded by two rows of trimmed privet hedges, and then his mother was opening the front door, beaming a smile of welcome at him. 'Hello love! What a nice surprise.' He got his colouring from her, although her once raven-black hair was now grey.

'Hello Mum,' he said briefly, pausing to brush her cheek with a kiss as he stepped past her into the hall. 'Dad at work?'

'Where else would he be?' Sandra Gillingham asked primly.

Duncan smiled amiably. His father, Gordon, had always been a 'good provider' for himself and his sister Lily, and in his mother's eyes, there was no higher praise than that.

'Is Lily in?' he asked mildly. 'I wanted to ask her if she wanted to go to the pictures tonight. I think there's a Doris Day feature on that she wanted to see.'

'Oh, I'm sure she'll like that. Yes, she's upstairs. She doesn't start work until lunchtime today. Go on up, I dare say she heard you arrive.'

Duncan again brushed her cheek then charged up the stairs, taking them two at a time, as he'd done as a teenager. The family called it 'gallumping' about, and he knew his mother would be smiling and shaking her head behind him.

However, once on the landing, he became still for a moment, then walked more quietly to his sister's room and tapped on it. 'Lil, you in?' he called softly through the door.

A moment later, the door was pulled open, and his little sister was staring up at him. Lily, at twenty-two, had blossomed from a rather gawky teenager, into a rare beauty. She had the same 'black Irish' colouring as himself, only her eyes were more blue than his own green. She was wearing a long, shapeless winter woollen dress and house slippers, but no amount of camouflage could hide the attractive shape of her figure or distract from her flawless complexion.

'Hello, I thought I heard the car,' she said flatly, holding the door open to allow him in. Her bedroom was small, with one single bed, a dressing table and a single chair. He pulled the chair out and sat on it with the same force of habit that his sister used when she perched on the side of the bed.

As children, they'd often assumed the same pose, talking and amicably arguing. Perhaps because there had only been the two of them (for some reason, the Gillinghams hadn't had a large family, unlike most of their neighbours) the two of them had been relatively close. There'd certainly been none of the sibling rivalry that plagued quite a number of his school friends.

'So, how's the new job?' he asked. His sister had re-trained as a hairdresser recently and now worked part-time at a local

171

salon. With her good looks and long black hair as a free advertisement, she was an asset to the shop, and all concerned knew it.

She shrugged listlessly. 'Fine. The pay's good.'

Duncan nodded, but he was watching her closely. She'd put a little much-needed weight back in the last few months, and some of the deep shadows around her eyes had gone. Either that, or she was wearing make-up.

'You feeling better nowadays?' he asked tentatively.

His sister, who'd been staring absently out of the window, shifted her gaze to him for a moment, then returned to her perusal of the housing on the other side of the street. Her face, Duncan realised with a pang, was totally expressionless.

'I'm fine. Like I was last week and the week before when you asked,' Lily said flatly. 'I wish you'd stop worrying about me.'

Duncan nodded, but it was meaningless. Of course he was worried about her. And of course she wasn't fine. How could she be?

He wanted to ask her if she'd been to a doctor recently – a proper doctor – and if she had, had she allowed him to examine her thoroughly. Just to see make sure that there had been no complications from … from what had happened.

But he knew he couldn't do that. It would only embarrass her and make her angry. Or cry.

'Seen the papers lately?' he said instead, turning to look casually out of the window himself now.

'We always have the *Tribune* now, you know that,' Lily said, by way of answer.

Duncan nodded. He knew, of course, that his parents read every article he ever wrote. In fact, he was sure his mother cut them out and kept them in a scrapbook. By the street's standards, he was a success story, and they never let anyone forget it. What they'd do when he finally told them he was engaged to the daughter of Sir Basil Fletcher, he didn't know. For some reason, he was holding that back until he and Glenda made it official, with an engagement party somewhere swanky. The Randolph, maybe.

'So you know about this Thomas Hughes bloke dying then?' Duncan carried on carefully. 'You know who he was, right?' he added blandly.

Lily shifted slightly on the edge of the bed and transferred her gaze to the slippers on her feet. 'Yeah, I know who he was,' she said quietly.

Duncan nodded. For a few moments, the room was totally silent. Then he said, 'I'm going to go the office now and write the next article for the evening edition. The police are investigating the family properly now. I've been speaking to the one they put in charge. You wouldn't believe it, but it's a woman, and she's younger than you! What do you think of that?'

Lily slowly flexed one foot and shrugged. 'Good for her,' she said vaguely.

'I'm going to point her in the right direction, sis, I promise,' Duncan said softly.

Lily shrugged one shoulder.

For another minute there was silence again. Then Duncan sighed. 'I told you I'd get him, Lil. And I will. I swear.'

Suddenly he saw her shoulders go tight and tense, and her chin shot up as she looked at him with the first sign of real emotion he'd seen in her since she'd had to kill the baby that had been growing inside her. 'Dunc.' She used the abbreviation of his first name without thinking, a throw-over from their childhood days. 'You haven't done anything *stupid*, have you?' she asked urgently. Her voice was tense, and her wide blue eyes were bright with alarm.

'Of course not,' Duncan denied firmly. 'You know me, sis. I'm never stupid.'

For a few moments, brother and sister stared silently at one another, then Lily's shoulders relaxed, and she returned her gaze

173

to the window. 'Just be careful, Duncan, that's all,' she finally said.

'Always,' Duncan promised. He got up, kissed the top of her head lightly, and walked downstairs, his heart heavy and thumping sickeningly in his chest. He wanted his young, care-free, happy and innocent sister back. But he knew she was gone forever.

'Just off, Mum. Got an article to write,' he called through the empty hallway.

'OK son, come by again soon,' the answer echoed from the kitchen.

Duncan walked back down the garden path, knowing his sister's eyes were on his back. He didn't turn around to look up however, but got in the car and turned the ignition.

He caught his reflection in the driving mirror, and the man reflected back at him looked perfectly calm. Only on the inside was he aware of a cold, relentless rage.

Most of his anger, he knew, was aimed at himself. He should have looked out for Lily better. But after he'd left home, it was inevitable that he wouldn't see quite so much of her, and thus wouldn't know what was happening in her life.

He'd simply had no idea how bad things were until it was too late. Until, one night, when he'd received that frantic phone call from her and he'd met her in their local churchyard. It was there, amongst the tombstones that she'd confessed to him that she'd gone to a back-street abortionist. That, after a few days, she was still bleeding a little. That she felt so unwell. That she was getting scared. And, most of all, that she was adamant that no one else could know.

Going to their regular doctor was out of the question.

So he'd asked around in places where people would know about such things, and had found out about the 'Friday clinics'. Some hospitals had decided to open a Friday clinic – Friday being pay day – in order to treat women who were either septic or bleeding. He'd paid for her treatment, of course.

And physically she'd healed. But there was still no sign of life behind her eyes.

As he finally drove away from the house, Duncan renewed his promise to himself that Kenneth Wilcox was going to pay for what he'd done to Lily. One way or another.

Chapter 27

Kenneth Wilcox looked surprised to find the WPC and coroner returning to his shop, but he hid his impatience well as he invited them into his office and asked them to sit down. His secretary, hovering uncertainly in the doorway, waited for instructions, but Kenneth was in no mood to offer them hospitality. If they wanted a cup of tea they could go to a café. He dismissed the pretty blonde girl with a simple nod and smile and then turned his attention to his unwanted visitors.

'So, has anything new turned up in your investigations, Constable?' he asked boldly. 'Only I'm rather surprised to see you back again. I'd have thought your superiors would have been convinced by now that my father-in-law's death was nothing more than an unfortunate accident.'

Trudy smiled blandly. 'We were just wondering if you'd thought of anything else that we should know, sir. Very often, after a little while has passed, people remember things that had previously slipped their minds.'

Kenneth looked at her sceptically, and Trudy wondered why Duncan had warned her about him. On the face of it, he was an attractive, successful, middle-aged, happily married man. He had no criminal record, and so far, she'd found nobody who had a bad word to say about him.

Now that she was here, she was wondering if a certain reporter hadn't been leading her up the garden path in more ways than one. It was more than possible that Duncan had given her bad information, although she couldn't quite see what he'd have to gain from that.

Still, she might as well push Kenneth a bit and see what happened.

She led with, 'I understand your father-in-law's will has now been read, Mr Wilcox. I think I'm right in saying that your wife gets the house in Headington – but nothing more?'

Kenneth's face went slightly tight, but he managed a nonchalant shrug. 'We never expected any great legacy,' he said flatly. 'Thomas always did think that his daughters should be provided for by their husbands.'

'So the fact that Matthew Hughes got so much, relatively speaking, and the rest of you almost nothing, doesn't worry you?'

'My son has a trust fund so his future's sorted, that's the main thing. And we have the house, as you say. Plus I have my own money – and plans for a new shop in town. All in all, I'm well content with my lot, I assure you.'

'Did you *like* Thomas Hughes sir?' she asked mildly. 'Only we've been hearing, from various sources, that he was a bit of a trial to your wife. Treating her more as a servant than a daughter, it seems,' she exaggerated a little. 'It must have been a bit of a strain sir. Living with him, I mean.'

Kenneth's eyes flickered slightly, but his vague smile remained firmly in place. 'He was sometimes hard to live with, yes. But he was family. You put up with it, when it's family, don't you?'

He looked to Clement and gave a small man-to-man shrug.

And suddenly Trudy just knew that she was wasting her time. This man would not be baited into saying something unwise –

and certainly not to her. She had the feeling that Mr Wilcox had women firmly filed away in certain categories, and that none of these categories included treating them as his equal.

She also felt as if Duncan, as annoying as he was, was on to something.

There was something about this man that she didn't like. Something hard and calculating – something that belied his affable charms and ageing good looks.

'Well, thank you Mr Wilcox, that's all for now,' she said, surprising both Clement and Kenneth alike. She stood up abruptly, and as the coroner stepped forward to shake the other man's out-thrust hand, she turned away, pretending not to notice when Kenneth offered his hand to her.

They found the outer office empty, and as Trudy shut the door firmly behind her, she sighed. 'I just don't like that man,' she said quietly, not wanting her voice to carry. 'And much as I'm loath to admit it, I think Mr Gillingham might be right about him being a "wrong 'un." I just think we're wasting our time tackling him head on though.'

'I agree,' Clement said, surprising her a little by agreeing so promptly. 'Men like that never give themselves away. Too damned smart by half. Which is why it's a good thing we have another option open to us.'

'We do?' Trudy said, baffled. 'What's that then?'

Clement grinned then nodded down at the empty desk beside them. Beside the typewriter and files, the telephone and a vase of rather wilted chrysanthemums, was one of those blocks of wood, with a metal nameplate attached. 'We ask Miss Susan Royal. Has nobody told you, if you want to know everything there is to know about a man, you can either ask his wife, his valet or his secretary?'

Trudy grinned back. 'Good idea! I wonder where she is? Perhaps she'd agree to let us take her out for a coffee break?'

Just then Miss Royal herself made an appearance. From the

way she was patting her newly brushed hair and the pristine patina of her lipstick, Trudy guessed that she'd just come from the ladies', after freshening herself up. She was only just out of her teens, Trudy judged, and froze like a rabbit caught in headlights as she saw them watching her with such concentration.

She almost gulped.

Then Clement put on his most avuncular smile and stepped towards her. 'Ah, Miss Royal, just the young lady we were looking for,' he reached out to the coat stand beside him, and before she knew what was happening, he was helping her into her woollen overcoat. 'My companion and myself would like to take you out for coffee.'

'Oh but …' She cast a quick, helpless look at her boss's closed door. 'I don't think …'

'Oh, Mr Wilcox won't mind,' Clement lied smoothly. 'Now, where's the best coffee shop around these parts, hmm?'

Whilst Trudy and Clement set about learning all they could about her boss from Miss Royal, over at the *Tribune*'s office, Duncan Gillingham, his face set and cold, typed furiously on his Remington typewriter. He'd pause every now and then to think. Around him, his fellow scribes typed, smoked, typed, chatted, and typed some more, but most of them left him alone.

He had the look of a man who wouldn't appreciate the latest joke or dirty talk surrounding someone's less-than-faithful wife.

'Police admit the Thomas Hughes case is far from closed.' He contemplated without enthusiasm the headline he'd chosen (surely it needed more punch?) and then the few paragraphs he'd written so far. It was all good solid stuff, but if he was going to skew the focus of the piece from the death of the local bigwig, and turn the spotlight onto his son-in-law he was going to have to be careful.

Tonight, he'd ring up Trudy Loveday and see what progress she was making. And if she hadn't unearthed any dirt on Wilcox yet, he'd be happy to help her out. It wasn't as if he didn't have plenty to spare, since Duncan had made it his mission to know all he could about the man.

Without mentioning Lily at all, he had enough on his private life to do the man's reputation some serious damage. He just needed a legitimate forum from which to do it. And a murder case, reported in the press, was ideal. He just needed that final push …

With a grim smile he hunched over his typewriter, ramping up the innuendo and narrowing the spotlight from the family as a whole to just one individual. Or maybe, for form's sake, it might be more prudent to chuck in another suspect as well? Say the other son, Godfrey? Yes, that would make sense. When he'd been doing his research into the family, he'd come across certain rumours that Godfrey had a rather smutty hobby, which his father might not have liked very much. But he mustn't smear the dirt on Godfrey took thickly – it was vital that Wilcox took the brunt of it.

It really was true, Duncan mused, that the pen was mightier than the sword. A fact that Kenneth Wilcox was soon going to understand better than anyone.

Chapter 28

'Oh, Mr Wilcox is all right. I suppose,' Susan Royal said a little uncertainly. They were sitting in a tiny tea room at the back of a local cake shop, which felt rather stuffy and over-warm, but the scent of freshly-baked bread and pastries, in Clement's opinion, more than made up for it.

'You don't sound that sure,' Trudy said with a friendly smile. 'Been working for him long?'

'Oh no. Just a few weeks, actually. The last girl left without giving her notice, so the agency I worked for sent me over to cover for her,' Susan said, her pretty face going from one to the other of them, as if she couldn't make up her mind which of them fascinated her most. 'I was only meant to be a temp, you see, but he hasn't started advertising for a permanent replacement yet. I suppose that's a good sign, isn't it?' she asked them, somewhat naively. 'I mean, that usually means that they're happy with you and might keep you on, like.'

Susan lifted her cup of tea to her mouth, but didn't drink from it. She probably didn't want to smudge her lipstick, Trudy thought with an inner smile. Although the secretary was probably around the same age as herself, Trudy couldn't help but feel that there was still something very young and childlike about her. It made the police officer in her feel protective of the other woman, somehow.

'Would you *like* to have a permanent job as his secretary?' Trudy asked gently.

'Oh yes,' Susan said at once, her pretty face lighting up. 'Or maybe … I'm not sure,' she added, confusingly.

'It's all right,' Clement said. 'You can say anything to us, and we'll understand and it'll go no further. We're not trying to trick you into doing or saying anything you don't want to,' he added, reaching for his own cup and saucer and adding a sugar cube into the steaming tea.

'Sorry, I know I don't always make myself clear. Take working for Mr Wilcox – sometimes it's good, and sometimes it's not.' Susan sighed and tried again. 'It's just that working for the agency's all very well, but you never know where you'll be working from one day to the next, you see?' She looked at them anxiously, and was relieve when they both nodded encouragingly. 'Always having to get to know new people and figure out their systems, and what have you. It's hard sometimes, and people can get so impatient if you don't work things out right away, can't they?' Her eyes opened widely. 'And then, after a week or so – or even only a few days sometimes, off you have to go and start all over again with someone else.'

Trudy nodded. 'It sounds a bit frantic,' she admitted. 'So to save all that palaver, you'll take the permanent job, if Mr Wilcox offers it to you?'

Again, the girl hesitated. Trudy glanced at Clement, who was watching Susan with a slightly bemused, slightly benevolent smile. He was obviously thinking the same thing as she was. Miss Royal wasn't particularly bright, and she probably wasn't a particularly efficient secretary. But she *was* very pretty.

'Oh yes. I suppose I will,' Susan muttered, putting down her cup and fiddling nervously with a teaspoon.

'You still don't sound very sure,' Trudy probed delicately. 'Is there something wrong? I think you said his previous secretary left without serving notice. That's unusual isn't it? Do you know why?'

'Oh, not really. Well, only from listening to the others talk, and all that. But, I got the feeling that Angela and Mr Wilcox had a row of some kind.'

'Really? What kind of a row?' Trudy was careful to keep her voice light and casual. 'It must have been a bad one if Angela … what was her last name?'

'Er … Not sure I remember … oh, Calver. Yes, I'm sure it was Calver.' Susan beamed.

'Well done – I often have trouble remembering names too,' Trudy lied. 'So, did the others say what the row was about? People who work in small businesses always seem to know each other's business too if you know what I mean,' Trudy grinned encouragingly. 'But I suppose you of all people would know that – doing the job you do.'

Susan smiled. 'Oh yes. You're so right, they do. A hotbed of gossip some places, I can tell you. The things I've heard in some offices …' Susan shook her head wonderingly.

'So what was the gossip about Angela?' Trudy lifted her cup and took a sip of tea, and when Susan looked at her with troubled eyes, smiled blandly back. 'It's all right, like Dr Ryder said before, it won't go any further I promise. The *police* don't go around gossiping,' she added, guessing that it wouldn't hurt to remind the secretary that she was speaking to the 'authorities' and as such, needed to pay attention and co-operate.

Susan shot a quick look at Clement, then looked away. 'Well, they said that Mr Wilcox and Angela … well, that they were friendly, like. You know … very *good* friends. Even though Mr Wilcox is a married man.'

She stared resolutely down into her teacup.

'Oh, like that, is he? Yes, I thought he was that type,' Trudy said careful to keep her voice light and free from shock. 'He's good-looking in a way, isn't he? And I suppose some girls seem to go for the older man, don't they?'

Susan nodded, clearly relieved that they were all being so grown-up and sophisticated about things.

'He hasn't tried to get very friendly with you, has he Susan?' Trudy asked gently.

'What? Oh no … oooh, that's a horrible thought, isn't it?' The blonde girl shuddered theatrically. 'I mean, I suppose he's all right, but he's so *old*! Besides, I've already got a steady boyfriend. My Tarquin plays rugby and works for an insurance company. He won't stand for no nonsense from the likes of Mr Wilcox,' Susan said, with evident satisfaction, tossing her hair for good measure. 'No, if *he* tries anything on, my Tarquin will soon sort him out.'

Trudy glanced at Clement, who was doing a very good job of keeping a straight face. But underneath their shared levity, Trudy knew that they were both feeling better for the fact that this pretty young girl had a jealous boyfriend to watch out for her.

'You know, if I were you Susan, I would ask the agency to find you a new position,' Trudy advised gently. 'When your boss has a bit of a reputation for being a ladies' man, it can lead to all sorts of trouble. Believe me, I've seen it all before.'

Susan nodded and sighed. 'Yeah,' she admitted. 'I've been thinking the same thing really. Only I've been putting it off, because Mr Wilcox does pay well, and he's being ever so nice to me.'

I'll bet he is, Trudy thought sourly, remembering the way Kenneth Wilcox had been eyeing her own figure on the sly throughout their interview. 'But it's not worth running the risk of upsetting Tarquin, is it?' she said. 'And if Mr Wilcox does make a pass at you, think how embarrassing that would be.'

'Oh, don't!' Susan pleaded, and again gave a shudder. 'You're right. I wouldn't be able to carry on working for him then anyway, would I?' She sighed heavily. 'I'll talk to the agency then,' she said, a shade despondently.

'I think that's a good idea,' Trudy said. 'You do that. I don't suppose you know where Angela's working now do you?' she added with cunning idleness.

But there, it seemed, the pretty Miss Susan Royal couldn't help them.

'That girl worries me,' Trudy said a few minutes later, as they stood on the pavement outside the cake shop watching her walk back to work. 'She strikes me as the sort who could get easily hurt.'

'Not with her Tarquin around to sort things out,' Clement reminded with a grin. In his mind, he was picturing some hulking, not-too-bright or particularly handsome scion of an upper-middle class family, pleased as punch to have landed himself such a pretty girlfriend, and determined to look after her.

Trudy laughed, but quickly grew more sombre. 'I need to track down this Angela Calver and see what she has to say for herself. Reading between the lines, I think our Mr Wilcox goes through pretty secretaries like most men go through a box of cigars.'

'Hmmm. But is that relevant to our case?' Clement asked.

'It is if Thomas Hughes knew about it and was threatening to do something about it,' Trudy shot back promptly. 'We already know that he was fond of throwing his weight around in that family. What if Kenneth, aggravated by having to live with the man all those years, decided he'd simply had enough and was going to do something about it.'

Clement nodded. It sounded feasible enough. 'OK. I've got to get back to the office and do some "proper" work. You track down this Angela woman and we'll meet up again tomorrow. Say, ten o'clock?'

'Fine. But I'm not sure how much longer Inspector Jennings is going to let me carry on with all this. If we don't have something by the end of the week, I think we'll have to close the file,' Trudy predicted glumly.

Clement sighed. 'It'll probably come to that. We're not exactly getting anywhere, are we?'

'No. It doesn't feel like it, does it?'

The evening edition of the *Oxford Tribune* was available at the news-stands and in the shops by five o'clock that evening, ideal for people who were leaving work to pick up a copy to read over their supper.

In the living room of her home, listening vaguely to her flatmate moan about the mess the bin men had made outside the door that morning, Caroline Benham read the leading article. It was by that man Gillingham again, and he seemed to be hinting that the police investigation into her father's death was speeding up.

As she read, she leaned forward in her chair a little. Was she mistaken, or did it sound as if Kenneth and, perhaps Godfrey, were coming under the most suspicion?

Caroline smiled grimly. What an idiot that reporter must be, she thought scornfully. Godfrey didn't have the guts to commit murder, and Kenneth was far too fond of his own skin to put it in jeopardy.

No. It would take someone very different from either of those two to kill somebody. It would take, she thought grimly and with considerable approbation, someone who knew all there was to know about hate or desperation.

With a smile, she tossed the paper aside. The police could investigate all they liked, for all the good it would do them.

In his study, surrounded by his erotic art, Godfrey Hughes alternately fretted and fumed and paced about, flinging the newspaper on the sofa in disgust. He'd sue – that's what he would do. Why, reading between the lines, this reporter fellow was all but accusing him of murdering his own father! Him or Kenneth.

Weren't there libel laws to prevent this sort of thing? He'd contact his solicitor in the morning and jolly well …

But then, pursuing a legal action would mean paying the legal chaps a veritable fortune, wouldn't it? And it wasn't as if he could afford to finance a court case.

He glanced around the room at his beloved pieces of art, and sighed heavily, his shoulders slumping. Perhaps he wouldn't sue then. After all, nobody was taking it seriously, were they? And the newspaper would very soon regard his late unlamented father as old news and then they'd forget about it and go on to bother someone else.

No, all he had to do was wait it out, he decided. And it wasn't as if he was in any danger, he reassured himself. Even if the police *were* to be so foolish as to arrest him … Well, he could always point them in the right direction, if needs be. Although everyone was keeping quiet out of loyalty, no one would blame him if he were to be forced to spill the beans.

It wasn't as if all the family hadn't guessed the truth from the moment the first sparks began to rise from the garden shed …

Chapter 29

Frank Loveday came home that night to be greeted by the smell of toad-in-the-hole, one of his favourite dinners, emanating from the kitchen. Also coming from the kitchen he heard the conversation of the two most important women in his life and as he hung up his coat in the hall, he was already smiling as he walked in to join them.

He lightly tossed the evening paper onto the table, and walked over to kiss his wife, who was draining potatoes for mashing.

'Evening love,' he said, then smiled across at his daughter. 'You managing to keep dry on the beat?'

Trudy nodded. She hadn't told them she was working on a special case with the coroner again, because she knew how much they worried about her.

'Yes, the weather's not too bad if you keep moving,' she hedged. After all, she *was* doing her regular duties part of the time as well. 'How's Bertha?' she asked teasingly.

Her father called all the buses he drove Bertha, and invariably they displeased him in some way or other.

'She's guzzling oil like's there no tomorrow,' her father predictably complained, but the twinkle in his eye let on to the fact that he knew he was the butt of the joke.

'Trudy, would you mind stirring the gravy, love?' her mother said. 'It'll go lumpy whilst I'm cutting up the toad-in-the-hole otherwise.'

Trudy obligingly went over to stand by the cooker and started stirring the wooden spoon around in the gravy saucepan. Her mother had just started to open the oven door when the telephone bell went.

They'd had a telephone installed in the hall only a month ago, and it was still something of an 'event' to hear it ring. But once Trudy had made it clear that she was going to carry on working for the police after her probationary period finished, her parents had decided the instrument was going to become more and more of a necessity. Besides, it beat walking down to the bottom of the street to use the public phone box all the time – especially in the rain!

'I'll get it,' Trudy said, turning the heat off from under the now bubbling gravy, and walking quickly out into the hall.

'Hello?' She knew that proper telephone etiquette demanded that she was supposed to cite the number now, but before she could even start to remember what it was, a familiar voice cut across the ether.

'Well, I *am* in luck, it's the lady herself! I was half-expecting to have to sweet talk my way past your father.' Duncan Gillingham's cheeky tones filled her ear.

'Humph, you'd never have managed it,' Trudy shot back acerbically. She had a bone to pick with this particular man, but even as she felt her anger begin to ignite, she remembered that her parents were sitting just through the open doorway, which meant that having an argument on the telephone now was out of the question.

'How can I help you, Mr Gillingham?' she forced herself to say politely instead.

'Well, you can start by agreeing to meet up with me to swap information again,' he responded, and Trudy could have sworn she could hear laughter lurking behind his tone. No doubt he thought it very funny that she was being so prim and formal with him.

'I'm afraid that's out of the question,' she said, and this time was able to smile happily. If this brash reporter thought she was going to fall for the same trick twice, he could damned well think again.

Duncan sighed slightly. He didn't know what had happened to put him in the doghouse, but something clearly had. And that could be a problem. He needed this particular member of the law firmly on his side.

He changed tactics. 'Oh? I thought we had the makings of a good team. Don't tell me you ignored my tip about Kenneth Wilcox?'

'I'm afraid I can't give out sensitive information over the telephone, Mr Gillingham,' Trudy said, again with a smile. Thwarting him at every turn was turning out to be a pleasant game.

'Ahh, so you *did* go and talk to him!' Duncan interpreted, and Trudy felt herself scowl. 'And don't tell me that a sensible, sensitive girl like you didn't pick up on something being off about him, because I won't believe you. The things I could tell you about him would make your hair curl – which is another good reason why we should meet up again for a cup of tea soon.'

He waited hopefully, but there was only a long, speaking silence.

Duncan sighed. 'All right, all right, have it your way.' He sought out a bone to throw her so that he could get back in her good books. He didn't really want to do it, as he wanted her concentrating all her efforts on the baby-killer, but as his old granny would have said, needs must when the devil drives. 'I take it you don't want to know why the old man was so down on his little sister then?' He selected a victim at random.

In her hallway, Trudy felt herself stiffen. 'You're talking about Mary Everly?' she asked cautiously.

190

'Yes, that's her – the merry widow,' Duncan confirmed irreverently. He had, as a matter of course, done his homework on all the Hughes family, mainly to see if he could dig up any more dirt on Kenneth. But in the process, he'd learned all sorts of things.

'What about her?' Trudy asked cagily, making him smile in triumph. Yes, she was back in the fold. He was not at all surprised that she'd hadn't been able to ferret out the existence of Mary Everly's new fiancé. People often told things to reporters that they'd never dream of telling the coppers, especially if a little money helped to grease the way.

'Why don't we meet up tomorrow and I'll tell you,' he wheedled.

'Why don't you tell me now,' Trudy shot back.

'On an open line? Tut, tut, WPC Loveday, surely you know better than that?'

Trudy heaved a massive sigh. 'All right. Tomorrow morning, first thing. Same place as before. You can buy me breakfast,' she added cheekily, and before he could make any retort, she hung up.

It wasn't until she returned to the kitchen, and saw both her parents looking her speculatively, that she realised she might have some explaining to do.

Barbara Loveday took one look at her daughter's flushed cheeks and sparkling eyes, and felt both worried and pleased. 'Who was that on the phone love?' she asked flat out.

'Oh. Nothing, it was work,' Trudy tried to dismiss the subject, but without much hope.

'It didn't sound like work,' Barbara pressed (just as Trudy had suspected she would), as she set about dishing out the meal.

'Well, it was,' Trudy insisted. Then, knowing of old that her mother wouldn't let it go until she was fully satisfied, she sighed. 'He's a reporter, that's all. He's the one doing those articles in the *Tribune* on that fatality up at Headington. I'm looking into the case, and he was just trying to get a quote from me.'

Her father, who'd been reading the *Tribune*, turned and tapped the latest evening headlines. 'This the chap?' he asked, pointing out Duncan's byline.

Trudy, who hadn't seen the latest edition, took the paper from him, and began to read the latest article. As she did so, her anger slowly returned and began to shimmer.

'POLICE ABOUT TO MAKE AN ARREST?'

Under this bold (and utterly inaccurate) headline was Duncan Gillingham's name and a speculative mishmash of speculation and innuendo that invited the reader to read between the lines and conclude that Thomas Hughes's son-in-law was about to be in for a rough ride from the police. And he didn't mean Caroline Benham's ex-husband either.

'That bloody man!' Trudy said, outraged. Just what game was he playing?

'Trudy!' her mother said sharply. 'Language!'

Trudy swallowed. 'Sorry Mum,' she mumbled. 'But honestly, he does make my blood boil sometimes. If DI Jennings reads this, he's going to haul me in and ask me what's going on, and I won't be able to tell him!'

Her father's lips twitched. 'You sound as if you know this reporter chap well,' he mused.

'No,' Trudy denied hotly and instantly. 'Why would you think that?' she added, not missing – or liking – the way her parents exchanged knowing looks.

'Well, strangers don't usually get under your skin the way this Duncan Gillingham chap seems to have done,' Frank Loveday explained with a knowing grin.

'I've met him once. Well, twice, technically,' Trudy said reluctantly.

'What's he like?' Barbara asked avidly, sitting down and reaching absently for the bottle of brown sauce to squirt over her sausages.

Trudy shrugged. 'Like most reporters, I suppose,' she said

insouciantly, as if she knew that many! 'Far too sure of himself for one thing, and determined to get under my feet.'

'Ah. How old is he?' Barbara asked casually.

'I don't know. Twenty-five or six perhaps.'

'Good-looking, is he?' her mother asked, and Trudy shot her a speaking look.

'I didn't notice,' she said flatly, trying to ignore the image of the handsome man with the black hair and intriguing cat-green eyes.

'Hmmm,' Barbara said thoughtfully.

Her father, wisely, retreated back behind the newspaper.

Trudy had just reached for the gravy saucepan to pour some over her mashed potatoes when her mother said, 'Why don't you invite him over for tea some time?'

'Mum!' Trudy wailed.

Chapter 30

The next morning Duncan was at the café bright and early and looking forward to seeing Trudy Loveday again. He wondered if she'd take her cap off today, and if she'd be wearing that light citrus-scented perfume she'd been wearing before.

Before drifting off to sleep last night he'd gone over how he'd play it today, and if he should ask her out on a date. A proper date, with none of this air of 'just business' to spoil things. He had to admit, there was something about her that nagged very pleasantly at him. She seemed such an odd contrast somehow. An innocent, but a copper, of all things. A natural beauty, who genuinely didn't seem to be aware of the fact. A little spitfire, but with a prim and proper attitude that made him want to shake her up a bit.

Of course, he'd have to be careful to take her somewhere where none of Glenda's friends were likely to frequent but that …

His pleasant thoughts skidded to a rather abrupt halt as Trudy walked through the door – closely followed by an older man. It took Duncan only a few seconds to remember where he'd seen him before – which had been residing over the inquest into Thomas Hughes's death. In another moment, his formidable memory came up with the name.

'Constable Loveday, Dr Ryder, thank you for agreeing to see me,' he said formally, rising from his seat at the table he'd picked because it was furthest away from the window, and reaching out to shake their hands. None of his chagrin or displeasure at finding her accompanied was allowed to show on his face.

Clement nodded, looking at him curiously.

When Trudy had arrived at his office and told him they had to go somewhere else before interviewing Angela Calver (whom she'd tracked down to her job in a record shop in Little Clarendon Street) he'd been amenable. And when she'd told him about the phone call to her home from Duncan Gillingham last night, he'd been very amenable indeed.

He'd been intending to make this particular young man's acquaintance as soon as possible, and now he wouldn't have to think up excuses.

Trudy, who'd been watching Duncan closely from the moment she'd walked in, was sure that she'd seen a flicker of disappointment and anger in his eyes over the fact that she wasn't alone, and she felt a distinctly feminine and near-spiteful pleasure at having put a spoke in his wheel.

When she'd got up that morning, she'd hadn't wanted to have to lie to her friend and mentor again. Also, she just had a feeling that meeting this man alone again would be a mistake. She was acting purely on instinct – an instinct that she didn't fully understand, but which warned her that this man was dangerous to her somehow – and it was all making her feel a little uneasy.

'We could hardly turn down such a kind invitation,' Clement responded to his opening with a formal smile of his own as they all sat down. 'After all, it's not every journalist who's willing to share his research,' he said mildly, well aware that the younger man had shot him a keen glance. 'Shall we treat ourselves to the full English?' he asked blandly, after giving the menu a quick perusal.

'Just toast and scrambled egg for me,' Trudy said hastily.

'Yes, why not?' Duncan said, meeting the coroner's eyes with a level gaze. 'Sounds like just the thing on a wet and cold winter's day.'

The same waitress as their previous visit approached and took their orders, her eyes again lingering on Duncan wistfully. All three of them noticed it. Trudy's lips thinned, Clement's twitched and Duncan merely sighed.

'So, what do you know about Thomas Hughes's argument with his sister?' Trudy asked crisply, getting straight down to business.

Duncan, realising that all his plans about making this a more personal and friendly meeting would have to be shelved, took her lead. 'It seems that he didn't like his sister's choice for her second husband. You were aware that she was widowed some time ago?'

Trudy nodded, rapidly scribbling away in her notebook.

'Well, last year, she re-connected with a friend from the old days, a chap called Captain Rupert Burrows. The "Captain" part is purely an honorary title these days, since he's no longer in the army. He, Mary, and Mary's first husband all ran around in the same set when they were "up" at Oxford here. Anyway, after she was widowed and returned home from all that gallivanting about abroad, she met up with this Burrows chap again, and they became an item. I believe they're what's known as "unofficially" engaged.'

'Why unofficially?' Clement asked curiously.

'Ah, that's the thing,' Duncan said. 'It seems Mary's big brother didn't approve of the match.'

'Why not?' Trudy asked bluntly. 'Is there something wrong with him?'

'Well, nothing that's very obvious,' Duncan said, breaking off the conversation and then leaning back in his chair a little as the waitress delivered two plates. The first, Trudy noticed, she put in front of Duncan – naturally – and the second plateful of the full English was given to Clement.

She had to wait a minute for her own order to be set down in front of her.

196

When the waitress finally left, Duncan picked up where he'd left off. 'Oh, he's a few years younger than his intended, but nothing to raise the eyebrows over. And he's a bit of looker too – you know, one of those fair-haired, blue-eyed boys that seem to make feminine hearts flutter,' Duncan said with a smile, sawing into a slice of bacon with his knife.

'And that's why her brother didn't like him?' Trudy asked sceptically.

'Oh no. Not entirely,' Duncan said. 'I asked around a few people in the know, and it seems our Captain Burrows didn't exactly cover himself in glory in the war.'

Clement, cutting into a kidney and spearing half a mushroom, shrugged slightly. 'A lot of men didn't. I take it Burrows must have done something *specific* to make Hughes take so firmly against him?'

Duncan nodded, making a mental note. There were certainly no flies on *this* man. From now on in, he was going to have to watch Dr Ryder very closely. 'Oh yes. It seems he made a bad decision, arrived at under stress. Men under his command died, when, perhaps, they needn't have.'

'A court martial offence?' Clement asked sharply.

'Oh no, nothing like that,' Duncan said. 'There was no question of cowardice. More a lack of judgement, or competence, I think. It's not always easy to get the truth out of the army,' he admitted with a wry grimace. 'Let's just say that he was shuffled sideways into a desk job and quietly put away where he couldn't do any more damage.'

Trudy quickly scrambled through her notes. Yes, she'd thought so. 'When I did background checks on Thomas Hughes, I found out that he'd worked for the War Office in London,' she said. 'So I suppose it would have been easy for him to find out all about the scandal, if he'd decided to check up on sister's beau. Or he might have heard the gossip about it at the time, and then remembered the name when his sister introduced him.'

'Either way, he definitely didn't want his sister marrying the man,' Duncan said firmly. 'It's amazing what the neighbours know and are prepared to talk about.'

Trudy looked across at Clement. So that's what the massive argument had been all about, she mused. 'Does he have any money?' she asked quietly.

'Clever girl,' Duncan complimented her. 'And you're right – not so's you notice. He's getting by on his pension and a bit of savings. It's Mrs Everly who has the comfortable income, thanks to her late husband's life insurance.'

All three of them digested this for a moment.

'But Thomas couldn't really have stopped her from marrying this Captain Burrows, could he?' Trudy pointed out logically. 'I mean, *legally* there was nothing to stop it? This Captain Burrows isn't married already and can't get divorced because he's a Catholic or anything?'

Duncan paused, his fork holding half a tomato hovering just in front of his lips. 'Oh no, nothing that romantic,' he teased her.

Trudy shot him a fuming look and turned back to her notes. 'So, although Mr Hughes might have been *against* it, there was nothing he could really do to stop them marrying if they were determined to go ahead with it?'

'Not on the face of it, anyway,' Clement said. 'But I get the feeling, from all that we've learned about him so far, that Thomas Hughes liked to have his own way. And had a nasty habit of getting it.'

Trudy nodded. 'Yes. But I got the same feeling from Mrs Everly – that she liked to get her own way too,' she clarified, as both men looked at her questioningly. 'And I don't think she would have let her brother get in her way if she really wanted something.'

'You think she might have killed her own brother to stop him interfering?' Clement asked, clearly surprised.

But Trudy was already shaking her head. 'No, I'm not saying that exactly. I'm just saying, I think she's going to marry who she wants to, and family approval – or not – can go hang, as far as she's concerned. She struck me as a strong-minded and confident woman.'

'I agree,' Duncan said cheerfully. 'Besides, I've thought all along that this was a man's crime.'

'Oh, did you?' Trudy said archly. 'And from last night's newspaper story, you seem to think it was either Godfrey or Kenneth Wilcox.'

Clement, who'd also read the latest story, looked at Duncan Gillingham thoughtfully. 'You do seem to have someone in your sights,' he observed.

Duncan felt himself stiffen in alarm, and forced himself to smile and look relaxed. It was one thing to gently manipulate a pretty young girl into doing his bidding, but it had become rapidly obvious that it would be pointless trying the same trick on this wily old duffer.

'I think there are things going on in that family that we don't know about, that's all,' he said mildly. 'So, what's your next move?' He reached for his mug of tea and looked at them guilelessly.

'As if we're going to tell you,' Trudy snorted.

Duncan looked abashed. 'Oh come on! I've done my bit – saved you some legwork by finding out about Captain Burrows and the little sister. Play fair!'

Trudy, finishing the last of her eggs and toast, pushed her plate away. 'I'm a police officer, Mr Gillingham,' she said magnificently. 'I don't have to play fair.'

It was, Clement thought, a perfect exit line. It was such a pity he hadn't finished his breakfast yet, forcing her to remain in her seat.

Duncan's laughing eyes told the coroner that he appreciated the joke too, and something about his smugness caught Clement on the raw. He didn't like the way he was treating Trudy – teasing her, complimenting her, and all but flirting with her. Remembering how convinced Sir Basil bad been that this man was only marrying

Glenda Fletcher in order to further his own ambition, he couldn't help but wonder if he was doing the same thing to Trudy.

After all, it was clear (to him at least) that this brash and cocky young man had an agenda of his own, and didn't care who he trampled on in pursuit of it. Clement didn't want Trudy's career to take a hit because of him, when she already had so many things going against her.

Carefully, he speared his fried egg with a slice of fried bread, and said casually, 'So what does your fiancée make of your latest scoop?'

Chapter 31

As Clement drove slowly down St Giles, keeping a wary eye out for a parking space as he did so, he was careful not to look too closely at his companion.

She had been silent since getting into the car, and it was clear that she was in no mood for social chatter.

He sighed a little, aware that he was feeling just a little guilty – which wasn't something that happened to him often, and he didn't appreciate being made to feel like the bad guy. But it didn't take a genius to surmise that the chances of her knowing about Duncan Gillingham's engagement to another woman were all but nil, leaving him with no other choice but to make her aware of it.

But had he been too brutal and abrupt about it, he wondered uneasily. He could have waited until they were alone and broken it to her more gently. He pulled into the last parking space and said abruptly, 'I'm sorry.'

They weren't words he used very often, and many of his friends had probably never heard him say them.

Trudy, frowning out the window, looked at him in astonishment. 'What for?'

'Blurting it out like that,' Clement said. 'About Mr Gillingham's engagement to Sir Basil's daughter, I mean. I could see that it upset you.'

'It didn't upset me,' Trudy lied automatically, her heart falling to her boots at the realisation that Dr Ryder had been able to read her reaction so easily. 'Why should it? I've only just met the man,' she heard herself insisting shrilly.

But in truth, the coroner's words had hit her like a pile driver, making her go momentarily light-headed. And when she'd looked at Duncan for confirmation, the look of anger and embarrassment on his face had made her feel faintly sick.

Which was silly, wasn't it? After all, what did it really matter? So he hadn't told her about Glenda Fletcher. Why would he?

'He's just an informant, Dr Ryder,' she said firmly. And from now on, she was going to make sure that she always bore that in mind.

'Oh well, that's all right then,' Clement said, rather weakly. The last time he'd had to deal with young women and their emotions was when his daughter Julia had had her heart broken by a telephone engineer shortly before she left for university. And if he remembered rightly, he probably hadn't been of much use to her then either!

'Well, let's go and see what Angela Calver has to say for herself, shall we?' he said with some relief. He knew where he was when it came to business.

As they climbed from the car and turned off to walk down Little Clarendon Street, neither of them noticed Duncan Gillingham pull his own car up onto a nearby kerb and then watch them closely.

From the somewhat stilted conversation that had taken place at the café after that damned old man had let the cat out of the bag about Glenda, the reporter had got the distinct impression that the pair of them were off to talk to an important witness. And he wanted to know who it was, and if there was anything in it for him.

He was slightly surprised to see them enter a record shop, but he settled in to wait them out.

Angela Calver was one of two girls in the shop, a tall attractive brunette with big grey eyes marred by a rather hard and cynical expression. About twenty-three or four, Clement guessed, she was older than the other shop assistant, an obvious teenager who was clearly pleased as punch to have found her first job in a record shop. Trudy guessed at once that the younger girl probably spent more time listening to the latest pop records in the booth than actually working.

She wasn't surprised, therefore, when it had been Angela who'd first approached them, and then rather warily confirmed her name, when asked.

'What's this all about then?' she asked now, eyeing Trudy nervously.

'Oh, it's nothing to worry about, Miss Calver,' Trudy assured her instantly. 'We're just conducting routine inquiries. Am I right in thinking that you used to work for Mr Kenneth Wilcox?'

At the mention of the man's name, she seemed to lose a little colour, and she shot Clement a sharp glance. Then she glanced swiftly around the shop, but apart from a gang of teenage boys over in the back, noisily perusing the latest albums, they had the place to themselves.

'Yes,' she agreed shortly.

'Can I ask why you left?' Trudy asked. 'It seems a step down from working as a secretary, to working in a shop.' Perhaps it was because she was feeling angry with herself for letting Duncan Gillingham almost make a fool of her, but right now she simply couldn't be bothered to soft-soap Angela along. She just wanted simple and straightforward answers to simple and straightforward questions, and she was going to get them. Or else.

Perhaps their witness sensed something of this uncompromising mood, because Angela suddenly seemed to slump slightly in defeat. 'I left because I didn't feel comfortable there,' she admitted.

Trudy nodded. 'His current secretary intimated that Mr Wilcox has a nasty habit of getting, shall we say, rather *close* to his female staff?' she said delicately.

Angela flushed violently. 'I'll say. He thinks he's some great Casanova, you know the type? He thinks because he's got a bit of money, and is reasonably good-looking, that he can just …' She broke off abruptly and shrugged.

Something about the other woman's ire made Trudy wonder what the specific problem had been. Had Kenneth Wilcox's advances simply been unwelcome, and she had left rather than allow herself to be constantly pestered? Or had Angela been only too happy to accept them – and more – and then got angry when his interest waned? That would certainly bruise her ego and could make her testimony suspect.

And then Trudy realised that it hardly mattered. Unless his father-in-law had known about Kenneth's activities, then they were irrelevant. With that in mind, she smiled gently. 'Do you think the man's poor wife knew about all his affairs?'

Angela gave a bitter smile. 'If she did, she turned a blind eye. But I think she must have known.'

'Did he ever talk about his father-in-law?'

'Only to complain about him.'

'Anything specific?'

'No. Well, something about money, maybe,' Angela frowned in thought. 'He wanted Kenneth to invest his money in some scheme or other, and Kenneth didn't want to. Not that I'm surprised about *that*! He had other *expenses* that had to be paid for,' she added, so viciously, that Clement actually blinked.

Trudy too, tensed, like a gun dog spotting a fall pheasant. 'Oh? What sort of things?'

But Angela went rather pale, and then shrugged, clearing backing down. 'I don't know. Nothing, forget I mentioned it,' she muttered uneasily.

'Please, Miss Calver, need I remind you this is a police matter?'

Trudy pressed, her own voice going hard. 'It's your duty as a citizen to help us with our inquiries. Now, exactly what did you mean by that remark?'

Angela shot another quick glance around the shop, then leaned closer, lowering her voice. 'I know he had to pay for some poor kid to have an … abortion.' She all but whispered the last word.

Trudy drew in a sharp breath. 'Do you know who?'

'No, I don't, and that's the honest truth,' Angela said. 'But I suspect it was probably the secretary before me – or some other poor girl he employed to work in the shop. There was gossip, but nobody was willing to … you know … actually come right out and talk about it. From what I heard, though, the poor girl didn't want to go through with it – you know, getting rid of it – but that bast … Mr Wilcox bullied her into it. Told her he'd deny it was his, and put it about that … you know, that she was no better than a … well, you know. And she'd never get another job because he wouldn't give her a reference, and, oh, all sorts of things. In the end, they say she gave in and had it done, but she's never been the same since.'

'The poor thing!' Trudy gasped. 'Are you sure you don't know who it was they were talking about?'

'No,' Angela said.

Her voice was just a shade regretful, Clement thought cynically.

'But I think it was some girl with the name of a flower – you know, Violet or Rose, or something.'

Trudy nodded, thinking rapidly. If Thomas Hughes had found out about this, and had confronted Kenneth, then they might finally have a proper motive for murder at last. Alice might have divorced him and taken the kids had she been told about it. His father-in-law would have chucked him out of the house. His reputation would have been in ruins – he'd have been a social pariah, and without doubt, custom at his shop would have fallen away. Given all that, a man might well contemplate committing murder.

Was it possible that Duncan had been right after all?

'I see. Well, thank you for your help Miss Calver,' Trudy said abruptly. The curt dismissal made Angela look both surprised and a little chagrined.

Clement thought that, given the chance, she'd have liked to dish out far more dirt on her former boss, but he agreed with Trudy. They had more than enough now to be going on with.

Back in the Rover, Clement popped another breath mint into his mouth and said, 'I think we need to talk to Alice, don't you?'

Trudy shot him a quick glance. 'Alice? Not Kenneth?'

Clement shrugged. 'No point, really is there? He'll only deny it. And if pushed, he can always say he had a fling with Angela, and that she's just spreading lies about him now because she's bitter. A woman scorned, and all that. No, it's been my experience that wives often know more about their husbands than their husbands like to think.'

Trudy slowly nodded. 'And if you think about it, *Alice* had almost as much to lose as Kenneth if there was a scandal,' she agreed. 'She wouldn't be the first wife willing to put up with her husband's wandering eye, so long as he was discreet. Or have to clean up after her husband's mess when he wasn't.'

Clement grunted in acknowledgement, turned the ignition and pulled out into the traffic.

Behind him, Duncan climbed out of his car and headed for the record shop.

Chapter 32

Caroline Benham watched her sister slump back wearily in her chair and frowned slightly. She'd been surprised when Alice had called and asked her to come up to Headington in her lunch hour, and she didn't like having to ask her boss for the extra half-hour or so to make it feasible, but she was glad now that she had. Alice looked to have aged about ten years in as many days, and something was clearly bothering her.

'You look terrible,' Caroline said, with her usual lack of tact.

Alice heaved a massive sigh. 'Oh, Caro, it's that wretched newspaper!' she blurted out. 'Did you read the latest assault on us? They all but outright accused either Godfrey or Kenneth of killing Father!' She looked at her sister with big, indignant and worried eyes.

'So? Do you think one of them did?' Caroline asked bluntly, watching her sister's face twitch in shock. She'd never had much patience with Alice's slavish devotion to convention, but she was curious to see what her sister made of it all. For, in spite of everything, Alice had quite a good brain inside her head. When she chose to use it.

'Oh Caroline, don't start,' Alice wailed. 'I can't cope with you right now when you're in one of *these* moods.'

'What moods?' her younger sibling asked, genuinely unaware what she meant by the remark.

'You know … saying outrageous things. I always said you did it just to show off.'

'Oh, you mean being honest,' Caroline interpreted bluntly, then seeing her sister wince, sighed heavily. 'All right, all right, I'll go along with it, and keep on pretending that everything's just fine,' she promised.

Alice passed a hand across her forehead, wondering somewhat belatedly, what on earth had possessed her to reach out to her sister of all people for some succour and support. She should have known it would be like this. Only the morning had been dragging on so, and it had been so quiet in the house with the children at school and Kenneth at work, and her nerves had been stretching out like piano wires being tuned. She'd simply had to talk to somebody or go mad.

And Kenneth was no use as a sounding board. Last night, he'd just read the paper in grim silence and then, when she'd become indignant on his behalf, had told her to ignore it. *Ignore it*! As if it would all just go away if they pretended it wasn't happening.

'I dare say Godfrey's in a tizzy right about now,' Caroline couldn't help but say, and smiled a smile that would have impressed the Cheshire Cat. Catching it, Alice almost felt like smiling too.

Then she shook her head, unwilling to be made to feel better. 'Oh Godfrey,' she said carelessly, dismissing her brother with a vague wave of her hand. 'What I'm worried about is *Kenneth*. Oh, I know he's just shrugging it all off, but the neighbours are beginning to talk. And it can't be good for the business either. You mark my words, soon the customers will stop coming into the shop. You know what people say – "there's no smoke without fire" and all that. Pretty soon that bloody reporter will have everyone thinking there was something … you know … wrong, about what happened that night.'

Caroline opened her mouth to say 'well, wasn't there?' but then – in a rare moment of finer feeling – closed it again before she could state the obvious. Nevertheless, she eyed her sister like a curious robin. Was it really possible, Caroline wondered, that Alice really *didn't* have any idea of what had happened that night the monster had got his just desserts?

She supposed, after a moment's thought, that it might just be so. After all, Alice seemed to have no idea about her husband's tom-catting around all these years, an activity he'd taken up almost since the night of their honeymoon. And just how she managed *that*, Caroline had no idea. Everyone in the family knew about it, and once or twice, lover-boy Kenneth had sailed very close to the wind indeed …

Then again, Caroline thought practically, Alice might well know all about it, but had chosen to pretend that she didn't. Her older sister had always been very good at seeing only what she wanted to see and ignoring everything else. Like the hell their mother had gone through, for instance.

'I'm thinking of selling this place and moving away,' Alice said abruptly, breaking into Caroline's bitter thoughts, and making Caroline look at her even more carefully.

'And what does Kenneth think about that?' she asked.

'Oh, I haven't mentioned it to him yet,' Alice floored her by saying. Catching the astonishment in her sister's expression, she added crossly 'Well, there's no reason why we shouldn't move, is there? The house is mine, in my name, I mean. I can sell it if I want to.'

Caroline, surprised though she was by this sudden flash of independent spirit in her doormat of a sister, thoroughly approved.

'Where were you thinking of going?' she asked curiously. 'Staying local, you know in this area or—'

'Oh no,' Alice interrupted. 'Going right away somewhere new. Dorset maybe, or Devon. I've always liked the West Country. Ever since we were children and used to go to Torquay for our holidays. Remember?'

Caroline did. But since those far-off days brought back memories of their mother, when she was still alive and healthy, she deliberately ignored the pull of the past.

'Speaking of holidays, I ran into Joan the day before yesterday,' Caroline said instead, deliberately changing the subject. 'They're off to America the day after tomorrow. I hope things go well over there for them,' she added pensively.

A shadow of anxiety flitted briefly across Alice's face, but just then the doorbell sounded. 'Oh bother! Who can that be now?' she grumbled, getting up and leaving the room. After a few moments, Caroline heard voices and then glanced up when the living room door opened again as Alice came back with their visitors.

The first thing she noticed was her sister, whose face had gone pale and blank, though her eyes were definitely frightened. Then Dr Clement Ryder and the pretty policewoman she'd met before followed on behind, and Alice was saying nervously, 'I think you've must have met my sister Caroline, Dr Ryder and … er …'

'WPC Loveday, Mrs Wilcox,' Trudy said with a smile. 'Yes, we have met. Hello Mrs Benham.'

Caroline nodded, then glanced at Alice. Did she want her to go? But the appeal in her sister's eyes when they looked at her told her that she was very much needed, so she made no move to rise.

'Would you like a cup of tea?' Alice asked, and was patently relieved when both Clement and Trudy accepted with thanks.

Alice all but ran out to the kitchen, leaving the other three alone.

'Well, don't stand on ceremony,' Caroline said robustly. 'Have a seat. Are you *still* going on about that man's death then?' she demanded flatly.

'Yes, I'm afraid we are. The more we look into things, the more things we seem to find that worry us,' Trudy said.

When she and Clement had arrived at the house, they'd agreed that Trudy should take the lead, but that Clement would come in if he heard or saw anything that he thought needed clarification. They had not expected to find two sisters for the price of one, but Trudy wasn't that dismayed. There was something very blunt and defiant about Caroline Benham that might work to their advantage. She'd met people like Caroline before – they seemed to have no sense of discretion or the ability to dissemble. They simply said the first thing that came into their heads, which could often be hideously embarrassing in a social situation, but which was manna from heaven for investigators like herself.

'Oh? Like what?' Caroline challenged fearlessly.

'Well, Mr Hughes seemed to be at loggerheads with almost everyone at the bonfire party that night for instance,' Trudy said. 'We know *your* grievance with him, of course, because you were kind enough to tell us, but we now have reason to believe that he'd quarrelled with, or upset, almost everyone else there – perhaps with the exception of the children.'

'Oh, I could have told you *that*,' Caroline said disparagingly. 'And don't think he hadn't quarrelled with the children either, because he probably had. The older ones, anyway. Make no mistake, nobody liked him.'

'*Caroline!*' This came from Alice, who had just entered with a tea tray, which she set down on the coffee table in front of the sofa. 'I can assure you, er, Constable, that *my* children had no quarrel with their grandfather!'

She shot her sister a furious look, then smiled and set about 'being mother.' And for a few moments, milk and sugar were added and cups passed around.

When she was finally seated and had had a chance to get some of her decorum back, Alice sighed gently. 'I was just telling Caroline how upsetting the *Tribune* articles have been,' she offered as an opening gambit. 'I was even wondering if Kenneth and I should sue. That awful man, Mr Gillingham, is all but accusing him of … well, I'm not quite sure what, exactly,' Alice said hotly. 'Do you think we'd have a libel case, Dr Ryder?' she appealed to him.

'Oh, I'm not a solicitor,' Clement said with a vague smile. 'But I expect the newspaper would employ legal men on their staff whose job it is to make sure that nothing actually actionable is printed.'

Alice sighed angrily. 'Yes, I suppose that's true. It's all sly hints about this and nasty digs about that, but never actually having the courage to say things outright. But it's not nice – they still make it clear that we're all suspected of doing something ghastly. As I was just saying to Caroline, the neighbours are beginning to talk.'

'Yes, we've had to interview your husband a number of times now,' Trudy said, not missing the way Alice jerked nervously in her seat, almost spilling some tea into her saucer.

'Oh? Kenneth never said anything about that to me,' she quavered.

Caroline snorted. 'He wouldn't,' she muttered, causing all eyes to turn to her. She met her sister's pleading gaze first, and added, 'He's the quiet type,' rather unconvincingly.

Trudy could have sworn she'd wanted to say something else though, and would have bet a fair amount of her week's wages that her brother-in-law's affairs were no secret to Caroline. And that made her wonder. Did the rest of Alice's family know about his wandering ways too?

'Did your father get on well with Kenneth?' Trudy asked blandly.

'Oh yes,' Alice said, at the same time as Caroline gave another inelegant, but telling snort.

'Oh, come off it, Alice,' Caroline couldn't help but say, goaded beyond endurance by her sister's latest and colossal hypocrisy. 'That man argued with everyone, and you and Kenneth were no different. He treated Godfrey like something to be scraped off

212

his shoe, and he loathed the sight of me almost as much as I loathed the sight of him. The only one he had any time for was Matthew, but even then, just lately ...' She suddenly went a shade pale and broke off abruptly, before turning sharply to look angrily at Trudy. 'Don't you think it's time all this was decently laid to rest?' she challenged. 'If there was any evidence of foul play that night, you'd have found it by now, wouldn't you?'

Trudy, who was very aware that their lack of any forensic evidence whatsoever, due to the destroying nature of fire, was their weakest link, did her best to look casually away. 'There is still the question of motive, Mrs Benham,' she said instead. But she kept her eyes fixed on Alice, who began to squirm a little under the observation. 'It seems to me that your father was a very clever man, in many ways, and was the kind of man that kept his eyes and ears open. And he seemed very interested in the doings of his immediate family members. His sister, for instance.'

With this, the two sisters cast each other a quick glance, and Trudy knew she wasn't imagining it when she sensed a sudden lessening of the tension in the room. Whatever was worrying them, the cause of their anxiety didn't lie in that direction.

'Aunt Mary?' Alice said, sounding surprised.

'But she wasn't the only one, was she?' Trudy said, quickly abandoning that line, since it was clearly going to lead to a dead end. 'Your brother Godfrey did very badly out of the will, didn't he?'

Again, the two sisters seemed to communicate silently, but again it was clear to her that neither of the two women took Godfrey seriously. It was, she rather suspected, the story of the man's life.

'And then there's your husband, Mrs Wilcox,' Trudy said carefully, but was surprised, when, yet again, the two sisters showed no signs of increased strain. Especially when Trudy had expected the exact opposite to happen.

'Oh, Kenneth was used to Father's ways,' Alice said flatly, and without any apparent unease. 'We put him up with him because he was so generous with this place,' she added, glancing around at her spacious home. 'And with providing for Lucas, of course.'

'But your father didn't like the way your husband ran his private life, did he Mrs Wilcox?' Trudy asked, deciding there was no use tip-toeing around things any further. They'd come here to find out if this woman knew about her husband's many and ugly infidelities, and if she did, whether they'd provided either herself or her husband with a motive for murder.

Trudy tensed, waiting for and expecting fireworks. She didn't have any preconceived ideas, exactly, on how she expected Alice Wilcox to behave. Would she go down the scandalised route, and demand to know how she, Trudy, dared to cast aspersions? Or would she become all sophisticated and nonchalant, and explain to her condescendingly how marriages had to be conducted with a bit of give-and-take on both sides? What she hadn't expected was for Alice Wilcox to look at her with blank, slightly bewildered eyes.

'His private life? What on earth do you mean?' Alice asked.

Suddenly Caroline started coughing violently, and when Trudy glanced at her, under cover of putting her hand to her mouth and leaning forward to catch her breath, Caroline shook her head in a definite signal intended to convey that her sister was ignorant of her husband's conduct.

Trudy, unsure of what to do next, looked questioningly at Clement.

He caught his cue instantly and leaned forward a little in his chair. 'Your husband confided to us that his father-in-law had been badgering him quite ruthlessly about investing some money from a bequest into one of Thomas's business enterprises. And that he, your husband, had had to be … shall we say, quite robust, in turning him down. It made for bad blood between them, I think?'

'Oh, that,' Alice said, her brow clearing. 'Yes, Father wasn't very happy about that, but he understood.'

Caroline snorted again, but said nothing, and was clearly relieved that near-disaster had been diverted. 'That man was never happy about anything,' she said darkly. 'And I told you before, he died because he deserved to. You can't go around causing misery and destruction like he did and expect to get away with it forever,' she rushed on, her anger levels rising. 'He killed mother, and instead of being sorry or trying to make amends, he was willing to do the sa—'

'Caroline, don't!' Alice all but shouted, and her sister's eyes, which had become a little glazed, suddenly flickered, and she paused and took a deep breath.

'Yes, what was he willing to do?' Clement asked smoothly, but he already knew it was too late.

Caroline had got a hold on her runaway tongue and simply shrugged. 'I was going to say, he was willing to do far worse, so long as it meant he got his way. But that night, his sins found him out and he was required to pay for them. That's all. You know, you're just wasting your time,' she added, glancing at her watch at getting up. 'Your investigation will never come to anything, because it can't. Now, I have to get back to work. Alice, thanks for the lunch. Dr Ryder, Constable Loveday.' She nodded at them both briefly and marched out, her colour still dangerously high.

When the door shut noisily behind her, Alice let out a sigh. 'I'm sorry about my sister's behaviour. She still really hasn't come to terms with losing mother the way she did,' she explained weakly.

'That's all right,' Trudy said, glancing at Clement to see if he wanted to add anything. But when he got to his feet, indicating that he hadn't, they both took their leave of a very relieved Alice and headed back towards the city.

Chapter 33

Duncan Gillingham was typing furiously. He was, at that moment in time, a very happy man indeed.

When he'd gone into that record shop in Little Clarendon Street he'd had no idea what he might find, but a quick look around had told him that the most likely candidate to have crossed Dr Ryder and Trudy's radar was the rather good-looking shop assistant.

It hadn't been any great hardship to get chatting to her in a friendly sort of way as she'd helped him negotiate the stacks of pop records to hit the charts recently. He carefully expressed no interest in The Highwaymen's religious ditty, 'Michael (Row the Boat)' but admitted to rather being an admirer of Helen Shapiro, who'd just had a hit recently with 'Walkin' Back to Happiness.'

Naturally, he'd then told her how much better looking she was than Helen Shapiro, and did she sing too?

Alas, the lady did not.

But the moment he'd finally managed to wangle her name from her, he knew he'd hit the jackpot.

Naturally, during the course of his vendetta, he'd researched Kenneth Wilcox's former employees vigorously, paying especial attention to the pretty women who made up his secretarial staff, and so the name of Angela Calver wasn't new to him.

But he'd been having difficulties tracking her down. Firstly, she'd moved rooming houses after leaving Wilcox's employ, leaving no forwarding address and he'd also struck out when he'd searched for her amongst the secretarial bureaux and agencies. And now he knew why. She had changed careers as well residences.

As they flirted over the 45's, it hadn't taken him long to get some of her life story out of her, but she was a sharp little thing, and had soon realised that this wasn't just the usual run-of-the-mill attempted pick up that she was probably used to. When she'd challenged him outright about why he was so interested in her past, he had hesitated to tell her the truth, but only for a moment.

Normally, when delicately fishing for information from a potentially hostile witness, the last thing he would ever do was to admit to being a reporter. But something about Angela Calver's sharp, keen eyes and hard but curious stare told him that she was no shrinking violet.

So he had taken a chance and introduced himself. And once again, he knew it was truly his lucky day, because she admitted that she had read all the articles he'd written about the Thomas Hughes affair, and far from being wary or upset about his veiled attacks on Kenneth Wilcox, had started to smile instead.

From that point on, two things had very quickly become apparent. Firstly, she had indeed been another victim of that creep's libido, and, far more importantly, was now very much the woman scorned. But she was no innocent, unlike his sister, who had fallen for all the man's lies and charms and promises, and then found herself in an impossible situation.

No, Angela Calver was a much more hard-headed proposition all together. This much quickly became apparent, when, after persuading her to snatch a quick cup of coffee with him at a nearby café, she'd made it clear that she expected to be paid (and paid well) for her information.

At first, this had made him incredibly wary. For a start, Sir Basil didn't like paying for information, even if the *Tribune*'s editor had a much more pragmatic point of view about such things. Then there was always the question about just how much veracity could be attached to information that had been bought and paid for. It was not, after all, unheard of for people to say exactly what they thought a hot and eager reporter wanted to hear, and to hell with the truth.

But again, the lucky streak that had started for him when he'd walked into the record shop continued. Because whilst Angela was not willing to be portrayed in print for all to see as a secretary who had fallen prey to a lascivious boss (and who could blame her for *that*?) she had something even better to offer.

Something far more substantial, in fact, than a list of accusations concerning sexual advances and abuses of power that Wilcox might have been able to shrug off as female hysteria.

No, Angela, bless her, had hard evidence in her possession of something far more devastating. And for a price, she was willing to share it.

From the café, she'd taken him for a short walk down Walton Street, where she now lived, and from her room overlooking Worcester College, had produced an envelope of carbon copies of certain financial transactions.

It turned out that the excess cash that Wilcox had claimed was due to a 'legacy' from his 'late aunt' had, in fact, been no such thing. Rather, it could be put down to the clever and systematic accumulation of money illegally skimmed off taxes due to Her Majesty's Inland Revenue.

According to Angela Calver, she had begun to suspect some sort of chicanery not long after starting work there, and her curiosity had led her to investigating her boss's desk after hours. As an honest and good citizen, she naturally didn't approve of such goings on, and had taken to making carbon copies of the irregularities in his books. Luckily, she had worked for a firm of accountants before going to Wilcox, and she knew what she was seeing.

Reading between the lines though, Duncan was convinced that she'd only started looking through her boss's drawers when it became clear that their fling was coming to an end. And, naturally, a girl had to look after herself.

He wondered if Angela had originally intended to blackmail Wilcox – either into continuing their affair, or for money to help her fund her lifestyle after he'd grown tired of her.

But since she was willing to sell Duncan the evidence, rather than keep it and make use of it, for some reason she had obviously not gone down that particular route.

As he continued to type the article that would finally smash Kenneth Wilcox's cosy, hypocritical little world once and for all, he wondered again why Angela had sat on the evidence all these months instead of using it.

Perhaps she still had some residue of feelings for the man? Maybe she hoped they could get back together? Far more likely, perhaps she simply hadn't quite had the guts to go through with it. It was one thing to get something on a treacherous lover, and feel all vindicated and smug. But it was quite another to take that irrevocable leap into the sordid role of blackmailer.

Whatever the reason, she had certainly been happy enough to take advantage of his offer to buy the proof for a one-off (and very generous) payment – and why not? Not only would she benefit financially from it in a perfectly legal way, but she'd also get her revenge on the feckless Wilcox as well, and all without any risk to herself.

The article finally finished, Duncan sat back and read it through, then happily tapped on his editor's door. Regardless of whether or not the Thomas Hughes affair had been a crime or an accident, he'd achieved his goal – the ruination of the man who'd wrecked his sister's life.

With his 'source' and documentary proof to back her up, the editor congratulated him heartily on his scoop, and agreed to lead with it that evening. The story would be dynamite, for if there was one thing the *Tribune*'s working-class readers liked, it was to read about greedy and corrupt middle class bosses getting their just desserts.

The tax inspectors too, would swoop down on Wilcox like avenging furies. With a bit of luck, Duncan thought vindictively, he'd not only have to pay a massive fine that would wipe him out financially, but he might also get to serve some time in prison as well.

That would learn the baby-killing, sex-mad bastard! He couldn't wait for Lily to see the paper tonight and know that Wilcox would finally have to pay for what he'd done to her. In fact, he would leave early and let her know just what was about to happen.

Going back to his desk, and grinning in triumph, he sat back on his chair and contemplated just how sweet life was. The only fly in the ointment for Duncan now was the memory of the look that Trudy Loveday had given him earlier on in the café, and he felt the smile slowly fall off his face. He began to fidget moodily in his chair.

Of course, it was a shame to lose her. He'd had high hopes of spending some nice times with Trudy before gently letting her down. The challenge of discovering the real woman behind the police uniform had been truly piquant, of course, but there had been something more to it than that. The sweet anticipation of them becoming lovers had been steadily growing in him ever since he'd first seen her at the bus stop. That combination of innocence and asperity had been particularly delicious. It annoyed him considerably that he would have to give up the pleasure of the chase and the ultimate reward.

He cursed Clement Ryder roundly for his interference.

Then he began to wonder. Was the situation *really* beyond salvaging? All right, it would take some doing, but was it totally impossible that he might yet talk her around? Oh, he'd have to wait a good while and let the dust settle. Right now, as the fulminating look in her eyes had told him, she was as mad as a hornet.

But time had a way of dulling outrage. And women, he knew from experience, had a way of letting themselves be fooled, if they wanted it enough. He was confident that she *had* been attracted to him. All he had to do was plant a seed of doubt in her mind, and let it grow.

To accomplish this, there were several options he could choose from. He could always deny the engagement – it wasn't official yet after all. He could simply say that the rumours of his attachment had been greatly exaggerated. The problem with that was, she might just have the gumption to call on Glenda and ask her outright how things stood – and that would never do!

He could possibly appeal to her sense of justice by coming up with some yarn about how Glenda had used her power as Sir Basil's daughter to make his life difficult. He hadn't *wanted* to start going out with her, but he was in an impossible situation. It didn't do to say no to the boss's daughter, did it? And then Glenda began to take their dates far too seriously. He only ever intended to keep on her good side, but she misinterpreted what was happening, and suddenly he found out that everyone was thinking of them as a 'couple.' And now he found himself in the unenviable position of either having to throw her over (and almost certainly lose his job) or play along in the hopes that Glenda would get bored and find some other victim to latch on to.

Would Trudy fall for that? It was possible, he thought hopefully. For all her choice of difficult career, there was something kind and vulnerable in those big brown eyes of hers.

Yes, Duncan thought, flushed with his run of good luck and high on having finally brought down his enemy. He'd give it a bloody good go.

He wasn't about to give up his pursuit of a certain lady police officer just yet.

With that, he got up and drove to the hair salon to see his sister.

Lily was busy putting a blue rinse to some old lady's hair, when she saw Duncan's car pull up outside the window, before he got out and peered in.

Just one look at his radiant face had her heart accelerating in fear and alarm – and something else.

'This solution needs ten more minutes to set, Mrs Wilkins. I'll be right back,' she murmured to her customer, who was too busy reading a woman's magazine to care.

Outside, Duncan grinned at her and said, 'hop in. It's warmer in the car.'

Lily, feeling her shoulders begin to ache with tension, slipped in and looked at her brother fearfully. 'What's happened? Are you all right?' she whispered.

Duncan smiled grimly. 'Oh, I'm just great. I've just written the best article of my life.'

Lily frowned. 'Is that all? When I saw your face just now …' She trailed off, as that same look of glee, relief and satisfaction crossed his face. 'Oh Dunc, what have you done?' she wailed.

'I've done it, sis. For you,' Duncan said simply. 'I've brought the bastard down!'

Lily didn't need to ask who he was talking about. Instead, she simply looked at him, stunned. 'But how?' Kenneth Wilcox had always seemed so untouchable. A man of relative wealth and far more power than a simple working-class girl like her could hope to compete with. For months now she'd felt helpless and worthless, haunted by her decisions and simply unable to move on, or even contemplate any possible kind of worthwhile future.

Something inside her had died when Kenneth had been so brutal towards her, making it so scornfully clear that he didn't value their child anything like he valued his own reputation, and the continuation of his easy, comfortable life.

He'd made her feel worthless and all the time with that knowing look in his eye that made it clear that she could do nothing but go along with it, or be left with the scandal of a child out of wedlock, and the financial ruin that came with it.

'You weren't the first, Lily,' Duncan said softly. 'He did it with other girls too. But one of them … well, let's just say, she was a bit more hard-headed than most. She got the goods on him. And tonight, you'll be able to read all about in the papers. He's been fiddling his taxes.'

Lily blinked. Taxes? For some reason, that struck her as funny. The man ruined lives, was willing to toss aside his own child as if it were nothing, and he was going to suffer because he'd been cheating the tax man?

Wildly, she began to laugh. And then, just as wildly, she began to cry.

Wordlessly, Duncan Gillingham reached across and held her awkwardly in his arms. 'It's OK, sis,' he said gruffly. 'It's all over now. Don't think about him any more. He got what he deserved. You can get on with your life, now. Yeah?'

Wordlessly, Lily nodded. But she wondered. Would it really be that simple? Was *life* ever that simple?

Chapter 34

'You know, I was sure those two women were communicating silently between themselves all throughout that interview,' Trudy said grumpily.

They had returned to the comfort of the coroner's office, and were now sitting before the roaring fire, sipping tea and nibbling on digestive biscuits.

'Oh yes,' Clement agreed. 'Often brothers and sisters – and some husbands and wives – can hold whole conversations, as it were, without actually uttering a word. They just know each other – and their circumstances – so well, that a simple look or gesture will do it.'

Trudy sighed. 'Let's face it, Caroline Benham had a point,' she said gloomily. 'We might just as well admit defeat and close the case. It's been nearly a week, and we've still got nothing solid to go on. Unless you can think of anything we've missed?' she added hopefully.

Clement sighed. 'Like you, I think there's *something* there, and that the whole Hughes family – perhaps in its entirety – might know what it is, but it's for sure that they won't tell *us*.' He was thinking of the silent children with knowing eyes as he spoke, and he wondered just what it was they were holding back. 'Of course, Thomas Hughes's death may still have been accidental, and all they're keeping quiet about is the fact that he died totally unloved and unmourned.'

'Yes. It's not nice to admit that you couldn't love your own parent, isn't it?' Trudy said, unable to really imagine it. Her own mother and father were an integral part of her life.

'Well, if there *was* anything going on,' Clement said, 'neither Alice or Caroline thought it had anything to do with Mary Everly.'

'Or poor Godfrey,' Trudy said with a grin.

'And I'd bet my last Trilby hat that Alice Wilcox has no idea what her husband gets up to with his female staff.'

Trudy shuddered. 'Can you imagine that poor girl, being forced to have an abortion? I almost wish we *could* pin it on Kenneth.'

Clement shook his head. 'No you don't,' he warned her softly.

Trudy sighed and nodded.

The only member of the family no one had mentioned was Matthew, Trudy thought. Which was odd, really, when you considered the fact that he'd come in for the bulk of the family fortune. You'd have thought there would be *some* sort of resentment in the family over that, even if the siblings were close and loving. It was human nature, after all, to expect fair treatment.

Unless …

Suddenly, Trudy felt herself sitting forward in her chair. Something someone had said in passing was urgently trying to find its way back into the forefront of her mind. Something really off-hand, that couldn't possibly mean anything important … and yet …

Holidays? No, not that. Or yes, maybe something to do with that, but not really … what on earth was it? And why was her heart thumping so hard suddenly?

Why did nobody resent Matthew, the favoured son …

And then she knew.

Just like that, the whole picture became crystal clear to her. Just as, when a child, she'd looked down the tube of a kaleidoscope and all the multiple coloured pieces suddenly coalesced into a proper pattern. She could see the picture clearly, in all its terrible, tragic, remorseless inevitability.

'Trudy, are you all right?' she heard Clement ask, but his voice sounded far away. 'You've gone really pale. Here, sit forward and put your head between your knees and take a deep breath.'

Trudy turned to face him, but she had no interest in taking his advice. Instead she looked at him with such an expression of horror in her big, velvety brown eyes, that Clement felt his own heartbeat begin to race.

'Doctor Ryder,' she whispered urgently, 'that disease, the one that killed Thomas Hughes's wife? Could it run in the family?'

Chapter 35

It was starting to get dark by the time they returned to Matthew Hughes's house, though it was barely four o'clock in the afternoon. They had, by mutual and tacit consent, remained silent on the journey, both caught up in their thoughts, and neither of them looking forward to the interview that lay ahead.

Once again it was Joan, Matthew's wife who answered the door. This time she looked flustered and distracted, and was clearly not happy to see them on her doorstep again.

'Oh, hello again. I'm so sorry, but this is a really bad time to call, I'm afraid. We're all at sixes and sevens packing for one thing. We're going abroad tomorrow, and it's such a palaver! And then I'm having to get the children's tea on, and we've just had Godfrey round, complaining.' Joan sighed. 'I think he's trying to persuade Matthew to give him some more money from their father's estate, since he's not happy with the small pension Thomas left him, and he's only just left and—'

'I'm so sorry, Mrs Hughes,' Trudy broke into her rush of words with gentle but firm insistence, 'but we're actually here to speak to your husband. We know he's not at work because we tried there first, and they told us he was no longer employed there.'

'Oh yes, Matthew handed in his notice,' she muttered. Trudy

pricked up her ears at this, for she had assumed that he'd simply walked away from his job without so much as a by-your-leave. But if he'd actually worked out at least the requisite week's notice, then he must have resigned his post as soon as his father had died. Which indicated, if nothing else, that Matthew Hughes had acted with considerable foresight.

'Oh dear, well, I suppose you'd better come in then,' Joan said reluctantly. 'My husband is in the study. Please, follow me.'

She led them quickly down a short corridor to a door at the far end. This she tapped on briefly, then stuck her head around and announced nervously, 'Matt, it's the police.' She moved aside to let them in. 'I have to see to the children,' she said, avoiding looking at them as she scuttled away.

Trudy carefully closed the door behind the departing woman, her big brown eyes troubled. When she turned around, she found herself in a pleasant but compact, book-lined room. A single window, with the curtains already closed against the November gloom, overlooked a small desk. There were only three chairs in the room and from a chair in front of the desk, Matthew Hughes was swivelling around to look at them.

He looked visibly older than the last time Trudy had seen him, and his thin frame seemed to droop a little, as if the weight of the world was pressing down on his shoulders and bending him in the middle. Dark smudges under his eyes were clearly notice-able in the artificial light.

He smiled at them without humour. 'Constable Loveday, Dr Ryder. Please, sit down.' He indicated the two wing-backed chairs that flanked a fireplace where a small gas fire hissed and popped occasionally. 'What can I do for you this time? You're lucky to catch us in. We have several errands to run before the children's bedtime.'

'Yes, your wife told us you were due to go abroad shortly,' Trudy said, taking one of the chairs and digging into her satchel for her notebook. 'You're going to the United States of America I understand?' she asked quietly.

She looked up at him and he nodded silently, his eyes going from her to Clement and then back to her again. He looked tired and wary and oddly detached. It puzzled her slightly, since she was used to people finding her official presence alarming, or sometimes amusing, or (in the case of the drunk and the habitually criminal) annoying. But she had the feeling that Matthew Hughes wasn't feeling much of anything right then. Perhaps he simply didn't have the energy for it. Which wouldn't have been surprising, given what they now knew.

'The last time I was here I spoke to your wife. She had to leave us for a while to check on your youngest – Helen, isn't it?' she began, determined to keep her voice calm and steady.

'Yes, Helen. She's four years old. She has a birthday coming up in February,' he added, his eyes flickering to the slight gap where the curtains met in the middle. Outside, a streetlamp was casting a smoky yellow glow into the darkening street.

Trudy swallowed hard. Was he wondering if his little girl would live to see her fifth birthday? Somehow, she thought that he was.

She caught Clement's gentle, encouraging gaze, and took a deep breath. 'At the time, I assumed your little girl had one of the usual childhood ailments. Chickenpox, or maybe measles,' Trudy went on gently. 'But since then, we've been pursuing our inquiries, and have discovered that her condition is much more serious. Isn't it?'

Dr Ryder had, in fact, only managed to track down and discuss the little girl's condition with her physician less than an hour ago.

When Trudy had first asked him if the illness that had killed Mildred Hughes was one of those that could be inherited, he'd quickly consulted some of his medical tomes and found out that it could. It had then been a simple matter for a man with his contacts, to find and locate the doctor treating Matthew Hughes's family.

And he had confirmed their worst fears.

229

Now the dying girl's father sighed heavily and shifted his gaze from the light shining through the curtains, and back to her. He smiled wearily, but again without humour. 'You have been busy, it seems.' His tone was not so much accusatory as uninterested.

Trudy swallowed hard, aware that her heart was pounding. For a moment, her mind went blank, as she found it impossible to think of what to say next. What *did* you say to the father of a little girl who was almost certainly going to die very soon? And at such a heart-breakingly young age?

She licked her dry lips, and stared down at her notebook and pencil. She didn't want to continue, but knew that she must. Eventually, she sighed gently. 'Did your father refuse to give you the money for her treatment, Mr Hughes?'

Matthew turned and looked once more at the curtains. His brown hair caught some of the light slipping in from outside, turning one half of it almost white. His face was flat and expressionless. When he spoke, his voice was so low they had to strain to hear.

'Of course he did,' Matthew whispered before continuing more robustly. 'If he wasn't willing to give half his bloody precious fortune to save his wife, why should he give it to save one of his grandchildren?'

Matthew laughed suddenly, not loudly or hard, but it was made unbearably ugly by the quiet desperation and weary hatred that forced it from his mouth. 'It wasn't as if Helen was his only grandchild, you see? He had plenty of spares – and she was not even a boy. He still had Lucas, Alice's child, and our own Ben.' He paused, then shrugged. 'To my father, Constable Loveday, trying to save my Helen simply wasn't worth the bother or the effort,' he said shockingly.

Trudy again had to swallow hard. A painful lump in her throat made it hard to breathe, and she had to clear her throat.

Matthew continued to speak, still in that same flat, uninterested voice, still staring out of the gap in the curtain. 'Do you know what he actually said to me? When, after all the tests were done and the doctors finally confirmed our worst fears – that Helen had the same condition that had killed Mother?'

He turned briefly to look at her, but Trudy, knowing what she must do next, couldn't meet his eyes and continued to stare miserably down at her notebook.

Matthew's lips twisted into a grim smile. 'He told me that if the doctors in the United States could *guarantee* that the treatment would work, he would loan me the money. *Loan* me it, mark you, not give it to us.' Matthew laughed softly. 'But of course, there are no guarantees to be had. You would know that, Dr Ryder, being a medical man,' he added, turning to look at Clement curiously.

Clement, feeling sick at heart, slowly nodded. 'I'm not on expert on rare conditions, Mr Hughes, but I understand after consulting with my colleagues, that with this particular disease, in a very small number of cases concerning children under the age of seven, it's possible that life expectancy can be prolonged by as much as ten years. With extensive treatment and an expensive array of drugs.'

Matthew nodded. 'Yes. That's what they told us too. But the chances are astronomical. Most children die within a year of diagnosis. That's why the NHS won't fund the treatment. And that's why my father refused to help us. Just like he refused to help mother. He said we had to face facts.' Matthew smiled bitterly. 'That life could be hard sometimes, and we had to grow a backbone and face up to it, like he'd had to, and get on with things. He even told us we could have more children if we wanted them.'

Trudy caught her breath at this particular piece of cruelty, but Matthew heard it. He glanced at her, too weary to feel any justification because of her reaction, and simply shrugged. 'That was the way he thought. To him, life was one big profit and loss sheet, and accumulating wealth and power was all that mattered. And if you were unprofitable …'

But even the numbness that had been mercifully enfolding him, wasn't up to allowing him to follow through on that particular thought, and he trailed off and simply shrugged again.

'I understand. And that's why you had to kill him,' Trudy said softly, still staring at the blank page of her notebook.

For a brief, breathless moment, she expected him to confess. The room was so silent that even Clement seemed to be holding his breath. Trudy waited, and waited, and eventually was forced to look up at him.

And when their eyes met, she realised just how foolish she had been to think this man would ever confess. His eyes, blank, remote, tired and almost amused, looked back at her unwaveringly.

'Is it?' he said softly. 'What an odd thing to say. Of course I didn't kill my father.'

As if he hadn't spoken, Trudy looked away from him and closed the pages together on her notebook. 'You knew that your father, once he'd made a decision, wouldn't be persuaded to change his mind.' She opened the flap of her satchel. 'And you knew that your little girl was fast running out of time. If she was to start treatment – and if it was to have any chance of prolonging her life – she would have to start it soon.' She slipped the notebook carefully inside the leather bag. 'And for that you needed money. Money you simply didn't have, but knew you would inherit when your father died.' She snapped the metal clasp on the side of the satchel, and the small 'snick' of sound seemed to ricochet around the room with unnatural force. 'And so, on the night of the bonfire, you waited until he went to the shed, and then you followed him.'

Trudy turned the satchel to her lap, and then, still incapable of looking Matthew Hughes in the eye, she too turned to stare at the chink in the curtain, where the persistent, incongruous light continued seeping through. 'It wasn't hard, was it? It was dark, and everyone was watching the bonfire. You just walked in and … what … picked up something hard, a gardening tool maybe and hit him over the head?'

She didn't expect an answer, and she didn't get one.

For some reason, she noticed at that moment that the curtains were chintz ones, with big pink and white tea roses marching across them. Odd, she hadn't realised that before.

'He probably didn't even get the chance to cry out,' she carried on thoughtfully. 'Did he start to turn around? Did he see it was you? Not that it matters,' Trudy went on quietly. 'You wouldn't have stopped, even if he had. It was either him or your daughter, wasn't it? It was as simple as that. And it was all his own doing too. That was the real pity of it. If he'd only shown some common decency – just a smidgen of love or compassion for you or your child, you wouldn't have had to do it, would you? But the truth was, he loved himself and his money, more than anything or anyone in the world. And that proved fatal.'

She slowly turned her eyes from the curtains and met those of the man sitting opposite her. 'All you had to do then was light the fuse of a firework and leave him, making sure you got out of the shed before it started to go off and drew attention your way.' She paused and shook her head. 'The whole thing wouldn't have taken you more than a minute, even if anyone had noticed your absence. And in the dark, who would? All you had to do then was wait for the shed to catch alight and do its worst, and it would all be done. By then you were back at the fire, as if nothing had happened. Did you go into the shed sometime beforehand and spread around a little paraffin? I think you must have done, otherwise how sure could you have been that the firework would do the trick?'

He had listened to her as quietly as he'd watched her, and when she had finished, he nodded almost approvingly.

'You'll never be able to prove a word of it, you know,' he said, almost sadly.

And Trudy knew that he was right.

Chapter 36

Matthew Hughes showed them politely to the door a few minutes later. Clement noticed that he shut the door behind them the moment they were off the stoop, in a hurry, no doubt, to help his wife with the packing.

Again, in tacit mutual silence, Trudy and Clement walked back to the car. Once inside, however, Clement didn't reach immediately for the ignition key, but sat instead contemplating the darkening night and the horror of the last ten minutes.

'Should I have stayed and tried to talk to Mrs Hughes?' Trudy asked. 'It's possible that she knew what he'd done. And she might not be such a hard nut to crack.'

But she was hoping that Clement would dissuade her, and she let out her breath in a sigh of relief as he did just that.

'No, I don't think that would help,' Clement said heavily. 'For a start, there's no way he would have told her beforehand what he was going to do. He wouldn't want to involve her,' he said confidently. 'It would make her an accessory before the fact, and he'd never risk doing that. If anything had gone wrong – if he'd been caught … well, the children would have needed her.'

Trudy swallowed hard as she contemplated how high the stakes had been for Matthew Hughes, that night when the fireworks had soared through the sky.

'Plus, there's the fact that she might have tried to talk him out of it,' Clement swept on. 'No, he would have felt that it was up to him to protect his family, and that it was a matter to be kept strictly between him and his father and no one else. And I don't think he would have told her about it afterwards, either. What would be the good of that? She would then have to share the guilt and the pain, and that man is determined to keep all of that to himself. Couldn't you tell?'

Trudy though back to the image of that aged, stooped, dead-eyed man, and nodded wordlessly. Yes. She could tell.

'But she might have guessed what he did,' Trudy argued list-lessly. 'Women very often know what their husbands have been up to, you said as much yourself. After the shock of the fire had worn off, and then inheriting all that much needed money … Well, she wouldn't have been human if she hadn't begun to *wonder*,' Trudy speculated, but her heart just wasn't in it.

'So what if she did?' Clement responded, his voice sounding calm and reassuring. 'Suppose you got her to admit that she suspected her husband had killed his father, would it really make any difference? There's no forensic proof that Thomas Hughes was murdered. There are no witnesses willing to come forward, though it wouldn't surprise me one bit if every single one of that family – including the children – all half-suspected or were convinced of the truth of what had happened. And Matthew himself isn't going to confess – not now, how can he? Don't you see the position he's in? His family need him so much. He *has* to go to America with his wife and child in the hope that little Helen will be the one in a thousand who'll be blessed with at least a partial cure – to gain a stay of execution for a while, if nothing else. Otherwise what he did on Bonfire Night will have been for nothing. Imagine the nightmares *that* thought must give him.'

'Oh don't,' Trudy said, her voice breaking at last. 'That poor little girl. Her poor mother. And her poor father,' she added quietly.

For a moment, she battled against the hot tears that swamped her eyes, and when she lost and felt them rolling down her cheeks, she turned a little aside and stared out of the window, trying to surreptitiously wipe them from her cheeks with the back of her hand.

Clement silently offered her the plain white handkerchief that lived in his jacket pocket.

She took it and sniffled for a while, struggling to get her emotions under control.

'Of course, there's another reason that he can't admit to what he's done, even if he'd wanted to,' Clement said, with forced practicality, pretending not to hear her distress. 'Because, as you would know only too well, by law, a person can't be allowed to profit from the proceeds of a crime.'

Trudy sighed and shook her head at the sheer futility of it all. 'You're right. If he confesses, they'll lose the money.'

'Which means that he'll now be forced to live for the rest of his life with what he's done, and never be able to relieve his soul with a confession,' Clement said soberly.

In the dark and cold car, Trudy shuddered. Whilst it might be true that the law couldn't touch Matthew Hughes – and as a police officer that thought still rankled a little – it was also true that the man could in no way be said to be getting away with murder.

At the police station, DI Jennings called somewhat impatiently 'Come in,' when the tentative knock sounded on the door to his office. A quick glance at the clock told him that it was nearly time for him to clock off, but when he saw WPC Loveday, and right behind her, Dr Clement Ryder step inside, he had the sudden feeling that his supper was going to have to wait.

There was something white and tight about his constable's face that told him there'd been trouble, and when he transferred his gaze to the coroner, a similar pale tautness marred his own handsome features. And it must be something pretty bad to rattle the old vulture, that was for sure!

In spite of the warmth of his office, the Inspector felt a cool trickle of unease run down the back of his spine. Instinctively he sat straighter in his chair.

'Sir, we've come to tell you that our investigations into the Thomas Hughes case are now over,' Trudy said crisply, all but standing to attention in front of his desk.

Jennings slowly leaned back in his chair. 'Are they now?' he said quietly. 'And what have you found?'

Trudy blinked, fixed her gaze on the wall somewhere just beyond his head, and said emotionlessly, 'We think that the case can be closed permanently, sir.'

On the way over here, they had discussed the situation between themselves and had finally concluded that there was no point in apprising her superior officer of all the details. Whilst they believed that there was simply no evidence to support a case for trial, they were both worried that DI Jennings and the powers that be might try to stop the Hughes from leaving the country whilst the prosecution service made up its own mind on that score. And that could take weeks – if not months, robbing little Helen of precious time.

And neither one of them wanted that on their consciences.

But if they had confidently expected DI Jennings would greet this news with enthusiasm and a certain amount of satisfied gloating, they were in for a rude awakening.

'Oh, do you?' Jennings said flatly – which was their first warning. 'Let me be the judge of that. Constable.' He fixed her with a beady glare. 'Your report please?'

'Sir?' Trudy prevaricated.

Beside her, Clement sighed and sat down heavily, a look of

resignation on his face. He might not like the man, but there were no flies on Harry Jennings.

'What have you been doing today, Constable Loveday?' Jennings asked silkily.

'We've finished questioning the family sir, and have concluded …'

'Tell me everything,' Jennings snapped, genuinely angry at her obvious prevarication. 'Do you think I don't have eyes in my head, Constable? Or do you think I was born yesterday?' He spared a brief glance for the grim-faced coroner, and wished that he had the authority to light a fire under the old vulture as well, but knew he'd have to content himself with dragging the truth from his officer. 'You've clearly discovered something unsavoury. Now out with it,' he rapped.

For a moment Trudy still hesitated. But then Clement said wearily, 'You'll have to tell him, Trudy.' And to Jennings he added warningly, 'Not that you'll wish you hadn't allowed her to keep quiet. Believe me, knowing what *we* know isn't going to make you any happier.'

Jennings rolled his eyes bitterly. 'Marvellous,' he said. 'Just bloody marvellous.' He heaved a massive sigh. 'All right, come on then – out with it.'

So Trudy told him everything.

Once or twice during the sorry, sad, and horrific recital, it looked as if Jennings was about to interrupt, but he never actually did so. Clement, watching the Inspector's face transform from an expression of impatient anger to dawning understanding and subsequent distaste and horror, couldn't help but feel sorry for the man. They, at least, had had some time to acclimatise themselves to the whole sorry mess, whereas Jennings was having it all dumped into his lap. Not only that, but now that he'd demanded the truth, he was the one who was going to have to decide what to do about it.

Clement could only hope the man did the right thing.

Finally, when Trudy's report was finished, there was silence for a long, long time.

Eventually, DI Jennings shuffled in his seat. 'There's no forensic evidence to be had at all, you say?' he asked finally.

'No, the fire destroyed it all, as you know,' Clement said flatly.

'And you don't believe that any member of the Hughes family can be persuaded to tell the truth? That they saw Mr Matthew Hughes enter the shed after Thomas Hughes had entered?' he asked next.

'We don't even know if any of them *did*, sir,' Trudy pointed out prosaically. 'And even if one or more of them had, I can't see them testifying against Matthew. Not under the circumstances. Can you?'

Jennings nodded perfunctory. 'And you're sure that there's no chance that you could get a confession from the man himself?'

Clement wearily went through the reasons why it was so unlikely that the killer of Thomas Hughes would ever admit to what he'd done.

'And the dead man was actually willing to let his own grand-kiddie die, just to save himself from spending a few pounds?' Jennings asked, but it was clear from the disbelief in his voice that the question was all but rhetorical. 'Well,' he said briskly, rousing himself and shaking off the nightmare world of the Hughes family. 'It's quite clear to me that since there's no possible case for the prosecution to get its teeth into, I think we should just quietly close the Hughes case once and for all, as you initially suggested, and file it away. The original findings at the inquest can remain unchallenged.'

Clement smiled a shade cynically. He had no doubt that Jennings's superiors wouldn't have thanked him for landing such a mess of a case in their laps, and by neatly sweeping it all the under the carpet, the Inspector was doing himself a favour, as much as anything else.

But perhaps he was doing the man an injustice?

Clement sighed, stood up and almost stumbled as his left foot began to tremble violently. He cursed his tiredness, which had almost certainly been instrumental in bringing on the latest bout of weakness, and tested his weight on his legs carefully, before he felt safe enough to actually step away from the support of his chair.

'Well, it's been a long day,' he said in massive understatement. He felt absolutely wrung out. 'So I'll bid you goodnight. Inspector.' He shot a knowing glance at Jennings, who smiled blandly back at him.

'Dr Ryder.'

Clement turned and smiled gently at Trudy. 'Trudy, my dear, as always, it's been a pleasure and a delight working with you. Until the next time, then?'

Trudy smiled and nodded. And it was only then that she recalled, at the beginning of the case, how worried she'd been that she might not be able to cope with working with this man again. How long ago that now seemed! And how absurd her lack of self-confidence seemed now.

If she could cope with the pity and the horror of a case like this, she felt like she could cope with anything!

'Dr Ryder,' she said warmly. 'Thank you.'

'I don't think I did much this time Trudy,' Clement said, meaning it. 'It was all down to you.' And if he'd deliberately held himself back, giving her all the room she needed in order to shine, he was confident that she had no suspicion of it.

When the door had closed behind the old vulture, Jennings looked at his officer thoughtfully. Without doubt, this had been as nasty a case as he'd ever come across.

No wonder she looked pale and hollow-eyed – especially if, as the old vulture had acknowledged, she'd carried most of the weight of it herself.

He grunted a little and then took a deep breath. 'You did well, Constable Loveday,' he said gruffly. 'This Hughes affair was a bad piece of work, and you met the challenge admirably. Well done.'

Trudy stared at him, her jaw falling open. Had the unthinkable really just happened? Had DI Jennings actually complimented her?

Jennings eyes sharpened on her. 'Well, don't just stand there looking like a stunned mullet, WPC Loveday,' he said acerbically. 'Don't you have work to be getting on with?'

'Yes sir!' Trudy responded instantly, and turned and walked stiffly to the door.

But as she reached for the handle, she was grinning widely.

Keep reading for an excerpt from the first book in the Ryder and Loveday series, *A Fatal Obsession* …

PROLOGUE

Oxford, July 1955

The body on the bed lay sedate and demurely silent as the middle-aged man looked slowly around the room. It was a lovely room – large, well-proportioned and lavishly decorated in tones of blue and silver. One of two large sash windows was partly open, allowing a warm summer breeze to blow in, gently wafting the fine net curtains and bringing with it a faint scent of honeysuckle from the lush and well-tended gardens below.

The man wandered slowly around the opulent bedroom, his eyes greedily taking in everything from the quality of the silk bedsheets to the bottles of expensive perfume on an ornate antique dresser, while being careful not to touch anything. Having been born into a working-class family, he knew nothing about the pedigree of the paintings that adorned the walls. But he would have been willing to bet a week's wages that the sale of just one of them would be more than enough to set him and his family up for life.

He'd never before had cause to visit any of the mansions that proliferated in the swanky streets that stretched between the Woodstock and Banbury Roads in the north of the city, or any of the leafy avenues in the area. So now he took his time, and a considerable amount of pleasure, in looking around him, luxuriating in the deep tread of the plush blue Axminster carpet beneath his feet, which was so reminiscent of walking on mossy lawns.

His eyes turned wistfully to the jewellery box on a walnut bedside table, left carelessly open. Gold, pearls and a few sparkling gemstones winked in the summer sun, making his fingers positively itch.

'Very nice,' he muttered quietly to himself. But he knew better than to slip even a modest ring or two into his pocket. Not this time – and certainly not with *these* people. The man hadn't reached his half century without learning there was one law for the rich, and one for everyone else.

Thoughtfully, his eyes turned once more to the body on the bed. A pretty little thing she was. Young too. Just out of her teens, perhaps?

What a damned shame, he thought vaguely.

Then the breeze caused something on the bedside table to flutter slightly, the movement instantly catching his eye. He walked closer to the bed and the dead girl, again careful where he put his feet, and saw what it was that had been disturbed. It had clearly been deliberately propped up among the pots of face cream and powder compacts, lipsticks and boxes of pills.

Bending ponderously at the waist, the man, who was definitely beginning to run to fat, squinted down at it and read some of the words written there.

And slowly, a large, beaming smile spread over his not particularly attractive face. He gave a long, slow, near-silent whistle and then looked sharply over his shoulder to make sure nobody from the house had come upstairs behind him and could see what he was about to do. Confident he remained alone and unobserved, he reached out for the item and put it safely away in his large inside jacket pocket.

Then he lovingly patted the place over his heart where it lay. For, unless he was very much mistaken, this precious little find was the best bit of luck he'd had for many a year – if not in his whole life. And it was certainly going to make his imminently approaching retirement years far more pleasant than he'd ever previously anticipated.

He walked jauntily to the door, leaving the dead girl behind him without a second thought, and stepped out confidently onto the landing.

Time, he rather thought, to tackle the man of the house.

CHAPTER ONE

Oxford, January 1960

Probationary WPC Trudy Loveday shouted, 'Oi, you, stop right there. Police!' at the top of her lungs, and took off at a racing sprint.

Needless to say, the young lad she'd just seen snatch a woman's handbag as she was standing below the clock face on Carfax Tower did nothing of the kind. She just had time to catch a fleeting impression of a panic-stricken young face as he shot a quick look at her over his shoulder, and then took off down The High, like a whippet after a hare.

He nearly got run over by a taxi as he crossed the main road at the intersection but, luckily for Trudy, the traffic that had screeched to a halt to allow him to cross meant she could take advantage of the gap to race across herself, in rather more safety.

On her face, had she but known it, was a look of sheer joy.

Sergeant O'Grady had given her the task of trying to find the man responsible for a spate of bag-snatching in the city centre that had been going on since before the Christmas rush, but this was the first time she'd actually caught sight of her quarry in all that time. Though the thief had been active enough, and the list of outraged complaints from housewives and shoppers had grown steadily longer, neither she nor any of her fellow constables walking the beat had yet been lucky enough to be in the right spot at the right time.

Until now.

And a month of pounding the freezing pavements, taking statements from enraged or tearful women, and hiding behind shop doors on increasingly aching feet while keeping her eyes peeled for mischief, had left Trudy with a proper grudge against this particular villain.

Which meant she was in no mood to lose him now.

She was aware that many of the people in the streets were watching her race by with open mouths and round, astonished eyes. Some of the men, indeed, looked as if they were going to try and interfere, and she could only hope and pray that they wouldn't. Although they no doubt meant well, the last thing she needed was for some chivalrous, middle-aged bank manager to try and stop the fleeing thief for her, only to be roughly tossed to the floor, punched, or worse.

The paperwork involved in that was something she definitely didn't want to think about. Not to mention the look of resigned fury that would cross DI Jennings's face when he learned she'd somehow managed to muck up such a simple arrest.

Less than a minute of mad chasing had passed so far, and rather belatedly she remembered her whistle and debated whether or not she should use it.

At nineteen (nearly twenty), Trudy Loveday still remembered her glory days at the track and field events at her school where she'd always won cups on sports day for her racing – be it sprinting or cross-country. And she could still run like the wind, even in her neat black shoes and police uniform, with her leather satchel of accoutrements bouncing on her hip. Moreover, she could tell she was gaining ground on the little villain in front of her, who had to deal with the added obstacle of shouldering pedestrians out of his way as he ran, leaving the pavements rather less clogged for her.

Her legs and arms were pumping away in that satisfying and remembered rhythm that allowed her to eat up the yards, and she was reluctant to alter that flow, but training and good sense told her she must. So, trying not to lose momentum, she reached her hand across her chest, swung the silver whistle on its chain up to her lips, and blew hard on the outward, expelling breath.

The distinctive, loud-pitched whistle promptly resounded in the cold, frost-laden air, and would, she knew, bring any of her colleagues within hearing distance running to her aid. Which might be just as well if the bag-snatcher decided to give up his attempt at a straight flight and tried to lose himself in the city's narrow, medieval back streets, or by dodging in and out of the shops.

But so far he was intent on just running down The High, no doubt confident he could outrun a mere woman. But this hardly made him the first man to underestimate her.

With a confident grin, Trudy put on an extra burst of speed. He was so close now, she could almost feel the moment when she'd rugby-tackle him to the ground, hear him grunt with surprise and then see the look of dismay on his cocky little face as she slipped her handcuffs on him and gave him his caution.

And at that moment, just as she was reaching out and getting ready to grab him, he turned and glanced over his shoulder, saw her and swore. And immediately began to dodge to his right, between two parked cars.

Trudy cast a swift look over her shoulder, saw that the road was clear, then looked ahead as far as Magdalen Bridge, noticing the familiar outline of a red bus chugging along, coming towards her. But she had plenty of time before it reached them.

Anticipating the fleeing thief's intention of crossing the road and trying to lose her down one of the side streets opposite,

Trudy gave a final blast on her whistle. This was as much to warn the gaping, watching public to keep out of the way as it was an attempt to attract further help from her colleagues.

Then she leapt sideways.

Her timing, as she'd known it would be, was near perfect, and before he could gain the middle of the road, she was on him, swinging him around and back towards the pavement. She hit him hard, putting all of her slight weight into it. Luckily, at five feet ten, she was a tall girl, and had a long reach.

The thief landed unluckily on his nose on the icy tarmac, and yelped in shock. He was a skinny, wiry specimen, all arms and legs, and already his nose was bleeding profusely. Comically, he was still clutching the lady's handbag he'd snatched back at Carfax.

Trudy felt her police cap fall off as she landed on top of him but, mercifully, her long, wavy, dark-brown hair was held up in such a tight bun by a plethora of hair pins and elastic bands that it remained contained.

Reaching behind her, with one knee firmly positioned in the middle of the thief's back, she groped for her handcuffs. She was vaguely aware of a male voice shouting something only a short distance away, and that the public, who had begun gathering in a curious little knot around her, were now moving back, when the thief beneath her suddenly bucked and twisted violently.

And before she could even open her mouth to begin to caution him, his elbow shot upwards, smacking her firmly in the eye.

'Owwww!' she yelled, one hand going up instinctively to cup her throbbing cheekbone. This provided the bag-snatcher with the opportunity he'd been waiting for, and he gave another massive heave, sending her sprawling.

Nevertheless, she had enough presence of mind to reach out and grab him by the foot as he attempted to get up. He turned, drew back his free leg and was clearly about to kick her in the face when she became aware of another figure looming over her.

'All right, matey, hold it right there! You ain't going nowhere,' a triumphant voice said. And a pair of large male hands came into her view, hauling the bag-snatcher to his feet. 'I'm arresting you for assaulting a police officer in the course of her duty. I must caution you that anything you say will be taken down and may be given in evidence.'

Trudy, her large, dark-brown eyes watering as much in frustration as in pain, watched as PC Rodney Broadstairs – the Lothario of St Aldates police station – slipped his handcuffs onto *her* suspect. Stiffly, she got to her feet. Only now that the adrenaline was wearing off was she beginning to feel the scrapes and bruises she'd sustained in the tackle. Although, fortunately, her gloves, uniform, and the heavy black serge greatcoat she wore over it had saved her from losing any actual skin.

A brief and polite smattering of applause from the public rang out as PC Broadstairs began frogmarching the thief back to the pavement. One member of the public diffidently offered Trudy her cap back, which she took with a smile and a weary word of thanks.

She also retrieved the lady's handbag for evidence.

But the admiring looks from the bystanders and the murmuring of approval for 'the plucky little thing' as she limped grimly after PC Broadstairs and the bag-snatcher did little to improve her now sour mood. Because she knew, after nearly a year's bitter experience, just how things were going to go now.

Broadstairs, having been the one to deliver the caution and put on the cuffs, would be accredited with the arrest. It would be the good-looking PC, not the humble probationary WPC, who would get the nod of approval from her superior officers.

She would no doubt be told to go home to her mum and dad and get some rest, nurse her burgeoning black eye and then type up her report first thing in the morning. Oh, and to go and get the deposition of the woman whose bag had been snatched. And all the time having to endure the whispers and snide asides about how that was all WPCs were good for.

Disconsolately, as she trooped back to St Aldates, she could only hope that DI Jennings wouldn't use her minor injuries as an excuse to put her back on desk duty again.

In front of her, PC Rodney Broadstairs looked over his shoulder at her and winked.

As WPC Trudy Loveday wrestled with the desire to swear in a most unladylike manner at her male colleague, five miles away, in the small and pretty village of Hampton Poyle, Sir Marcus Deering had stopped work for his elevenses.

Although he was still nominally in charge of the large chain of department stores that had made his fortune, at the age of sixty-three he now worked two days a week from the study in his large country residence in Oxfordshire. He was confident his managing directors, plus a whole board of other executives, could safely be left to do the bulk of the work without any major mishaps, and now rarely travelled to the main offices in Birmingham.

He sighed with pleasure as his secretary came into the book-lined room with a coffee tray laden with fresh-baked biscuits and that morning's post. A rather portly man, with thinning grey hair, a neatly trimmed moustache and large, hazel-green eyes, Sir Marcus liked to eat.

His appetite, however, instantly fled as he recognised the writing on one large, plain-white envelope. Addressed to him in block capital letters, it had been written in a rather bilious shade of green.

His secretary deposited the tray on his desk and, noticing the way his lips had thinned into a very displeased line, hastily beat a retreat.

Sir Marcus scowled at the pile of correspondence and took a desultory sip of his coffee, telling himself that this latest in a line of recent anonymous letters was nothing more than a nuisance. No doubt written by some crackpot with nothing better to do with his time, it was hardly worth the effort of opening and reading it. He should just consign it straight to the wastepaper basket instead.

But he knew he wouldn't do that. Human nature wouldn't let him. The cat wasn't the only creature curiosity was capable of killing, after all. And so, with a slight sneer of distaste, he snatched the offending envelope from the pile of correspondence, reached for his silver paper knife, and neatly slit it open. He then pulled out the single piece of paper within, knowing what it would say without even having to look at it. For the letters always made the same preposterous, ambiguous, infuriatingly meaningless demand.

He'd received the first one a little under a month ago. Just a few lines, the implication of a veiled threat, and unsigned, of course. Nonsense, through and through, he remembered thinking at the time. It was just one of the many things a man of his standing – a self-made, very wealthy man – had to put up with.

He'd crumpled it up and tossed it away without a second thought.

Then, only a week later, another one had come.

And, oddly enough, it hadn't been more threatening, or more explicit, or even more crudely written. The message had been exactly the same. Which was unusual in itself. Sir Marcus had always assumed that nasty anonymous letters became more and more vile and explicit as time progressed.

Whether it was this anomaly, or sheer instinct, he couldn't now say, but something about it had made him pause. And this time, instead of throwing it away, he'd kept it. Not that it really worried him, naturally.

But he'd kept the one that had come last week too, even though it had said exactly the same thing. And he'd probably slip this one, also, into the top drawer of his desk and carefully lock it. After all, he didn't want his wife finding them. The wretched things would only scare her.

With a sigh, he unfolded the piece of paper and read it.

Yes, as he'd thought – the same wording, almost exactly.

DO THE RIGHT THING. I'M WATCHING YOU. IF YOU DON'T, YOU'LL BE SORRY.

But this letter had one final sentence – something that was new.

YOU HAVE ONE LAST CHANCE.

Sir Marcus Deering felt his heart thump sickeningly in his chest. One last chance? What was that supposed to mean?

With a grunt of annoyance, he threw the paper down onto his desk and stood up, walking over to the set of French windows that gave him a view of a large, well-maintained lawn. A small brook cut across the stretch of grass marking the boundary where the formal flower garden began, and his eyes restlessly followed the skeletal forms of the weeping willows that lined it.

Beyond the house and large gardens, which were so colourful and full of scent in the summer (and the pride and joy of his wife, Martha) came yet more evidence of his wealth and prestige, in the form of the fertile acres being run by his farm manager.

Normally, the experience of looking out over his land soothed Sir Marcus, reassuring him and reminding him of just how far he'd come in life.

It was stupid to feel so bloody … well, not frightened by the letters exactly; Sir Marcus wouldn't admit to being quite *that*. But unsettled. Yes, he supposed that was fair. He definitely felt uneasy.

On the face of it, they were nothing. The threat was meaningless and tame. There wasn't even any foul language involved. As far as nasty anonymous notes went, they were rather pathetic really. And yet there was something about them …

He gave himself a little mental shake and tramped determinedly back to his desk, sitting down heavily in his chair. And with a look of distaste on his face, he swept the letter into a drawer along with all the others, and locked it firmly.

He had better things to do with his time than worry about

such stupid nonsense. No doubt the mentally deficient individual who'd written them was sitting somewhere right this moment, chortling away and imagining he'd managed to put the wind up him.

But Sir Marcus Deering was made of sterner stuff than that!

Do the right thing … Surely, it couldn't be referring to the fire, could it? A spasm of anxiety shot through him. That was all so long ago, and had had nothing to do with him. He'd been young, still working in his first executive position, and had no doubt been wet behind the ears; but the fire hadn't even occurred on his watch, and certainly hadn't been his responsibility.

No. It couldn't be about that.

Defiantly, he reached for a biscuit, bit into it, opened the first of his business letters and pondered whether or not he should introduce a new line in wireless sets into his stores. The manager at the Leamington Spa emporium was all for ordering in a large batch of sets in cream Bakelite.

Sir Marcus snorted. Cream! What was wrong with Bakelite that was made to look like good solid mahogany? And what did it matter if it *was* 1960 now, and the start of a whole new exciting decade, as the manager's letter insisted? Would housewives really fork out their husband's hard-earned money on cream Bakelite?

But at the back of his mind, even as he called in his secretary and began to dictate a reprimand to his forward-thinking executive in the spa town, his mind was furiously churning.

Just what the devil did the letter mean by 'do the right thing'? What *was* the right thing? And what would happen if he, Sir Marcus, *didn't* do the right thing?

Dear Reader,

We hope you enjoyed reading this book. If you did, we'd be so appreciative if you left a review. It really helps us and the author to bring more books like this to you.

Here at HQ Digital we are dedicated to publishing fiction that will keep you turning the pages into the early hours. Don't want to miss a thing? To find out more about our books, promotions, discover exclusive content and enter competitions you can keep in touch in the following ways:

JOIN OUR COMMUNITY:

Sign up to our new email newsletter:
hyperurl.co/hqnewsletter

Read our new blog www.hqstories.co.uk

: *https://twitter.com/HQDigitalUK*

: *www.facebook.com/HQStories*

BUDDING WRITER?

We're also looking for authors to join the HQ Digital family!
Find out more here:

https://www.hqstories.co.uk/want-to-write-for-us/
Thanks for reading, from the HQ Digital team

If you enjoyed *A Fatal Truth*, then why not try another unputdownable thriller from HQ Digital?